AS TARTARY BURNS

AIRSHIP 27 PRODUCTIONS

As Tartary Burns
© 2014 Riley Hogan

Published by Airship 27 Productions
www.airship27.com
www.airship27hangar.com

Interior & Cover illustration © 2014 James Conahan

Editor: Ron Fortier
Associate Editor: Ilena George
Production and design: Rob Davis.
Promotions and marketing: Michael Vance

ISBN-13: 978-0615955230
ISBN-10: 0615955231

Printed in the United States of America

10 9 8 7 6 5 4 3 2 1

AS TARTARY BURNS

By Riley Hogan

CHAPTER 1

The Early Seventeenth Century in a world that could have been our own.

"Sorcerer?" Vasyl said as he opened the oak door, he had explored caves that were brighter than the shadow shrouded home before him.

"Aye?" Came a raspy voice from the shadows.

"Are you Aleksandr, the sorcerer?"

Aleksandr drew himself up from a bunk, "Who are you?"

"I am Vasyl Graboy," he said, staring at the silhouetted man in front of him "My daughter is dying."

Aleksandr yawned. "We have doctors in the Sich."

Many medical men had fled to become Cossacks to avoid punishment for experimenting on corpses. Their surgical skills made them invaluable to the Zaporozhian host.

"She suffers from a curse." He paused for breath. "Please help! I lost my wife to plague years ago; I can't lose my daughter! I've heard of your great skill and power; name any fee."

Aleksandr packed his grimoires. "I'll do it for free."

It would be dishonorable to take ducats for helping a fellow Cossack.

"Thank you sir!"

Aleksandr stepped into the light. He wore a simple shirt, Turkish trousers, and cavalry boots, while his smooth head was topped by an oseledet scalp lock and a thin mustache. He studied his latest client. This was obviously a settled Cossack, judging by his girth and expensive clothing. Vasyl had a smooth face with full brown hair.

The two men left the sorcerer's home, which contained only a bunk, clothes, and arcane tools. They walked through the Sich, the heart of the Zaporozhian host. The Sich dwarfed several cities in sheer scale; many young recruits would wander through it for hours staring in wonder at its dark towering structures. Aleksandr's home was located near the vast wooden wall, a line of spikes that encircled the Sich to protect against Crimean Tatar raiders and other menaces.

Aleksandr and Vasyl walked into the space near the gates. Since it was midday the area was only partly crowded with Cossacks practicing swordplay, cooking meals over fires or gambling. The men made a fearsome sight with their scalp locks twisting in the wind, drooping mustaches and coarse clothing. Many Zaporozhians wore only wool shirts, pants and sheepskin shoes, some men preferred to wear English clothing that they acquired through trade, while others wore Turkish garb complete with turbans.

The two men went to their separate horses. Aleksandr passed a group of men bartering with meat and Turkish swords obviously taken from a raid. He thought of the day that he had stolen his horse as he mounted and rode out to meet Vasyl, who was already waiting in his saddle near the massive gates.

"Can't you fly?" Vasyl asked, as they galloped past men trading tobacco and wines.

"Impossible," barked Aleksandr; sorcery could not break natural laws.

The horsemen rode out of the gates, Aleksandr directed his horse to the left to allow a patrol party of four men to pass. Vasyl waved at men in homes located around the Sich; most Cossacks lived in kuren, barracks, those who wanted better conditions built homes. Aleksandr's home had been built with money he had earned by using sorcery to curse a rich merchant's rival; though his fee had been lowered since he had refused to curse the target's children.

❦ ❦ ❦

"Follow me," Vasyl said.

As their beasts climbed a hill, Aleksandr paused to stare at boats in the Dnieper and thought of Marko's foolish expedition. Cossacks had gained infamy thanks to their skill as mounted infantrymen, but they were also talented pirates who dominated the Dnieper and the Black Sea with their chaika boats. Chaika boats were built to cut across the water swiftly and were too low to spot; they could be as short as a rowboat or longer than a Venetian ship.

Ruthenia opened before them; the bronze hued steppe and the dark green forests filled with oaks curving up to the pure blue sky.

"I couldn't locate your ataman, is he hunting boar in the woods or raiding villages?"

Aleksandr grimaced, "Marko sailed off with two chaiki under his command, on a foolish expedition."

"Fishing?"

Aleksandr laughed. "No, nothing so sane." The sorcerer wondered how his ataman had convinced brave Bohun, Andriy and other men of great skill and courage to follow him. Marko had spent weeks planning the expedition and convincing countless young men to join him on an enterprise which he promised would establish the Zaporozhians as a major power. The young ataman actually believed his mad scheme would succeed, turning him and his men into heroes who would be admired for centuries!

"You dislike your ataman?" Vasyl asked, as the riders turned, passing animal bones.

He shook his head. "I love Marko more than any brother," not that Aleksandr ever had a brother, "but my ataman can be foolish and headstrong."

Vasyl's laugh rang out. "When I was a young chern my ataman was just the opposite, he was meek as a kitten, only ordering us to launch small raids against Turkish towns."

"You were a lucky chern then."

"Aye," Vasyl said, pulling his reigns to slow his mount's pace.

Aleksandr followed his client through patches of forest so thick and dark that it was not unlike riding through a mountain valley. Out of habit, both men were alert to spot boar or stags. Vasyl kicked his mount, which carried him through the woods; he swiftly ducked his head under an arching oak limb as his horse leapt over a log.

"Well done!" Aleksandr said, picking thorns out of his leg.

"Thanks," his client replied as a wind swept past.

"Is Baranko still the Sich priest?" Vasyl asked as the sorcerer caught up to him.

"Yes; the pious old goat will probably spend centuries saving souls," quipped Aleksandr as they left the woods behind and entered the steppe plains.

Vasyl chortled, then said, "Do you know how he came to be our priest?"

Aleksandr shook his head.

"At first he was going to become a holy man in the Novgorod republic." It was a very comfortable position. "Then, while traveling, his party was attacked by raiders from the Crimean Khanate. They took Baranko hostage, knowing that a priest would fetch a high ransom."

Vasyl continued, "Baranko's holy order approached the Cossack Hetman." This was the elected leader of all Zaporozhian Cossacks. "They promised any favors in addition to a handsome sum for his return."

"Continue," Aleksandr said, watching Cossack patrols in the distant and seemingly endless steppe.

"Through spies, atamans learned where the Tatars were holding Baranko; hungry Muslims have no loyalty."

Aleksandr nodded in agreement.

"Eight of the best men from different kurens were assembled; four traveled by chaika, the others by horse." Vasyl paused for breath. "They liberated Baranko without losing a single man."

"Were you among them?"

"Oh no."

"Then what?" Aleksandr asked whipping his horse forward.

"Baranko chose to stay; he thought that God's plan was for him to minister to us and that the Tatars had placed him in our hands."

Aleksandr snorted. "Fool!"

Vasyl fingered the cross swinging at his neck. "I admire his faith. A true Christian, he represents the people we defend."

Aleksandr had no reply. He followed his client toward a stretch of hills near thickets. He noticed clothing shreds on thorns as he kicked his horse up the first hill.

Horsemen sped past. It was a Zaporozhian patrol leaving to protect the frontier of settled families and those who paid tribute, defending them from roving Tatar slavers out to harvest the steppe for souls to sell in their evil capital of Kaffa. Kaffa was the capital of the Crimean Khanate: a state of great power whose slave raids terrified every decent Christian. The Khanate was enemy of every Cossack who longed for the day they could destroy Kaffa.

Vasyl held his sabre tightly as his beast climbed the hill. A typical Zaporozhian sabre had an almost identical appearance to the kilij swords of the Turkish hordes.

Aleksandr had only brought a flintlock pistol with him. Were Marko and his men engaged in battle by now?

"Look!" Vasyl exclaimed, stabbing a finger at the settled Cossacks' homes. Any Zaporozhian who chose to marry and produce offspring built a home outside the Sich. They were still members, but had become settled Cossacks. The homes were built from mighty timber and topped with triangular roofs, with chimneys in the center made from stones gathered on Dnieper's banks. Settled men raised livestock in addition to how most Cossacks made their money; raiding and extorting money from smugglers who wanted to pass through lands they controlled.

"Be as swift as the thunder," Aleksandr said, whipping his horse. "Your daughter's life rests on our skill as horsemen!"

As the two men raced for Vasyl's home, he tried to guess the sorcerer's age. While Aleksandr had a youthful face, his voice and mannerisms made him seem as ancient as the waves. Men who fled to the Sich developed bonds that went beyond any ties of blood or friendship, but few revealed what had drove them to become Cossacks, even though any man was welcome to join. Vasyl stared at the bag bouncing across Aleksandr's back as they galloped across the plain that separated them from a child in need. What secrets lay within those books? He had grown up hearing tales of tomes so evil that touching their pages would destroy souls, condemning the reader to a fate worse than hell. Any literate man could purchase or steal a grimoire to learn methods of summoning angels or demons through holy names and the vast preternatural hierarchies that such beings belonged to. Sorcery was not an inborn talent confined to a precious few; it was a skill that anyone could learn, thus occult texts were a tightly controlled resource. How had Aleksandr gained his books of sorcery?

Finally they reached the settled homes. Vasyl jumped off his horse, almost falling into mud, and lead his new friend into his home. Aleksandr was impressed, the house had two rooms, beds, and tables displaying Circassian pottery; clearly his client traded with Kavkaz mountaineers. Vasyl lead the sorcerer past the red stone fireplace to his daughter's bed. The child had a pure face and dark blonde hair.

"Her name?"

"Bohdanna."

He nodded and took her pulse. "Your daughter shall live to see her wedding day and her grandchildren!"

"Praise God!"

Aleksandr took a seat in a chair; he would have to enter the Unseen Realms to find out what plagued sweet young Bohdanna. "Remain silent and do not touch me."

Vasyl nodded, left the room.

Aleksandr began the process of leaving his body.

❦ ❦ ❦

Aleksandr felt his body fade away, for a second it felt like he was drifting in the Azov Sea. He felt pain as he took his spirit form. Fire seemed to speed through him as he took the body of a snake. Ideas become real in the Unseen Realms, concepts are its building blocks, and therefore people exploring the infinite invisible world take shapes that match their personalities. Pain of a sort exists in the Unseen Realms since its travelers cannot leave their bodies completely, so a connection to fleshly agony remains in the way that the mind interprets arcane attacks as pain. Aleksandr was still in Vasyl's room, only now he saw whatever occult realities that could not be detected by the material body; namely the daemonic parasites feasting on Bohdanna's spirit body, which was a dove. There were three of them, each identical, and they had small dark green 'bodies' and rows of eyes beneath gaping mouths lined with razor sharp 'teeth', which symbolized their predatory nature.

"Who are you to interrupt our meal?" came from one vile creature.

"He's a man of power!" squealed another.

Aleksandr knew that parasites were at the lowest end of the demonic hierarchies; it would be simple to return to his body and banish them. Any ritual affecting both the physical and spiritual had to be done from his flesh body.

"Attack him!"

The sorcerer had much practice with arcane combat. Sorcerous attacks took the form of assaults from whatever concept a spirit form was centered around. While in the physical, a curse would be something in line with natural law such as pain or disease. Aleksandr lashed back with a spray of 'venom' and the powerful magic attack banished the petty demon who instantly disappeared back to his realm. He attacked the second one with venom, which the demon managed to dodge; it sprang forward with fangs. The sorcerer used his tail to whip the demon back then attacked with venom again, banishing the vile imp.

"Farewell," spat the last demon, which chose to leave instead of being forced back to his hell realm.

❦ ❦ ❦

Vasyl watched in shock as the young sorcerer returned to his senses. "Bohdanna's awake!"

Aleksandr stumbled out of the chair. The room spun as though he was dangling from a hemp rope. He gasped for, "Beer."

Vasyl quickly brought a glass which his guest downed quickly; it helped restore Aleksandr to the physical.

"Thank you!"

Aleksandr rubbed his aching forehead. "It's not over yet."

"What?"

"Only a ritual will protect her for good." The demons could return.

"I'll get your bag."

"Keep your fingers off of it!" Aleksandr barked, still adjusting.

Vasyl drew back; shocked at the display of rage. The sorcerer seized his books and approached the child.

"Who are you?" Bohdanna asked. Hadn't she only been asleep for a few minutes?

"The man who saved your life," quipped the sorcerer.

He thumbed through a book older than several royal dynasties, until he came to the headless one ritual.

"Subject to me all daimons so that every daimon, whether heavenly or aerial, or earthly or subterranean, or terrestrial or aquatic, might be obedient to me; and every enchantment and scourge which is from God."

Aleksandr placed his hand upon the child's brow and continued, "I summon you, headless one, who created earth and heaven, who created day and night, you are Osoronnophris whom none have ever seen; you are Iabas, you are Iapos, you have provided for discrimination between that which is just and unjust; you have made female and male; you have revealed both the seed and fruit; you have made humans love each other and hate each other.

"I am Hermes Trismegistos your prophet to whom you have transmitted your mysteries celebrated by Khem. You have revealed the moist and the dry and all nourishment. Hear me!

"I am the messenger of pharaoh Osoronnophris; this is your true name which has been transmitted to the prophets of Khem. Hear me, ΑΡΒΑΘΙΑΩ ΡΕΙΒΕΤ ΑΘΕΛΕΒΕΡΣΗΘ ΑΡΑ ΒΛΑΘΑ ΑΛΒΕΥ ΕΒΕΝΦΧΙ ΧΙΤΑΣΓΟΗ ΙΒΑΩΘ ΙΑΩ! Listen to me and turn away this daimon!

"I call upon thee, awesome and invisible god, with an empty spirit, ΑΡΟΓΟΓΟΡΟΒΡΑΩ ΣΟΧΟΥ ΜΟΔΟΡΙΩ ΦΑΛΑΡΧΑΩ ΟΟΟ. Holy headless one, deliver me, from the daimon which restraineth me! ΜΑΡΑΡΡΑΙΩ ΙΟΗΛ ΚΟΘΑ ΑΘΟΡΕΒΑΛΩ ΑΒΡΑΩΘ, deliver me, ΑΩΘ ΑΒΡΑΩΘ ΒΑΥΣΜ ΙΣΑΚ ΣΑΒΑΩΘ ΙΑΩ.

"He is the lord of the gods. He is the lord of the inhabited world. He is the one whom the winds fear. He is the one who made all things by the command of his voice.

"Lord, king, master, helper, empower my soul, ΙΕΟΥ ΠΥΡ ΙΟΥ ΠΥΡ ΙΑΩΤ ΙΑΗΩ ΙΟΟΥ ΑΒΡΑΣΑΞ ΣΑΒΡΙΑΜ ΟΟ ΥΥ ΕΥ ΟΟ ΥΥ ΑΔΩΝΑΙΕ, immediately, immediately, messenger of god ΑΝΛΑΛΑ ΛΑΙ ΓΑΙΑ ΑΠΑ ΔΙΑΧΑΝΝΑ ΧΟΡΥΝ.

"I am the headless daimon with sight in my feet. I am the mighty one who possesses the immortal fire. I am the truth who hates the fact that unjust deeds are done in the world; I am the one that makes the lightning flash and the thunder roll. I am the one whose sweat is the heavy rain which falls upon the earth that it might be inseminated. I am the one whose mouth is utterly aflame. I am the one who begets and destroys; I am the favor of the Aion; my name is a heart encircled by a serpent. Come forth and follow."

❀ ❀ ❀

Bohdanna and her father were stunned, a presence older than time had spread through the house; both felt sick yet safe.

"Will my daughter be safe for now?"

"Aye," Aleksandr said, stumbling out the door to his horse. He tried to adjust to the physical with thoughts of friends. Would sly Andriy avoid combat? What of Joseph and Noman? Would ataman Marko survive his own insane raid?

❀ ❀ ❀

"They say there were wizards among the Cossacks, sorcerers, supernatural people. They would take a pinch of native earth and hide it under their cap and in battle this earth gave them the power to become invisible when they came face to face with the enemy. The Mussulman could hear the Cossack laugh, could hear his horse neigh but neither was to be seen; invisible as a ghost and laughing!"

-Oles Honchar, the Cathedral

CHAPTER 2

Capture meant impalement. Marko purged thoughts about hell on a stake from his mind as a gale from the Thracian plains filled the sail.

"The canon is loaded," said Bohun Rutschke. His beard masked battle scars; unlike most Cossacks his blond hair dangled down to his neck. The gunner wore a disguise: a round red tarbouz cap, a yellow shirt, green trousers, and mest ankle boots. Bohun's garments were taken from slain Turks, stripped and left to cook under the sun.

Marko Storozhenko nodded. He had a handsome, smooth face, thus his sobriquet Хлопчик: the boy. The young Ataman's disguise was maddening; the turban made his dark hair itch, the cloak that hid his Cossack garb stunk of vomit. Like most Zaporozhians, Marko was of average height and thin; only settled Cossacks had time to gain fat.

The Ataman turned to Noman Firqa. Son of a Szlachic rapist and a Tatar victim, he abandoned Lipka Tatar life in favor of the Cossacks where he was judged on merit rather than birth. The warrior's unique skin tone reflected his heritage. He was tuma, of mixed Turkic and Slavic blood. His hair was always neatly trimmed and a thin mustache rested over his lip. Noman wore Tatar costume: a kalpak fur hat, a cloak, Turkish trousers and pointed mest shoes. He hadn't worn such clothing since childhood.

Marko left the vessel's tented half to be greeted by a view of the city of seven hills: Tsargrad, Constantinople. The sight of the Hagia Sophia electrified him. No Turk could build such a thing!

Empty galleys, a mere two guards. According to Noman, Friday was their Sabbath; an ideal day to strike! The tiny fleet halted at the main dock. Noman called out to sentries in Turkish, but there was no response. The guards slowly advanced. Marko felt panic, as if he had downed a mug of traditional Tatar drink, horse blood and milk.

With the grace of an Alevi, Noman leapt on deck. Noman told tales; they were but poor merchants come to sell wares! He presented a handsome Persian knife, a prize from a ship they took last year, as proof. As Bohun nocked an arrow, Marko watched greed overpower suspicion; the sentries were locked in a bidding duel. One held up a light sack while the other pulled off a ring and held it up, letting a gem catch the fading sun beams.

Marko seized a compound bow, fitted a shaft, and let fly! Arrows jutted through throat flesh; the first guard fell dead. The second Turk dodged the missiles. Marko tossed the bow and sprinted, hand on sabre. The guard rushed him, kilij sword out, howling. Marko drew his blade. In one smooth motion, shining steel slashed through entrails.

The second sentry collapsed, spilling intestines. Noman grasped hair and opened the Turk's neck with a dagger. Cossacks stormed the deck, holding oil jars and blades.

They split up. Noman lead men towards the warships. Marko tore off his vile turban as he raced forward. Pirates followed, like hawks to carrion. Through a gate, down small narrow streets, Marko held up his sabre for silence.

A distant stamp of Janissary boots. Marko pointed at the night sky. Cossack pirates nodded in unison; climb roofs, pick them off at leisure. Marko crouched. A young Moldovian, doglock in hand, stepped onto his shoulders and leaped. Minutes later they stood on tiles, waiting.

Noman hurled jars. A warship got an oil coat, he touched a torch to it; flames devoured the hull. A squad stepped forward, releasing a barrage of flaming arrows. Direct hits, the ships were ablaze. Noman thought of Shadrach, Meshach, and Abednego.

Janissaries spilled into view with their silly hats, bright womanly clothes. Marko signaled and volleys of arrows skewered infidels. Survivors pointed muskets, too shocked to aim. Cossacks ran out of sight as janissaries fired, hitting air.

Marko drew a flintlock and jumped as his men rained down onto the Turks. The Zaporozhians had to finish the Muslims before they reloaded weapons. Bohun fired, a Janissary's face exploded. The Ruthenian fired his last pistol…a miss. A Janissary rushed at him waving a rifle, and Bohun froze.

Marko pulled his sword out of a Janissary skull and sprinted past Cossacks slaughtering infidels. A lunge and the infidel fell inches before Bohun, who nearly slipped on gore. Marko ignored Bohun's thanks and gave an order to, "Loot homes!"

Chern shattered doors. Marko savored the sweet melody of screams. Bohun held an empty musket on a family, his friends left a room, coins spilling out of hands. One Ruthenian reached for the mother's tit, the father started shouting. Bohun emptied a flintlock into his face and watched an old Turk's insides shift to mist. The bitch and her whelps moaned and cried. "Leave that whore," Bohun uttered, "No time for her." Cossacks left laughing.

There! A jewel crusted yatagan blade in the old man's robes! Since Bohun was the only Christian in the room he seized the knife, concealing it as he ran.

※ ※ ※

Noman reclined on a canon, admiring the view of a burning fleet. Cossacks crouched behind deck, natural cover, gripping weapons. Noman's task was finished; it was time to wait.

※ ※ ※

"Kâfir durdurmak!"

Marko turned. A Turkish officer stood with his back to the flaming harbor and raised his Kilij. The Ataman raised a flintlock, pulled the trigger. Misfire!

The Muslim cackled as he fingered amulets; sorcery. Marko heaved the pistol and lunged with his blood stained blade. His opponent parried the attack. The Cossack stepped back, sabre in a defensive position. His opponent advanced slashing wildly; a shot tore through a coffee house inches away from the arcane swordsman.

"Stand down, Bohun!" Marko feinted right, leaving the Turk unable to defend against his sword arm. Slash, blood spurted. Marko retreated.

For a second he saw fear in the Muslim's eyes as he sprang forward slashing. Marko easily countered and thrust; his sabre tore through rib cage. With a cry the Ottoman collapsed, his kilij fell to the cobbled pavement. Marko would not touch his enemy's weapon, the sword could have a death curse upon it. The Cossack put a boot on the Turk's throat; he was barely alive. "Sorcery is no substitute for skill."

Marko turned to a sudden thud; a rope. "Climb Ataman, half the Sultan's horde will soon be here," urged one of his men atop a roof. He scaled the wall, leaving his enemy to die slowly. Sheathing his sword, Marko saw chern on rooftops. Few people looking up. The Ruthenian ran for the harbor.

※ ※ ※

Noman's heart leaped, his friends were safe! "Orders, Ataman?"

"We sail for the Sich," Marko said as he threw bags of gold, taken from an imam's home, towards his brothers.

"Huzzah! Huzzah! Huzzah!"

Marko only smiled and sat on the ship's bench, "Fire the canon."

"Yes my ataman," Bohun said, brandishing a torch. There was an alien screech, and a faint light. Bohun pointed the torch at its general direction and stumbled. The Kerkes!

It was a giant scarlet heron with two long feathers jutting from its skull. The creature's red body glowed like coals in a heretic's execution pyre. Noman grabbed a torch and fired the falconet, hoping to silence that hellish roar. The canon ball struck the mortared wall in front of the harbor, missing the galleon-sized bird. No time to reload.

It made no sense! An empire only sent Great Beasts into the most vital battles! Clearly the sultan had no time to rally soldiers or they were making foolish use of precious weapons, for It couldn't be slain. The Kerkes flew out of range, wind from the wings almost made the chaika capsize. "Let the bay have the canon!"

Four chern dropped the weapon into the water, and the ship set sail. Noman nocked an arrow; he stood next to a Cossack gripping a torch. The Kerkes was circling, playing. Noman twisted his fingers into the Mongol draw, pulled the sinew bowstring to his cheek. As the beast flew down he released an arrow: a miss. Noman dove down as the creature passed and its harpoon sized beak narrowly missed the sail canvas. Bohun fired two flintlocks, hitting the Kerkes, which screeched!

Noman released arrows with no time to aim and the shafts struck waves. Bohun scrambled to reload in dim light, and his fingers shook. They were moments away from a second sky-daemon attack.

It gave a Luciferian howl, and dived. Bohun drew a weapon, and squeezed the trigger. Direct impact, blood streamed from blood red flesh.

Marko, sabre strapped across his shoulders, grabbed a line and began to climb with feet against wood. He reached the mast's peak with barely enough room to stand. "Fire a volley!" Noman's fellow archers obeyed but arrows fell short of the sky beast.

The demon dove. Marko swallowed fear and drew his sword, still drenched with Turkish blood. The young Cossack was eye level with the Kerkes; a mast sized beak, scimitar sharp mouth, horrible gaping eyes, and winding neck like a serpent. Marko slashed but his target easily dodged the clumsy stroke, and the ataman fell.

Marko smashed into the deck and pain exploded. Should he try to move?

Filthy water inflamed his wounds. Marko's plummet from the mast had holed the chaika. The winged beast began to descend; a struggle sweetened meat. Where was his sword?

With a yell Bohun fired his last fresh pistol; the shot punched through the Kerkes' wing. The entity screeched and flew away; wounded, yet far from death. Noman and Bohun hefted Marko into the second ship; his men had prepared a bed of skins. Noman muttered something in Tatar while Marko watched the waves claim his chaika. "Your wounds are survivable," Bohun informed his Ataman.

Marko thanked his fellow Ruthenian. "Any ships in pursuit?"

Noman shook his head. "The wind favors us; we will see the Sich in mere hours."

"Thank the Holy Father," Marko said, shedding soaked clothing.

❀ ❀ ❀

Morning.

Noman awoke to laughter. Someone was midway into telling jokes about Turkish women and well-hung oxen. He surveyed the vessel to find that men under his command were eating, talking, or going to sleep after a shift. Noman looked at Joseph, who was gorging himself on salt preserved sturgeon. The Tatar took a small sip of ale and walked over to Marko. "Can you move?"

"Easily; the pain has dulled."

"You didn't shatter anything," Bohun said, ripping off a piece of stag. "If I can fix muskets, I can repair flesh."

Marko only smiled. He stood up and tried to hide his pain.

A man from the far end called, "You will be able to sleep in your own bed tonight, honorable Ataman."

"According to who?"

"I am called Zhenya." He was tall, late twenties, a thick mustache blanketed his upper lip, and Zhenya's head was shaved save for an oseledet; a common Cossack style.

Marko chortled. "Well he who is called Zhenya, could you bring me ale?"

"Right away, glorious Ataman." He clearly wanted a considerable share of the spoils. Zhenya rushed across the ship with a cup, brimming with spirits.

"My thanks."

"Anything else, great Ataman?"

"No," Marko realized he had hours of this ahead of him. Centuries ago Ushkuiniks, ancestors of Cossacks, controlled these waters. Marko followed an ancient tradition.

❀ ❀ ❀

"...Cossacks dealt a most audacious blow when, within view of the sultan and a garrison of 30,000, Cossack chaiky managed to slip into Costantinople harbor, burn it and make their escape. In 1620 they repeated the same feat."
-Orest Subtelny

CHAPTER 3

TWO DAYS LATER: THE SICH.

"...I follow you to a life in Christ, Amen," Marko finished his prayer. Feeling at peace, went outdoors, his kuntush rippling in the wind.

Colossal timber walls concealed a dynamic warrior republic. The men who lived in the Sich were divided into countless barracks, kureni, each with an elected ataman.

Fortunately the men who had placed their trust in Marko demanded very little of their leader. Occasionally he would judge cases or mitigate personal feuds. Zaporozhia was lead by the hetman. Any Cossack could cast votes or stand as a candidate in the grand Hetman elections.

Marko walked by Cossacks trading valuables from ships, ports and homes; most men lived on plunder. Other chern ringed around dancing fires cooking flesh; horse, stag, and fish. Marko approached Ostap Chrobak, an ataman of advanced age who claimed to have fought alongside Vyshnevetsky. Ostap had spent much of his life in the saddle; a centaur of the steppe! He was busy training a recruit with blond hair and a smooth face; the youth wore sheepskin shoes, gray pants dotted by holes and a stained white shirt.

"You're not chopping wood!" he exclaimed. "Think of your weapon as a bird, hold it too tightly and you choke it, too lightly and it flies away." Only sparring was permitted; Cossacks could not fight each other, there was no place for Cain and Abel in the Eden of the Sich.

The recruit stared at Marko and stood at attention. Ostap laughed. "We're mere atamans; we have no great ones here."

"Sorry." The newcomer's cheeks burned.

"With a sword arm like that you won't have to apologize very often," Marko said with a reassuring smile.

"You're the hero who made the Sultan flee Tsargrad!"

Hero? Marko almost laughed, although it healed shame about his fall.

18

"Christian duty is far from heroism, but thank you. Your name?"

"Oleg Lozinski, I…" The bell sounded; a rada!

"Not now," Marko said, breaking into a sprint. Men swarmed to the Hetman's residence; no man was more respected. Hetman Samiylo Kishka emerged with his bulava-baton in hand, clad in opulent garments he looked like a Dacian senator. A sea of Cossacks cheered, jutting their sabres into the air!

Kishka had the worst job in the Sich; a hetman's privileges were few and he could be easily removed by the majority that elected him. Samiylo held up his hands, his rings sparkled. "Thank you my brothers!" he said, then explained, "A Liakh noble, who will remain nameless, asks us to exchange Tatar prisoners for captives held by the Khan. Who will lead?"

Aleksandr stepped forward, "Allow me, most serene hetman." If Samiylo was the most respected man in the Sich, Aleksandr held the most interest. The sorcerer wore a simple shirt, western style trousers, cavalry boots, and no hair save for an oseledet and a thin mustache. Like most men of the Sich, he went and came as he pleased, only without his possessions being put at risk.

"Are you certain?" Sorcerers were a precious resource.

"Yes."

"Very well then." A Commonwealth officer left Samiylo's home, hand on sword as if he was expecting to slash his way out any second. Bohun suppressed laughter; the Pole couldn't hide fear! "This is sergeant Piludski, your guide," the hetman explained, baton held high.

❀ ❀ ❀

Marko checked a pair of Turkish pistols; he had taken them off a Bosnian's corpse years ago at the siege of Akkerman. Aleksandr feared that he would have to put the sword dangling at his side to good use; he shivered at the thought and adjusted his fur cape. Bohun made sure that his powder was dry; it could rain and Aleksandr had no power over the weather. Andriy deposited tobacco into a pipe and lit it; he began to puff in relief.

Aleksandr glanced at the outsiders. The Liakhs rode ahead of them with three Tatar hostages leashed to horses. Piludski sat up straight as a hussar's lance. The sorcerer smirked; the sergeant was playing at being noble. The officer rode beside a pair of cavalrymen; Pancerni, and extra mounts. Clearly the hostages were of some importance, otherwise they'd have sent expendable men; mercenaries from the Gaelic Union, Pagan Lithuania, or Christian Spain.

The traffic of horses passed a hill and came to a river. Aleksandr leaned forward; a shallow stream, easy to cross. Bohun kept looking at their escorts; Cossacks had little trust for Liakhs.

Aleksandr faced Piludski. "Will we reach the meeting point soon?"

Piludski brushed water off his leg. "It shouldn't be much longer."

Annoyed at the officer's vague reply, Aleksandr probed further. "Who are the hostages?"

"Friends of mine," he said, staring at distant mountains.

A Tatar collapsed. His kalpak fell into mud; he coughed out words in an alien language.

Aleksandr gestured to Bohun. "He won't be of any value after being dragged for miles."

"Agreed," Bohun said, nudging his horse toward the Tatar. He disliked the idea of wasting water on a Muslim but was not foolish enough to disobey a temporary leader. Bohun tossed a water skin into the captive's hand and watched as he greedily sipped. The Cossack was ashamed to feel brief sympathy for the Crimean.

Marko rode by snatching the skin out of infidel hands. "Enough of that."

"Keep the skin," Bohun said, "I won't drink out of anything that has touched Mohametan lips."

"Wise man," Marko said hanging the skin beside his canteen. Aleksandr prodded the Tatar onto his feet with his sword, laughing at the Tatar's curses.

A small clearing with a group of Crimean horseman in the center appeared; the exchange point. "Stay in the woods," Aleksandr instructed Bohun and Marko. "If I throw my hat to the ground, shoot." They rode on.

The Tatars were a fearsome sight; kalpaks rested on their heads, fur cloaks covered their shoulders, scarred hands gripped lances.

Piludski held up his arm in greeting, Tatar horses parted to reveal two bound men. Marko assumed they were nobles; each hostage wore a dirty yet ornate kuntush. One of the Pancerni dismounted, drew a dagger from his boot, and slashed the bonds of a captive. The freed Tatar limped across the field to his fellow Muslims, massaging his wrists.

Andriy fidgeted in his saddle as he watched hostages walk to spare horses. He was too hungry to feel pity; besides, they were not his brothers. He considered asking Bohun for food when a sudden emerald flash caught his eyes. Did he actually see that?

"In the name of Michael I command you to halt!" Aleksandr commanded, shaping his hand into a position corresponding to the Angel's sphere.

Marko was in shock; mere feet separated him from a Lisovyk, a forest-demon! Aleksandr recited Latin; the pronunciation was of no importance.

Marko stared at the seven-foot-tall horned creature; a mass of undulating bark, vines, and leaves made up its body. A fleshy gap for a mouth, almost human eyes; the sound of it drawing breath was not unlike windstorms. "Release him," Aleksandr ordered pointing at the terrified men, Liakh and infidel both in the creature's grip.

"No." Not exactly shocking. "Why do you care about these two?"

"If my brothers and I do not see to their safe return there will be no money."

"Ah," the Lisovyk replied, stroking the Tatar's face.

"What interest could you possibly have in a petty noble and a Tatar?" The Lisovyk only growled.

Bohun latched his hand onto Andriy's arm. "Stay where you are."

"We must defend our Ataman!"

"The same Ataman who hasn't signaled us? That demon could have every wolf within miles upon us," Bohun replied.

"Allah!" came as a guttural cry; and with that the Tatar charged. The Lisovyk screeched, and a falcon dropped down; the bird thrust talons into Tatar eyes. Marko saw an eyeball fly into the air as he discharged his flintlock, killing the falcon. Aleksandr steadied his horse and tried to keep his hand in position; gunfire left him dizzy.

Hearing slowly returned. Marko sheathed his pistols and shouldered the Lisovyk's half-blind victim. He tore a spare shirt, and tied the cloth around the victim's head. If the Tatar had any sense he would flood the wound with alcohol. Liakhs were either in shock or simply too frightened to move.

"Take those two and let us leave," Aleksandr ordered, fumbling through a sack.

"Why?" How could such a simple word sound so bone wrenching? Aleksandr's fingers felt a knife, deer flesh, and the amulets!

Aleksandr felt no pride in his work; it looked as if the sigils had been scratched on with a yak hoof. He shouted Latin words, and hurled. As the amulet struck the forest demon it gave a sharp cry, releasing the hostages, who ran for horses. Aleksandr spurred his horse urging everyone, "Go!"

Marko held tight as his mount carried him off. He didn't dare to look back. The Pancerni covered Piludski's retreat with volleys of arrows. Aleksandr paused for one last look at the Lisovyk's captives and spurred his horse toward the forest, too. Piludski emptied his flintlock into horse meat and a Tatar smashed down; distraction for the demon.

No wolves. No armies of living birch trees. No hawk swarms.

Marko stopped shaking. Either they had escaped or the Lisovyk simply wasn't the master of nature from his grandfather's tales. Marko faced Andriy and pointed at his pipe. "Can I have that?"

"Enjoy," Andriy said, passing his ataman tobacco.

"Thank you," Marko was pleased to find that the instrument was still lit.

Bohun diverted his eyes from the Poles, who were deep in argument with the surviving Tatars, and turned to Aleksandr. "Why isn't he following?"

"Lisovyks rule limited areas so we are either out of his grasp or he has no interest in us."

"Why those two?"

Aleksandr twitched. "No idea."

"Oh," Bohun replied. There was awkward silence. The nobles rode between Pancerni gazing ahead; numbed by their taste of Tatary. Tatars rode in the middle, confident that Liakhs would risk war by attacking them.

❦ ❦ ❦

After many miles, the riders entered a village. Tatars rode east for the Khan's lands. Pancerni secured water and feed for horses while nobles stumbled into the tavern followed by Cossacks. Aleksandr took in the bar; a humble structure slightly larger than a hunting lodge, occupied by a handful of farmers. Marko ignored the scent of vomit and eased into a bench, a welcome comfort after hours in a saddle. Andriy scraped shit off his boots and ordered wine, hoping it wouldn't taste of vinegar.

Bohun sipped beer paid for with tribute from Kievan smugglers. He studied the nobles. One had blond hair, a face that was mostly smooth save for stubble, and wore a stained Kuntush which hung about the aristocrat's average-sized frame. The second was tall and wore a delia coat with a zupan hat over dark hair; both nobles wore fragmented cavalry boots. The Liakhs ignored the Zaporozhians, for the Cossacks were only mercenaries; probably Ruthenians or Vlachs, so no one of value.

"We should take another Turkish port," Marko suggested. Chaiki were the perfect war vessel; they sailed close to the waves, invisible to galleys.

"Eager to turn pirate again?" Bohun asked.

"Yes." A Cossack could be an infantryman one week and a corsair the next. Months ago Marko made a small fortune from the sale of a captured Muslim polacca ship. Why anyone would pay so much for half rotted wood was beyond him, but he didn't question the money.

Aleksandr spoke, "Those Tatars are weak and nearby; we can overtake them."

Andriy asked, "Do they have anything of value?"

"You would make a poor tradesman; their horses alone will fetch a small fortune," Bohun answered.

"You must forgive us, gentlemen," Marko said standing up with his brothers, "But we must depart." There were weak nods. The warriors left through the rear entrance to avoid pancerni. Aleksandr and his friends mounted quickly and within minutes they were out of the town, stalking Tatar prey.

❦ ❦ ❦

Andriy held his nadziak war hammer tightly; he had no fear left after his encounter with one of *Them*. Aleksandr rode in the front, eyes darting from the sun to the road ahead, fire tools in hand.

Bohun spotted a nearby hill, kicked his horse left toward the convenient look out point. He reached the top easily and was pleased by the view; fire from woods due east, a Tatar camp? Bohun returned and made his report.

"Keep your weapons close but not in hand," Marko ordered. No sense in sparking a battle with innocent pilgrims. Cossacks loaded muskets, readied sabres and tucked nadziaks into their cloaks, emptied pipes.

Aleksandr approached the tree line, shouting a Tatar greeting.

"Esselamu galeykum!"

No response. Andriy drew a sword; time for blood. The four raiders rode forward, hands filled with weapons.

Tatar corpses littered the crude campsite. They played with the bodies. A birch Lisovyk scratched its back with a hand and smiled. Domoviks danced on the one-eyed Tatar's body; they were albino-skinned, bald, and grinning. Aleksandr thought they were strictly household spirits. Thinking quickly he scooped up soil, poured it into a pouch.

Marko kicked his horse crying, "Ride for your very souls!" Bohun and Andriy snapped out of shock and panicking, they yanked reins like stranglers. Aleksandr leaped from his mount drawing a sword. Marko almost laughed, what use was steel against *Them*?

Aleksandr slashed out a circle. "In the name of the blessed Trinity, I consecrate this piece of ground for our defense; so that no spirit may have power to break these bounds prescribed here, through Jesus Christ our Lord."

"Ride!" Marko urged.

"Wait," Aleksandr pleaded, "we've never seen so many of *Them*." Aleksandr's friends halted, what sort of coward flees the unknown? A few Domoviks paced on the edge of Aleksandr's arcane border. The tiny ones laughed, it sounded like a frog gurgling.

"You think we are but petty demons? Oh, you have much to learn, hedge wizard."

"What are you?"

There was laughter. Andriy detected a more mundane sound, hoofs, a great number of riders. "Their friends," the Tiny Things stated, pointing at corpses.

"Spread out," Marko ordered as they ran for their horses, "Reunite at the hill!"

"Lighten supplies!" Aleksandr yelled; digging spurs into horseflesh. His mount sprang into a gallop. Andriy glanced south, saddle bags in the air. Five Tatars approached. Cossacks fanned out into the trees, as arrows hit bark.

Bohun rotated and fired a flintlock. A horse crashed down, spurting gore.

Marko gripped his horse's torso with his legs, turned and discharged a musket. A miss. The Tatars ceased shooting arrows and drew blades; they were gaining. As he seized the reins, the musket flew out of his hands, hitting the soil. The fear of death at infidel hands eclipsed the pain of losing a Vainakh rifle.

Branches whipped Aleksandr's face, and he nearly fell. Andriy squeezed his flintlock's trigger, but the shot soared over his target. "Shoot the horses!" Bohun advised, steed in midair.

"Right!" Andriy yanked himself down; a limb shot over his head. Feet separated him from a Tatar, sword shining. The infidel dropped arms, an invitation to duel!

No time for honor, Andriy threw his nadziak. A direct hit; the beak jutted from skull as blood splattered his opponent's kalpak. A quick blow sent his horse racing forward toward a clearing.

Aleksandr whipped his mount with a belt and turned a corner. "We're nearly out of the Khan's lands!"

Arrows rushed over the tree line, impacting dirt. The Tartars were away from home, and thanks to the sinking sun, their bows were useless. Cossack horses thundered towards the Dnieper, they had escaped!

❦ ❦ ❦

"A horse crashed down..."

Bohun rode in the center of their square holding a torch. Their sole source of illumination, he held it aloft like a Hetman's mace. Despite the apparent Tatar retreat, all four were prepared to receive cavalry and basic infantry tactics. Marko was in mourning for he had loved that musket's unrivaled accuracy, now an infidel was pawing it; assuming that the tool wasn't in pieces.

Aleksandr felt relief course through him; his book was still tucked away in the folds of his cloak. The text was a present from a Szlachic grateful for Aleksandr's help in banishing impotence. Over the years it became more than a tome, for he could recite the content from memory. It was effectively a talisman.

Months ago he had aided a cleric in the task of driving a demon, evoked by a young man, from Ternopil. The fool had attempted to summon a Goet to reveal the presence of hidden treasure; instead *It* was unleashed. Perhaps he hadn't drawn the appropriate sigils correctly, maybe the circles were imperfect, but the hell-beast plagued Ternopil. It infected dreams, stole infant souls, poisoned milk and corrupted innocents. Armed with the book, Aleksandr's banishing ritual required virtually no effort.

The men rode on, eager to return home to their beddings and furs.

"The Field of the Alans occupies a wide expanse. It is a wilderness in which there are no rulers...neither Alans nor others. Cossacks alone sometimes wander there 'searching' according to their custom for someone to devour. They live by booty and are subordinate to no one. They roam through the wide and empty steppe in detachments of three, six, ten, twenty or sixty persons and sometimes more."
-*Matvei Mekhovskii*

CHAPTER 4

"**f**or the crime of theft I sentence you to...," Marko glanced down at his worn copy of Russkaya Pravda, "...pay a fine of two ducats."

A young chern cursed and fished through a sack. "Here!" He tossed ducats at Marko's makeshift judge table: a plank balanced on logs.

"Dismissed." Marko's audience left 'court' in a small shed and back to work at shipmaking, herding, and sentry duty. The ataman gathered paper; the Sich used Russkaya Pravda and Marko's copy was rarely organized. The code was Novgorodian and punished crimes by fines, which provided atamans with additional money. If a man couldn't pay he had to work it off.

Bohun walked by Tatars; he was late. Riders galloped past and he stepped back from their hooves. Finally he ran, elbowing his way through chern.

He glanced east. Aleksandr was working near the wall. The sorcerer crouched over wood; a baidak was taking shape under his skilled carving hands. Aleksandr drove his shoulder into the work, stopping occasionally to brush off timber chips. Once the interior was complete he would bind reeds to the edge; soon the fleet would have a new addition.

As he approached the gate, Bohun waved. Aleksandr didn't glance up from carving. The gunman left the Sich; Ostap and Andriy stood outside, cloaked in smoke. "Ready lad?" Ostap asked, emptying his pipe.

Bohun suddenly realized that he had foolishly forgotten to load his rifle! After checking the lock and then the trigger, Bohun stood his half cocked musket on sand and began to load powder. He took a purse of powder measured out days ago from a pack across his shoulders and poured it down the barrel. Bohun gave the side of the barrel a sharp tap; the powder was set.

With the delicate touch of an icon painter, he placed a ball and patch on the muzzle and set both objects into the barrel. Bohun forced the ball down onto the charge and made sure it was firmly resting on top of the powder. He shouldered his rifle, ready to fire and kill any Turk or Tatar foolish enough to attack a Zaporozhian.

The party set off. Ostap wore faded riding boots, meat red Turkish trousers, and a linen shirt; an ataman should look his best. Andriy's costume was made up of a long shirt, pants from coarse fiber, leather shoes; all clothing that could survive a plunge. Bohun wore Western garb taken from an oak chest he had removed years ago from a smuggler's ship.

They arrived at the shore; savoring the river's sweet scents of seaweed and flowers while staring at the Dnieper gleaming under the sun like a newly forged blade. Ostap and the others walked across the crudely constructed dock to reach the line of chaiki boats bouncing on the waves. The trio entered a rowboat and pushed off from the docks; the swift current immediately dragged them into the Dnieper's center.

"We don't have to worry about rations," Andriy said tapping his pack "I brought nets."

Bohun leaned forward, "I've a deep hunger for sturgeon."

"Keep your mind on labor," Ostap barked.

"Yes, Ataman."

Ostap asked, "What did you take from Tsargrad?"

"Coins and a few rings," Bohun said, thinking of a bejeweled yatagan hidden in his kuren bunk.

"An Orta standard," Andriy answered, full of pride; he had humiliated a Janissary regiment through his theft of their prized banner.

"My compliments," the ataman replied, adjusting his hold on an oar.

"Look there!"

"I see it, Andriy," Bohun said, plunging his oar into rapids; the rock looked like a massive fragment blown off a castle wall by a siege cannon. All three put their shoulders into rowing. The current tossed them like whelps in a cradle. The boat narrowly slid past stone, and rock scratched hull wood.

"Fine job lads!" Ostap bellowed.

No response.

Bohun craned his neck for a view of glass clear water with steppe plains on either side where there was a lack of rocks. The current swiftness increased and all three were suddenly locked in clash with the river to keep their craft on course. Unlike a chaika, the rowboat had little weight. Ostap's thoughts turned to boyhood; throwing toy ships down into the falls. The current became gentle again. Cossacks lowered oars and enjoyed drifting.

The craft took a turn and land changed slightly; there were a few trees here and there. Bohun paddled left, to keep the boat on course, and his back throbbed. Ostap was smoking his reed pipe. Andriy counted flints with his weapon resting on a leg.

"Water?"

Bohun checked pockets, "Nothing; sorry."

Andriy handed Ostap a leather flask. "Take mine, ataman."

❦ ❦ ❦

Joseph motioned. "This way." The Sich had the appearance of a town emptied by plague; Cossacks were in church.

Knocking jolted Aleksandr awake; was all of Cossackdom trying to bring down his meager door? He rubbed eyes while adjusting his clothing and opened his door. It was Joseph and…

"We've met before," the guest stated, "may I come in?"

"Please, it would be an honor." Aleksandr tried to smile; he looked more like a rodent gnawing.

"Thank you," the man said, stepping into the cabin as if he had been incased into a box. "I was one of the hostages you aided."

The blond Szlachic! Aleksandr suddenly felt angry at how those nobles had ignored him and his fellow commoners.

"What brings you off the Rzeczpospolita's map Mister..?"

"Sapieha, Mecys Sapieha." He wore a jewel dotted cap, a fur coat stopping inches from the rough birch floor, and spotless boots.

Blood in the water! Joseph and Aleksandr locked eyes, and both understood the obvious; kill a noble, kill the Sich.

With gritted teeth, Aleksandr lied, "It's an honor to meet a member of such an illustrious house."

"I require your expertise and assistance."

"How so?" Aleksandr rolled his eyes towards heaven, had angels made him this whelp's guardian?

"That demon from the clearing…"

"They're not demons," Aleksandr interrupted, "demons can be controlled through holy names and formulae. They can only be banished."

"Those things stalk me, I need your help."

"How did you learn of me?"

"That isn't your concern. I'll pay the price of your choice."

"Shall we step outside?" Aleksandr turned from his Tatar acquaintance. "Joseph you're missing the service." Joseph hurried out; he had to report this to the hetman. Once Joseph was on Holy Ground, Aleksandr turned back to his aristocratic acquaintance. "Continue."

Mecys paced in imitation of the Sapieha patriarch's pose. "Those things torment me; they appear at random, cause pain, and take me places when I dream. Come to Kryvyi Rih, and help me." The Sapieha family clearly wanted their son away from politics; was Mecys a source of shame?

"I'll be ready to leave in minutes." Where was his saddle?

Mecys asked, "How do you command spirits?"

Aleksandr was turned with his back to the nobleman, "I use sacred names and formulae from a hierarchy that spirits are bound to spiritual authority. The problem is that your Antagonists may not be bound to that system."

Mecys paled. "You can't aid me?"

"I can shield you, but I may not be able to bind them; not without knowing their rules."

"I have a ship waiting." Color returned to Mecys' skin.

"I need to find my saddle."

❧ ❧ ❧

Bow wood dug into sand. Cossacks jumped out. As Bohun and Andriy pulled the craft out of water, Ostap enjoyed a smoke. The ataman sent up a silent prayer: Let the pleasure that tobacco brings ease the climb. A massive slope to the top of a cliff overlooking the meeting place between the Dnieper and sea; one of the many spy points the Cossacks used to maintain mastery over their waters.

Bohun volunteered, "I will go to the peak."

The others wished him well and settled into the beached chaika as he began his climb to the spy point's summit. Bohun's legs were weak from the river voyage so it was no surprise that he nearly tripped on the sharp rocks that lined the route up the steep hill thick with grass. He walked with an oar which he used for support and to sweep the ground in front of him for any vipers that could lay concealed in the yellow brush.

Pausing for breath, he turned around to stare at crystalline Dnieper surrounded by brown oaks and the sprawling steppe of waving yellow grass. He spotted distant bands of Zaporozhians on horseback; riding off to guard the steppe from Muslim predators or racing off in search off adventure. He was approaching the spy point's peak and the sheer height sent a brief wave of fear through him. Bohun felt like he was balancing on top of a guard tower. Finally, legs burning, he reached the summit and wearily stared at the vast dark sea that seemed to stretch on to the realms of ancient gods.

Terror. He couldn't breathe!

A galleot was flying the cursed crescent! An official member of the Ottoman navy, not a mere corsair polacca. Bohun fell several times as he ran downhill.

"The porogi are whirlpools or rocky places where the Dnieper continuously rolls over rock and boulders, some of which are underwater and others, just even with it. Several boulders are higher than the water level and make travel past them very dangerous, especially when the water is low. The travelers must leave their boats, at these extremely dangerous spots. Then getting into the water, by means of ropes or poles they lift the boats over the sharp rocks and carefully let them down on the other side. Those who are holding the boat with the ropes must pay great attention to those who are in the water, listening to their commands when to pull or releases the ropes so that the boat will not crash and be completely destroyed. There are at least twelve of these places."

-Erich Lassota Von Steblau, Hapsburg diplomat

CHAPTER 5

Aleksandr rushed out of the gates to join the rada assembly. Innumerable throngs were directly ahead, circled around the atamans and hetman, who stood on a large platform near the archery range. He stood at the back, next to a chern who held a torch. He struggled to hear the hetman's words over talk from the men around him.

"Ostap has already told you of the Turks in our waters, your vote?" Samiylo asked a formal, obvious question.

Cries filled the night air.

"Kill them!"

"War!"

"Skin Turks alive!"

Samiylo's mace went up for silence. The atamans would now withdraw to draw up battle plans.

Marko and Ostap joined a line into their Hetman's cabin. The door opened to reveal crude benches, and men entered and took seats. Samiylo was the last to go in; atamans stood at attention. The Hetman nodded, and everyone sat down.

"Marko, inform your fellow officers." 'The boy' only knew Ostap; atamans were elected and removed so frequently, he had no patience to keep up with the list.

"Turks are trying to contain us. An invasion would trigger war with Poles or the Novgorod republic."

Ostap stood. "It's only a group of builders with rowboats, why the fuss?"

Marko established eye contact with the elder warrior. "They didn't row here from Tsargrad. A ship could be in the Black Sea, maybe an entire fleet."

Ostap replied, "An idea." There was instant silence; the old man was a master tactician.

"These Cossacks serve for money almost all the states which call them, but also without money for robbery alone."
-Isaac Massa

CHAPTER 6

A boot smashed into his stomach. Aleksandr rolled off the bed groaning in pain. His eyes shot around the room, locked on a whelp in servant garb. "His grace requests your presence." A smug grin curved across his face.

Pure rage swept through Aleksandr at this wake up attack. "I'll be right there," he said wincing.

"Very well," the servant turned.

"One quick thing first." Aleksandr kicked legs and the lad hit the barge floor. Ignoring the agony, he grabbed hands and snapped fingers. The servant boy screamed like a whore giving birth.

"Stand up."

Terrified, the servant boy obeyed, where were the guards? Aleksandr drew his sword, the boy tried to shield himself with his arms as if he expected to be sliced to ribbons. The sorcerer swung the sword's blunt side into the boy's skull, he repeated the action several times; inflicting immense pain but failing to draw blood.

"Get out."

The servant boy crawled for dear life.

Aleksandr sat down, the pain was almost gone; beating that scum had produced a remarkable soothing effect. The mercenary sorcerer glanced out a window; Ternopil was nowhere in sight. There was time to sleep but he was far too awake. He dressed quickly; his client had provided trousers in English style, cavalry boots, even a linen shirt!

Aleksandr left the sleeping quarters. Mecys was waiting, flanked by guards. The nobleman held the servant boy by the collar. "I saw him kick you." He yawned. "Your verdict?"

"Sack the wretch."

"That's it?"

"Of course; the fool won't last a week on his own." The guards gasped, the master's strange friend was merciful and subtle!

"Wise choice." Mecys tossed servant boy to the guards. "One other thing."

"Yes?"

Mecys held up a feathered slouch hat. "To cover your top knot." The message was to blend in. A true noble cannot openly employ a dog from the Sich.

Aleksandr smiled at the insult. "Your Grace is far too generous."

"You'll find shaving utensils in sleeping quarters; I expect your beard to be gone by the time we dock."

"Of course."

Aleksandr retreated to his room, where were the tools? Soon he found an impressive kit: a marble case with multiple razors, a mirror, and a brush. The few times the magus shaved it was usually with a knife blade over a pool. After locating a pitcher of water he slathered cheeks with soap and began to slice off hair.

Minutes later Aleksandr was baby faced. He pressed a cloth scrap over cuts. The sorcerer took another glance at the kit; only a Liakh would own something so whorish and womanly! Fatigue washed over him. He lay down again; better to be asleep than to talk with Mecys.

Nearly an hour later Aleksandr stared at Ternopil, rubbing his eyes. Patches of two story homes, papist cathedrals, and well-dressed people filled the streets. The city's scope shocked him; he was raised on open plains, these narrow shit-slick roads were alien to him.

He left the boat with the entourage of his patron and walked toward the horses. "You will ride with me," Mecys called from a coach.

"Your grace is very generous," Aleksandr said, climbing into the carriage.

"No, I just don't want you to become lost, at least not until you rid me of these *Pests*." Aleksandr was planning to follow Mecys, but saw no reason to mention it. He settled in and avoided eye contact with the noble, preferring to stare out the window.

Up close the city wasn't impressive; the architecture differed little from that of settled Cossack towns. A young man was groping a prostitute like livestock; Aleksandr felt pangs of sympathy for the misguided girl. He tore his eyes away from child beggars to look at Mecys; so serene, calm, assured.

"Are your tools ready?"

Aleksandr hand instinctively reached for his sack of books. "Yes."

"Good, good," the Szlachic knocked on the ceiling with his ceremonial sword. "Faster! Put that whip to good use!"

Aleksandr scraped waste from his boots on the coach ladder, ignoring a frown writhing across Mecys' face. He turned around, what type of home did his client infest?

It was an apartment. Portraits covered walls, baroque furniture on oak floors, and a crude chandelier that evoked memories of brothels. It seemed that Mecys' father preferred to keep him away from court life. Was the young noble a source of shame?

"Please sit."

"Very generous of you." Aleksandr gently lowered himself into a very delicate looking chair.

"How do you begin?"

Stress hit. Aleksandr had no plan so he stalled. "Show me where they usually appear."

"Follow." Mecys lead him into the bedroom "Days ago I woke up with one perched on my knee. I passed out from shock."

"My sympathy," Aleksandr said, trying to appear concerned. What to do? Standard exorcism wouldn't take, and an amulet could protect Mecys but that wouldn't be enough to snare the noble.

Mecys lead him to the dining room. "They often jump on my plate."

"Do they interfere with your eating?"

"No, thankfully."

"Have they tried to murder you?"

"Not yet."

"That's a relief, at least until you pay my fee," he laughed. Silence. The frown grew.

"Let's go to the library," Mecys said with a growl. Aleksandr followed his client through an oak hallway lined with family portraits and entered the library. He gasped at shelf after shelf loaded with volumes; literacy was common in the Sich but they had few books. Most men learned letters to avoid relying on Jewish scribes.

"They appeared over there," Mecys pointed to the room's center, "Two times."

"Two is a very powerful number," Aleksandr almost laughed at the lie. "It's very significant." Mecys paled. Aleksandr smiled. "Is that all?"

"Yes."

Aleksandr opened an Angelic grimoire and spread out a cloth covered in sigils; his 'table' of practice. A slab of onyx did for a scrying medium; crystals shattered too easily. No wand; he didn't need toys for beginners. The magus emptied a pouch and small cuts of fabric fell; they were magical lamens.

Aleksandr sat down. Relaxation evaded his body: One mistake and he could bid farewell to a very profitable future relationship with a member of one of the commonwealth's greatest houses. He began to speak:

"In the name of the blessed Trinity, I consecrate this piece of ground for our defense; so that no evil spirit may have power to break these bounds prescribed here, through Jesus Christ our Lord."

Skipping an incense invocation, no Cossack had time for such womanly scents, he continued:

"In the name of the blessed and holy Trinity, I do desire thee, thou strong mighty angel, Michael, that if it be the divine will of him who is called Tetragrammaton and the Holy God, the Father, that thou take upon thee some shape as best becometh thy celestial nature, and appear to us visibly, and answer our demands in as far as we shall not transgress the bounds of the divine mercy and goodness, by requesting unlawful knowledge; but that thou wilt graciously shew us what things are most profitable for us to know and do, to the glory and honour of his divine Majesty, who liveth and reigneth, world without end. Amen.

"Lord, thy will be done on earth, as it is in heaven. Make clean our hearts within us, and take not thy Holy Spirit from us.

"O Lord, by thy name, we have called him, suffer him to administer unto us. And that all things may work together for thy honour and glory, to whom with thee, the Son, and blessed Spirit, be ascribed all might, majesty and dominion. Amen."

A presence filled the room, a light color tinted air. A strange sensation not unlike lightning coursed through each man. Mecys was elated; he stood with an Angel!

Aleksandr blinked at an image of Michael in his scrying stone; a proud figure clad in Greek fashion, standing behind a blend of colors. Aleksandr's emotional reaction was restrained; this was routine.

"Michael in the name of God the Father, the Son, the Holy Ghost and the Tetragrammaton. I ask that you protect Mecys and his home from all spirits save from the Angels of Heaven."

He paused for breath.

"Thou great and mighty spirit, inasmuch as thou camest in peace and in the name of the ever blessed and righteous Trinity, so in this name thou mayest depart, and return to us when we call thee in his name to whom every knee doth bow down. Fare thee well, Michael; peace be between us, through our blessed Lord Jesus Christ. Amen."

"To God the Father, eternal Spirit, fountain of Light, the Son, and Holy Ghost, be all honour and glory, world without end. Amen."

Michael's presence faded, Mecys and Aleksandr suddenly felt cold and frail. Mecys was filled by an impulse; retreat to bed, curl up and weep. Aleksandr was exhausted; apparent from the demanding nature evocation his throat ached.

"Could I have water?"

"Of course!" Mecys raced off to the kitchen. His servants left weeks ago; staff had little tolerance for a demon-infested home.

"Thank you!"

Mecys spoke: "What I saw…"

"You should keep to yourself."

Mecys shrugged. "The inquisition doesn't operate in Commonwealth lands."

"True." Not openly at least… "But please do not speak my name freely."

Mecys chortled. "You think I want friends to know I hired a Cossack heretic?"

"No sir," Aleksandr ignored thoughts of extortion.

"I feel better already!"

"Glad to hear it, sir."

"Now then your fee…."

"Yes?

"Name any sum."

"The passage from the common life of man unto a Magical life, is no other but a sleep, from that life; and an awaking to this life; for those things which happen to ignorant and unwise men in their common life, the same things happen to the willing and knowing Magician."

-Arbatel: of the Magic of the Ancient

CHAPTER 7

Bohun's hands were about to tear off, he was convinced of it. Cossacks hauled ships on a crude dirt path; atamans shouldered burdens. Smoke specked the midday sky: there were Turks.

Sheer rage drove Zaporozhians; Muslims defiling Ruthenian waters! Marko adjusted his hold on a rope; the chaiki balanced on crude wheels, men used cords thrust through oar holes to pull vessels. Ostap led the way on foot; using horses or the river would alert sentries.

Andriy dropped his sabre, panicking he reached for it, fingers fumbling wildly. He couldn't halt the formation and he couldn't face infidels unarmed. "Here," Noman held up his comrade's sword, a lovely piece of craftsmanship modeled after Vainakh blades.

"Thank you." Andriy held the sabre in one hand and a line in his left for there was no time to strap the sword to his waist.

"Halt!" Ostap held up his rapier, a war prize taken off a corpse after battling Venetian papists. "From here we lower our voices and speak only when necessary." His men nodded at the commands of their temporary commanding ataman. "Those who want to attack the Turks camped on the Dnieper's bank, step forward."

Noman and Andriy along with nine others walked toward Ostap; in one fluid motion the warriors took muskets off their backs. "The rest of you, continue toward the launch point. You already know when to act." Bohun ignored rope burns, blood lubricated lines, and trudged on.

Andriy sidestepped through brush; fellow gunmen moved through woods like Lisovyks. Evidence of a Turkish infestation grew with every step; small trails, feces, and garbage. Soon they heard voices and the camp came into view revealing Yaya infantry and Tufekci musketeers, napping civilian workers, and sentries that Noman could count on one hand. He spotted coils of great chain besides sleeping Muslims. Did they think that Cossacks could be fenced off?

Cossacks crouched into firing positions, ramrods and shot at their sides. The men slowly pulled back the hammers and aimed; enturbaned heads entered their sights.

Fire!

Turks fell like cattle; very few missed targets. With the deafening gun-fire Andriy was certain he would never enjoy music again. Zaporozhians dropped rifles and ran through water, blades swinging. The Turks had done one thing correctly: they had chosen a spot with little current; an easy cross.

Noman raced at an officer who frantically tried to load a musket; too late. Noman's sabre spilled entrails.

Andriy jumped back from a sword. He scrambled up from sand and lunged, and the Turk parried. The infidel looked half awake and he retreated, slashing wildly as if he was scrawling calligraphy in the wind. Andriy easily blocked his opponent's polyos and thrust. Ruthenian steel penetrated infidel ribs.

As Andriy lowered his sword, gore flew off the blade. His former opponent wore civilian clothes, in life he must have been a carpenter. Turks were suited for little else save labor.

❀ ❀ ❀

The camp was now a slaughter field. Albin pursued the only soldier left with a pulse.

"Wait," Noman called.

"My kill!" The stupid boy ignored orders! Albin sprinted across sand; his prey was seconds away from hell! Albin heard a click, and then everything became… pain. Lifeblood was everywhere as he fell.

Noman aimed, easy kill. Albin's comrades raced towards him. Andriy tried to feel pity for the fool writhing in dust which was quickly turning to muck from so much blood. Noman laid a finger on the Turk's neck. Flies covered his wounds, he was stone dead. Could the same be said of young Albin?

"Shoulder wound," Andriy said. "In and out."

"Does that…?"

"You'll live." Andriy paused to catch his breath, "Even longer if you learn to follow orders."

"S-s-sorry!" Albin clutched his shoulder, trying not to cry out.

Oleg spoke. "Who has ale?"

Noman held up leather flasks, "Will this do?"

"Perfect." Oleg poured beer into the wounded boy's mouth.

"Pour it on the wound," Andriy said, adding, "You can squeal if you want boy; time for silence is over."

N-n-no!" Albin gnashed his teeth as the liquid burned into his flesh, washing away sand.

"Bandage his wound, I have to signal." Andriy walked across corpses and accidentally stepped on a stomach; it felt like a brothel mattress. He fired two pistols, pried from rotting digits.

❦ ❦ ❦

Across the Dnieper, Marko, at the sound of twin pistol shots, dropped his sabre; this was the signal to begin rowing. The vessel soared through shallow waters; the Dnieper and Black sea met in area with coves, brush, creeks, and islands. A galley could become well hidden, a chaika would be invisible. Marko was part of the second step of Ostap's strategy: locate and take any Turkish ships. Ostap was in charge of the first boat, Marko had command of the second, both men stood at the helms of their vessels.

Chaiki left a cove and passed a swamp. Ahead was a maze of rocks and miniature islands.

"Slow now!" Ostap ordered. Even after all his years in the steppe and at sea, the sight of the Black Sea stones made him pour sweat.

Joseph turned in his seat, raised his oar and pushed off from a rock. Marko dipped a staff in front of the ship, testing for underwater boulders. The small flotilla inched through rocks and finally reached islands.

Ostap held up an arm and softly called to Bohun, "Go ashore, if there are Turks nearby they must have heard the battle."

"Yes, ataman," Bohun said as lowered himself into the surf, leaving all weapons behind except for a cheap sword; little more than a comfort. He waded past half-rotted entrenchments of logs and earthworks; a considerable defense against invasion.

Bohun reached a small moss-carpeted island. Turk spies could be anywhere. Or would a rusalka drag him down as swam?

He quickly searched the island, little more than a sand bar. No signs of past camps. He scanned, shielded by brush, but saw nothing, as more islands blocked his sight.

After securing the throwaway sabre across his shoulder blades, Bohun slid into the water and began to swim. He strained his ears for any sound, no matter how innocent, which could betray the presence of a galley waiting to destroy Cossacks. From a distance it would be easy to mistake him for a rock; only half of his head poked out of water.

Here Bohun was baptized. Here Bohun swam for the first time. Here he bed his first woman. It was his sea.

Bohun swallowed water and felt arm muscles burn as islands came closer. He climbed rocks and stumbled ashore, crouching; the moss felt like a noble's feather mattress. He became statue still and snake crawled behind a tree cluster. He lay still, taking time to catch his breath.

Terror rushed though Bohun; the smallest mistake would lead to his flaying or impalement. Years ago on a trading expedition he had viewed remains of impaled Klephs; stakes through carrion. Slowly he parted the brush.

A Turkish ship was just a fraction of a mile away: a galleot, crafted for swift raids, possessing one mast and few guns. This was a vessel of choice for scum like Murat Reis or Jack Ward. It was anchored off a tiny isle that was too small for battle.

❧ ❧ ❧

Minutes later:

"How many?" Marko and Ostap crowded Bohun, who looked half drowned.

"Five," the scout squinted, "at least."

"Fine," Ostap glanced at a cannon. "Continue as planned." The old man effortlessly leaped back to his chaika.

"Prepare muskets," Marko ordered. Cossacks lined up in front of a small compartment in the ship; a dry haven for paper and powder. Warriors withdrew bundles of ramrods and began loading rifles.

Bohun shed clothing; taking a ship required speed. Since a young recruit had volunteered to load a gun for him, he sorted through other weapons and chose a schiavona. He stabbed the sky to test his new blade; it was excellent.

Marko loaded cannon. He scraped the muzzle's interior clean with a rammer then untied a sack and filled the charger with powder, brushing any spill into the pouch. With the utmost care he loaded the charger into the gun and packed down power. Bohun's few dry garments on the floor caught 'the boy's' eye.

"Can I use those?" He gestured to cloth.

"Have them, I shall wear Turk silk this afternoon," Bohun said with a smile.

Marko mumbled his thanks and rammed fabric for a wad. He gripped drenched cloth and used it to mop out excess power. Delicately he laid a ball into the gun, completing his task.

Ostap finished supervising the loading of cannons and dropped his hand, which meant row!

Chaiki sped forward like ancient Varangian ships. They were clear of rocks, free to demonstrate mastery of the Dnieper and Black Sea.

The tiny fleet split into a hunting pattern. Marko's vessel went right. The chaika under Ostap's command look a left turn.

Cossacks dug their shoulders into oars and pine shards penetrated flesh. The ships darted from rocks to reeds to islands as camouflage. Bohun looked up from his oar and caught a sight of the enemy ship; such a clean vessel, it looked as though it had never seen combat.

Ostap peered out through reeds just moments way from entering cannon range. He thrust a piece of wood into a coal tin for a torch. As he gave the command to enter battle, fear touched every oarsman.

The chaika sped towards the rear of the targeted ship. Without thinking, no time, Ostap brought the torch down, firing the cannon. A direct impact and the stern exploded; timber flew, limbs floated. Deathly cries filled every ear.

As Marko's vessel entered open water, Muslims scrambled. The Cossacks weren't in range. A naval Janissary set off the bow's culverin. Oarsmen swerved left. It was a miss but water splashed Christian faces.

Marko almost fell as he discharged his pistol and the ball smashed through the bow. The galleot's crew had no choice but to stand and engage the enemy; the anchor chained them down and with both ends demolished the ship was trapped. Men under the ataman's command aimed and fired a thunderous volley that slaughtered Muslims; few Christians missed targets. Marko gave the order to retreat and his men had to reload then attack from a new position.

Ostap's chaika veered right, narrowly evading cannon fire. Now they knew the exact range! Ostap's second shot destroyed the main cabin but he was aiming for the mast. The elder warrior waved a pike as a signal for the third step.

۝ ۝ ۝

Marko stood by a loaded cannon and returned his fellow ataman's signal by throwing a hat. Ostap and Marko aimed cannons and fired. It was a direct center hit. The once mighty ship had the appearance raided serf village.

The cannon ball supply was exhausted. Chaiki cut through the Black Sea to take the galleot!

Ostap's ship went for the center. The last attack destroyed the enemy's main guns, leaving a vulnerable shell. The ataman caught sight of a gunner loading a falconet. Ostap drew a flintlock and fired, hitting the man in the shoulder. The chaika slammed into its target, Cossacks swarmed aboard climbing on ladders, jumping for ropes. A number of riflemen remained aboard to provide cover fire.

Marko's ship halted at the rear. Cossacks hurled grappling hooks, biting into wood. Joseph and other men scaled aboard, within minutes they stood on enemy ground.

Men drew sabres and jumped off quarter deck wood, to battle! A sailor in common Turk garb ran at Marko, who drew a pistol. No time to fire! Marko dodged a kilij slash and struck his enemy's forehead with the pistol butt and the Muslim hit wood. Marko stepped on his throat and watched the Mohammedan's face turn azure. A kick to the skull finished him.

Ostap emptied his flintlock into a naval Janissary's heart. Slowly he approached the slouching Ottoman; unarmed, barely breathing. Ostap gouged eyes and sank his sabre blade into entrails. No intoxicant like gore! The captain's quarters were not far.

Bohun blocked a thrust from a Yaya's yataghan. The soldier howled in Turk, alien chatter. Blades locked as both fighters rammed each other. For a split second he made eye contact with that infidel. Bohun swung a foot around his enemy's leg, and yanked. The Yaya stumbled down, thrusting his sword into air; the blade sliced into Bohun's forearm and metal scraped bone.

The Turk tried to stand on the quaking ship. Bohun jumped, dodging his enemy's swinging sword. The Cossack stamped a boot down on infidel wrist, disarming his opponent. Bohun stabbed down, the ship's lurching threw off his sabre. The blade dug into shoulder meat and the Turk howled like a trapped wolf cub. Quickly Bohun pulled his sword out of a bone, slashed the man's throat and took in his dying breaths.

Ostap grabbed braces and climbed onto the edge, away from battle, nearing the captain's cabin. With ropes in one hand and a flintlock in the other he slowly sidestepped across the edge, inches away from a fall onto rocks. Combat was starting to die down. The Turks were driven back, more and more fled below deck. A thrill coursed through Ostap: No Cossack had fallen!

Joseph stooped into a firing position and jabbed a pike at a charging Janissary who blocked the attack with a bayoneted musket. The Mohammedan counterattacked, stabbing Joseph's thigh. Writhing in agony, the Tatar screamed, but the Janissary stood there.

Joseph realized his Ottoman foe wanted to bask in Cossack pain. Wandering hands seized tackle block and Joseph threw it; the rigging smashed into skull, felling the Janissary.

"A kick to the skull finished him."

Joseph climbed up, ignoring his pain. Pike in hand he speared his enemy in the eye. Gargling cries, spasms, and then nothing.

The Tuma Cossack scanned the deck as he nursed his wound; the battle was almost over.

❧ ❧ ❧

Ostap dropped from the main boom; his bones felt like reeds under a carriage. Slumped against the wall, he wheezed and unbuckled his sabre. Standing out of way he pushed open the cabin door.

Pistol fire tore through paper thin walls; a Turkish greeting. Ostap crashed in. A short, skinny bearded man at a desk dropped his pistols then raised palms in surrender. A bulbous turban covered the captain's head, a small armor plate rested over robes and he wore patterned red trousers above boots.

Ostap exited the main cabin, pushing the bound captain forward. Apparently his name was Kutbeddin. The ship was theirs! The Cossack throng broke into cheer; they danced, stabbing sabres toward the sky!

❧ ❧ ❧

"Bohun!" Ostap yelled.

Bohun jogged across carrion. "Ataman?"

"Bring tools," he said, pointing with a dagger to a lower deck filled with Turks expecting Cossacks to rush down into musket fire.

"Yes, Ostap."

The elder ataman turned to Joseph. "The captain has alcohol in his quarters, pour spirits on your wound and bandage the flesh."

"Yes, ataman." Joseph almost ran; he would collapse on a Turk mattress!

Marko navigated through cheering Cossacks and approached Ostap. "Congratulations on a successful attack."

"It's too soon to celebrate."

"Right, right," Marko replied.

"Back to work," Bohun said as he dropped a sack. Hammer and spikes spilled out.

Cossacks hammered boards over exits; within minutes surviving Turks were entombed.

Other men collected enemy weapons, bayoneted corpses, stripped Kutbeddin's lavish cabin naked of anything valuable. Joseph joined the men, including the bound captain; leaving for the chaiki. Two remaining Cossacks flooded the decks with oil. Finally Ostap brought a torch, and ignited the deck.

The trio climbed down to waiting ships, most men either ignored the dangling corpse or joked about it. "The boy killed a lad," Bohun said, chortling; anything to take his mind off his forearm pain. Marko laughed as he stopped aboard Ostap's vessel, pausing to throw a jarrand. A torch touched the oil soaked wood and fire began to consume the hull.

They watched flames blanket the galleot. They heard screams of burning men. They smelled roasting flesh, a scent like boar on a spit.

ꙮ ꙮ ꙮ

Tears soaked the former captain's silks; he had failed. Elite troops of his imperial majesty slain by Christian pig-eaters in fishing boats! The spectacle brought him back to one of his first assignments as a soldier, guarding Hurufi infidels sentenced to execution. At the time Kutbeddin had thought heretics deserved death by fire; now his guilt was so overpowering, he could barely stand. A blow from one of his captors brought him back to the present.

"Careful," he said in Latin, a common language in the Rzeczpospolita, "No one ransoms a corpse."

"You think you're to be ransomed?" Ostap's laughter made Kutbeddin quake.

"I've been to Tsargrad, a boring town," Marko said, turning around. "Right, men?" There was jeering, laughter and random gunshots.

The chaika carrying atamans set off for the beach. Marko regretted burning the galleot but the hetman's orders were clear: it was far too dangerous to ransom men or sell ships at this time. Marko turned to their sole captive. Kutbeddin felt like meat on a hook. No sense in jumping overboard, musketeers would pick him off in seconds. "Can I have his rings?"

Ostap frowned, "Wait."

'The boy' called to Joseph, "How is your leg?"

Joseph sat up from his fur bed in the center deck. "I'm worried, the flesh could become corrupted."

ꙮ ꙮ ꙮ

"They're back!" A sentry shouted.

Andriy and his companions started yelling, "Huzzah! Huzzah! Huzzah!" Men would have fired muskets in jubilation if only they had shot and powder to waste. Only one chaika though?

The ship ran aground and Cossacks eagerly leaped for land. Andriy approached the atamans.

"What of the other ship?"

Ostap removed his cap and explained, "We didn't lose a single man; the other chaika remained to make sure no Turk will escape the fire." He kicked Kutbeddin into the mud. "Gentlemen, within moments the infidel ship will lie at the bottom of Ruthenian waters!"

"Huzzah! Huzzah!"

Marko stumbled out of the vessel. "We have one wounded." He noticed Oleg's cries of pain. "Construct a litter for both men."

Andriy nodded and he returned to camp. Where was that axe? "Noman," he cried, "We have wood to chop for a stretcher."

As Zaporozhians spilled out of the ship, Marko announced, "All bounty seized from the galleot will be divided once the last chaika returns!"

Ostap drew a kard dagger and shouted, "Kill this Turk, who would have shackled you to the Sultan's yoke!" Cossacks drew blades and waited; atamans should slash first.

Kutbeddin covered his face with hands; a weak flesh shield.

Men advanced with knives, eager for blood. Marko knew that the captain would die a brutal, agonizing death. Quickly he drew his pistol, stepped in front of his men, discharging his flintlock into his enemy's skull: a swift honorable death.

❀ ❀ ❀

No screaming? Were they dead, or merely unconsciousness from smoke? Water began to conquer the galleot and it slowly sank like a leaf floating off an oak. First the hull and then the mast became submerged. The keel went down, followed by the masts; finally the rudder disappeared. Within minutes a member of the sultan's armada, a vessel for Turk hordes lay among sea weed and sturgeon.

Bohun stared at mast tips, waiting to see if any lucky Ottomans had escaped. There were floating banners in calm waters.

The entertainment was over, so men returned to seats and began rowing; craving food or a kuren bunk. A sense of relief rather than victory hung over the chaika.

Without any reason to hide, Cossacks easily sped past islands, like mountain goats leaping from cliff to ledge. The ship halted as they entered the barriers of wood and stone. Zaporozhians slowly poled through the maze; any other vessel would have been lost. Bohun struggled to keep the chaika straight as he shielded guns from waves with his body. Soon oarsmen cleared the harrowing stretch of obstacles, and a straight route lay ahead!

❀ ❀ ❀

Kutbeddin was alive; was this an act of God? The former officer's captors had planned a slow death; after stabbing they lashed him to a pine to watch him bleed out like veal.

Were the Christians staring? Kutbeddin was close to death and his vision had become twisted. He focused and the infidels stood in a ring, inches away from the tide.

❦ ❦ ❦

"For Joseph, an extra share." Marko knelt to hand his friend a sack of daggers, ducats and rings. Honor was not the sole reward of being wounded in battle; atamans and chern received equal shares

Oleg rolled in his stretcher. "What about..?"

Ostap looked up from coins and precious silks. "You get the same share as the rest."

"My wound!"

Ostap fingered pockets, where was that tobacco? "In the process of failing to follow orders, you should thank the Father that you're not gull food. No Cossack rewards stupidity."

Marko counted ducats. The plunder was divided equally; the remaining money would be deposited into a common fund. He asked a question dancing through every Cossack head.

"What of the wine?"

Ostap glanced at Kutbeddin's considerable supply. "We save that for the Sich." It was motivation for the return voyage.

Marko approached Kutbeddin, fingers curled around an Ottoman pistol. He stopped in front of the captive, and after making eye contact, he began to slowly load the pistol, taking great care with wadding, powder. 'The boy' shot Kutbeddin again. There were rib shards, lung chunks, and muscle flew. Marko dragged a corpse back to camp; leaving a sinew trail. The camp broke quickly; Zaporozhians gently brought their wounded aboard ships, the ex-captain's body was set adrift in a boat for Turks to find.

"When they meet with any Galley or Vessel (which they discover at a better and greater distance than they can be discovered their boats being but two foot and a half above water) they approach towards them till night, keeping about a league's distance, and then well observing the place where they saw the vessel they begin to rowe about midnight with all their force and encompassing it about, take it unaware, it being impossible for a vessel beset with such a number of boats all at once to disengage or defend itself; they take out the money, guns and all merchandise which they can conveniently carry away and afterwards sink the ship, they being not dextrous enough to carry her off..."

-Pierre Chevalier, witness of Cossack piracy.

CHAPTER 9

Days later

Marko's head burned with pain! It was if a lytavr was being played in his skull! Where were his trousers? He dressed quietly then left his quarters. His kuren was graveyard silent with chern recovering from celebration. The ataman's memory was incomplete; something about leaping over a fire to win a bet, and a drunken horse race.

Marko wandered around in a haze. The rest of the Sich was humming with activity; recruits were leaving for patrol. Would they encounter Tatars? He walked into Ostap's kuren and found Bohun roasting boar for breakfast. "Sit," Bohun pointed at stumps around the cooking fire.

"My thanks," Marko replied, settling into a rough seat. Bohun handed him a slab of meat. It was greasy and overcooked but good.

"To our most generous hetman," Bohun said, referring to how Samiylo had agreed to temporarily allow women into the Sich for celebrations.

"Hear, hear," he replied, making a mock salute with his flask.

Bohun doused the flames with water from a bucket and carved flesh. Marko glanced left to see a pack of riders returning; since women were not normally allowed in the Sich, victorious men would ride out to towns to find women to bed.

"Did you have any a company last night?"

"A short girl in a tavern," Bohun replied, "with raven hair."

"I should launch another raid," Marko joked, "Just as an excuse to have her."

"You could always become settled," Bohun suggested.

"Leave the Sich for the villages of settled Cossacks? Balance raising whelps with raiding Tatars? You speak of hell!"

"Aleksandr," Bohun said pointing south.

Marko craned his neck; the sorcerer was walking near the church grounds.

Bohun spat gristle and stood up. "Join us! This pig won't last long."

49

Aleksandr broke into a sprint, eager for fresh meat.

He quickly passed kureni with lost belongings hanging from posts, pelts, and shit mounds. Zaporozhians were supposed to bury feces; one of the Sich's few rules but very difficult to enforce. Chern guilty of minor crimes were often sentenced to the duty of cleaning up shit.

Aleksandr took a seat, ignoring the moist wood.

Marko made eye contact. "When did you return?"

"I don't remember," Aleksandr lied.

"Too much beer, eh?"

"Something like that," the magus replied, lips twisting into a smirk. They wasted no time sharing accounts of recent exploits. Aleksandr felt a sting of shame at having been away.

Bohun dug a bork hat out of a pack. "I took this off a Janissary."

Aleksandr made a face. "You're not going to wear it?"

"No! I just want to have a collection of keepsakes lining the mantle once I'm settled with a hoard of whelps."

Marko swatted at cockroaches. "You're going to bind yourself to one girl?"

Bohun shrugged and sawed meat with a Persian dagger. "Not until I capture an orta's banner."

"Ah." Was the gunman serious? Marko had lost interest years ago. "If you're going to commit suicide, why not attack Liakh's fallen angels?"

Bohun chuckled at Marko's ignorance, sad that he didn't know the love of a good woman. "Tin wings would look lovely over a fireplace."

Aleksandr yanked fat off flesh. "Get me a pancerni helmet; the perfect soup bowl."

"Maybe this meat would taste better fried on an armor plate," Marko said, tossing bones.

"Make way!" Ostap's voice penetrated morning air. The ataman was dressed in mismatched silk with a chamber pot balanced on his skull; a parody of a noble.

"Forgive us, oh great one!" Cossacks stood up chortling, making pretend bows.

The elder reached for clouds. "Kiss my rings; it's the closest you get to what used to be your money." Marko thought his sides would split from laughing so hard.

Ostap made a face; mock-serious. "You dare giggle at me? Why...why I'll... do something that doesn't require stained palms!" Bohun howled, nearly falling into fire, in laughter.

Aleksandr smiled. "Come sit; eat what you've earned with that play acting."

As he took a seat, Ostap distributed valuables. "Take these trinkets; I'm years, at best, away from coffin worms."

"Nonsense."

"Don't say that!"

Eyes fell on Aleksandr. "You take on as if there is something that can kill you." That's better, everyone else glanced away. Eager to shift subjects he asked, "How are the wounded?"

Ostap sank his teeth into overcooked pig flesh. "Joseph's recovered. Oleg…" he gnashed his teeth, "Less so."

Bohun gathered infidel clothing, but Aleksandr collected personal debts. "What can I do?"

"The boy's in my kuren," Ostap said, leaping up. Aleksandr followed him on the short walk to his quarters.

"How critical is the wound?" the sorcerer asked, stepping through an entrance.

"You'll see in a few moments," the ataman said, ducking his head.

The kuren was empty; save for Oleg lying on a coat. Aleksandr stared at the young man. No sign of fever! "Show me the wound."

Oleg came to. Bleary, he squinted. "What?"

Ostap leaned over. "Lift up your shirt." Time to play the grandfather role. The recruit obeyed, displaying flesh bordering corruption.

"Your view?"

"Burn it out," Aleksandr stated. There was silence. "After he's drunk; I'll assist with my methods. Do you have a blade, Oleg?"

"Aye," he replied, fingering a skinning knife.

"Ostap, cleanse the knife with flame, cool it with water and drain the corrupted blood," Aleksandr said, gesturing to a torch.

Aleksandr drew a dagger and Oleg recoiled. "This isn't for you," the sorcerer explained, seizing a chunk of wood. Carefully he carved Jupiter's Seal, an X in the center of a circle, upon the object. "Hold this," he said tossing the fragment at the patient.

"The knife is prepared," the ataman announced.

Oleg spoke. "Cut." Aleksandr withdrew to a corner to ready himself as Ostap sliced through sick meat. Ignoring Oleg's squeals of pain, the sorcerer prayed, attaching himself to every word. He had to be *clean* to contact the forces he was about to call upon.

Ostap's voice said, "Finished."

Aleksandr pocketed his prayer rope, and approached the patient. "Prepare the blade to burn flesh again." Ostap nodded, reaching for the torch while Oleg began to greedily suckle at a flask. Seeing that Ostap was holding the knife over flame, Aleksandr began.

"In the name of the blessed Trinity, I consecrate this piece of ground for our defense; so that no evil spirit may have power to break these bounds prescribed here, through Jesus Christ our Lord."

A deep breath. Now the orphic hymn to open Jupiter to aid healing.

"O Jove much-honor'd, Jove supremely great, to thee our holy rites we consecrate..."

Was the room alive? Ostap felt as if he was standing in the belly of a giant while the Invisible Force flowed through Oleg, surging through his teeth and bones.

Aleksandr huffed in relief; an orphic hymn from memory, not a single error! He savored the sensation and presence of Jupiter; an ecstatic pulse coursed through him.

Ostap touched the dagger to flesh. A Don Cossack, one of the few survivors of Yermak's expedition, had taught him this crude treatment. Oleg howled, yet the pain was endurable, somewhat dulled. He squeezed the wood chunk, and relief increased. The timber scrap was not a talisman; it served to draw Jupiter to Oleg.

Ostap watched rot burn away. Oleg passed out. Aleksandr shut his eyes; a scene unfolded in his mind's eye, a vast tunnel! Light of every color blended together; a web in center.

"What do you think?" Ostap's voice snatched him back to earth.

Aleksandr rubbed tears out of his eyes and glanced at the wound, formerly infected flesh now fused together. "Good. Do you have any more beer?"

"Right here." Ostap reached for a flash.

"Drown the wound in alcohol."

"Aye," Ostap said, obeying.

Aleksandr began to close. "Thou great and mighty Jupiter, inasmuch as thou camest in peace and in the name of the ever blessed and righteous Trinity, so in this name thou may depart, and return to us when we call thee in his name to whom every knee doth bow down. Fare thee well, Jupiter; peace be between us, through our blessed Lord Jesus Christ. Amen."

"To God the Father, eternal Spirit, fountain of Light, the Son, and Holy

Ghost, be all honour and glory, world without end. Amen."

The room felt dead. Ostap felt hallow. He checked Oleg's wound. "Job well done."

"Thank you," Aleksandr replied, walking out. He hiked across the Sich; the cooking fire was abandoned and looked like the site of a wildcat kill. Turning right he continued toward his quarters, nodding at a passing Greek carrying an old doglock pistol, who grunted in return.

Aleksandr quickly entered his quarters. Where were the carving tools? He searched his small room; there was nothing under the bunk or next to his sabre. Finally Aleksandr located the carving instruments next to a femur bone.

He retrieved the curious object and tried to recall its origin. Was the bone animal or human? Judging by its size it could have come from a bird or child; but he didn't remember digging up graves belonging to children. Cemeteries were convenient for anyone requiring ritual materials. He thought of baby corpses, and felt a touch of The Fears.

Aleksandr grabbed tools and walked outdoors to his incomplete chaika. He flipped the craft so that its keel faced the sun. The chaika required a consistently smooth, level hull; a boat with an uneven bottom would pose a danger. Slowly he scraped off burls and knots, and he had to dig out other chunks with a dagger. Aleksandr carefully shaped the helms. Both points on a Cossack vessel were identical; a crew would not have to turn it around giving the ship great maneuverability.

❀ ❀ ❀

Bohun inspected a stone. Most flints could only take twenty firings, others could survive up to forty shots. A good flint is dense enough to handle repeat firing, flat on both sides and free of cracks. Usually he discarded spent flints; it made more sense to simply knap a new one. The flint in his palm was still in excellent condition; at least five more shots.

He sat up from his bunk, grabbed his half-assembled musket and walked out of the empty kuren to check the water. Bohun stared at the crude steel pot as he reached for his weapon, removed the lock and wiped it down with a wet rag. After running a dry cloth over the lock, he delicately set it down and picked up a ramrod.

Bohun stuck a patch through the instrument's point and sank it into bubbling water. Once it was soaked he coated the swab with a slab of soap taken from a merchant port they raided months ago, and ran it down the barrel. Thanks to the piece of wood blockading the barrel's end, water didn't flood the rest of the gun.

Bohun replaced a filthy swamped swab with a dry patch. He ran his ramrod down the barrel; no rust. Minutes later he checked a new swab. It was dry; a clean barrel.

He grabbed fresh cloth and began to clean the stock. Bohun cleaned wood with sweet oil, taking great care with the bright work, and rubbed it down with a dry rag. The musket had gained a pristine appearance, as if it was a display piece on a Szlachic mantle rather than a Cossack's tool. Bohun cleaned firearms with greater care than a mother bathing a child.

❦ ❦ ❦

Ignoring his craving for a pint, Marko entered 'court'. Ostap and Noman were locked into another argument. A small audience had congregated next to the shed; conflict between the ataman and the Tatar was entertaining.

"What now?"

Noman advanced, "Ostap stole my love!"

Ostap parried, "Yours? Those women were just toys."

Noman insisted, "You insulted me!"

The elder Cossack chortled, hacking up phlegm. "You want to marry the whore? Live in a shack and plow dirt like a serf?"

Marko seized his mace, signaling silence! "What am I supposed to do about this?"

Noman's hand darted to his sabre's pommel. "Allow us to duel."

Ostap's thick guttural laughter filled the shed. "I'm not in the mood for butchering a calf like you."

Marko could almost taste beer. "That's out of the question. The Sich has few rules but they won't be shattered over women."

Noman's fist smashed the shed walls, would the 'court' collapse? "I demand compensation!"

Marko sighed. "Ostap give him twenty ducats. Noman can buy at least two whores on his next trip to Kiev."

Ostap dug through cloak folds. "Any price for silence."

"Accepted." Noman was sated.

"Atamans?" The room turned. It was Albin. Marko and Ostap raised forearms. Ostap said, "Speak lad."

"You are required at an officer rada," Albin explained.

❦ ❦ ❦

The room almost shook from speech; atamans discussed raids, women, or trading, Aleksandr leaned against the doorway, keeping silent. Samiylo stood in centre right next to the bunhuck standard: a hetman's spear with a horse's tail. He raised his mace and there was instant silence. "You all know what Marko and his compatriots witnessed?"

Atamans stared at one another. Why ask a foolish question? Every chern talked of their adventures! They nodded in confirmation.

Samiylo spoke, "Who else has encountered such daemons?"

Ostap rose. "My boyhood home had a domovik." Eyes locked on the elder, Ostap could remember that much?

"Its appearance?"

"A tiny man in drab garb; it took the form of the previous owner."

"What did it do?"

Ostap's face went blank. "A moment please." He closed his eyes for a second. "It assisted with chores mainly, but whenever I would curse; events took place…"

Samiylo queried, "Events?"

Fear shined in Ostap's eyes. "Vile language angered it; such a gentle being. On the day I told my brother to eat his shit the Domovik appeared. One wave of his hand and I rose into the air!" The atamans reacted with shock, doubt, and boredom.

"What then?"

"Our most priceless vase; shattered. That's all I can recall."

Samiylo turned to the men assembled, "Has anyone else seen *Them*?"

Certain men had seen *something* out of the corner of their eyes years ago such as a small figure crouching on a tree. A few of the ataman knew families who knew other people who could have seen one of *Them* decades ago. There were stories of Rusalkas dragging a boy under. Unintentional falsehoods?

Samiylo made a flourish with his mace. "Are they a threat? Or a possible ally against Turks and Liakhs?"

"We have friends," Ostap said.

Samiylo grimaced. "The Novgorodians regard us as distant cousins, and they give us sellsword work, but that's all. The Sich has few contacts among the Szlachta, they would betray us in an instant; we are many yet very lonely."

"What of angels and demons?" Ostap asked.

"They are too distant; such beings will grant individual favors but they won't take sides. Imagine a grandfather miles away, who will send you money when you ask but won't assist you in a family argument," said Aleksandr. "I yield the floor to you, most honored commander."

"Marko, your task is to gather as much information about *Them* and locate *These Things* if you can. We need allies."

Marko fought to avoid writhing in fear. "How many men?"

"No more than five, and take Aleksandr." The hetman did not smile on sorcerers forming relationships with Liakh nobles behind his back.

Ostap jabbed an elbow at Marko. "Take me; Rusalkas would go mad with lust over my beard."

"I'll consider it," he said, chortling.

☙ ☙ ☙

"Hell."

"What?" Marko didn't understand; the three men stood outside the Sich near a deserted trail at the edge of the steppe.

"The penalty for suicide," Bohun explained.

Aleksandr stopped pacing. "There is no reason to be afraid; these *things* wouldn't leave souls for Satan."

A tiny smile, was he joking?

"This isn't suicide. With their allegiance we can build a Cossack empire!" Marko exclaimed.

Aleksandr interrupted. "I will go; we need to know more about *Them* than mere bedtime fables."

Bohun said, "I'll go too." He wasn't worried if the expedition would fail; he wanted a reprieve from routine.

"Cossacks are outlaws or banished men."
-Geoffrey Ducket

CHAPTER 10

The Sich church was humble, crude even, compared to proper urban chapels or simple peasant churches. Although any man: pagan, protestant, or papist, could join; apart from the Pagan idols erected by Baltic recruits, only Orthodox true Christians enjoyed places of worship. Noman entered reverently. As he approached icons, he crossed himself; no cross without the three fingers. He kissed one icon; it was the arrest of Saint George.

He sat next to Marko. The ataman seemed very bored. "Your legs are crossed."

Marko corrected his error.

"Do I have your support?"

"Worry about the kuren." Marko couldn't wait to leave on his mission. Every man in his kuren knew that a temporary ataman would have to be elected to govern while Marko was away. The victor of an election would govern for a full year if Marko perished.

"Understood, ataman," said Noman, sheathing his words in sarcasm.

"I think you would be an excellent ataman." The post and its risks did not attract incompetents.

"Thank you."

"Who else will stand?"

"Andriy and I think Albin might."

Marko's gentle laughter rang through the church. "The Liakh boy?"

"The same."

"He would last moments with an ataman's mace."

"If that."

Noman asked, "How do chern treat unpopular atamans?"

"Expulsion from his kuren if his fortune holds, usually hanging or being hurled into the rapids." In the silence church wood creaked.

"But Novgorodian code…"

Marko said, "Doesn't address our form of government. Chern decide."

Sickness seeped into Noman's abdomen, "I see…" Was he in the process of committing suicide?

Marko grew tired of the tuma's presence. "I must return to prayer."

"Of course," Noman said as he stood rose up to leave.

❧ ❧ ❧

The shooting range was a mud caked-plain with poorly constructed targets. Ammunition was virtually a currency; thus Cossacks honed their aims with archery. Most men used Tatar bows and closed quivers covered with oriental décor. They knew how to repair arrows. They practiced steppe traditions passed down from the Scythians to the Khans, though few men used the Mongol draw. Mounted archery competitions were common, but truly daring men discarded saddles, preferring to lock legs around mounts like Scythian warriors.

Marko aimed and let fly; his arrow flew past a scarecrow target. "Your shot."

Oleg nocked a shaft from the quiver at his hip. "Noman won't stand for ataman?"

Oleg's arrow hit a painted stump, Marko grimaced. "No."

The young man lowered his bow. "Your shot."

"You have a strong chance of winning," Marko said as he aimed, waiting for the wind to die down. The former ataman released his fingers, watching with pride as his arrow stabbed into stump bark.

"Really?"

"The election of young recruits is not uncommon." Once Marko tired of target practice he would return to his kuren.

❧ ❧ ❧

"You wanted to see me?"

The hetman stood up, pulling a scroll from his sash and pointing it at the sorcerer. "Information for your mission."

Aleksandr took the parchment. "Information?"

"A list of priests came in; anyone who has encountered such daemons would either seek comfort from clergy or remain forever silent," Samiylo explained.

"Silence from fear of ridicule or insanity?"

Samiylo's response was a shrug. "If you fail to forge relations with them you won't face any consequences."

"Other than disheartening the Sich."

Samiylo said, "The Turks have the Kerkes, the Liakhs possess Bialozars, the Novgorodians own great serpents."

"What about the Spaniards?" Aleksandr knew little of life beyond Novgorod or the Commonwealth.

"Christian Spain sends giants into the most dangerous battles."

"And the infidels?"

"The Andalusians have the nanas; born of demon and woman it has a half -body and hideous features."

"You've seen it?"

"Nay, but a merchant from the Gaelic union told me of such wonders; he served in the armies of Christian Spain in his youth."

"Is there anything else, Most Serene Hetman?"

"No, you should leave; you'll miss your kuren's election."

☙ ☙ ☙

Marko balanced on a rooftop. The rada stared up at him; it was time for what could be his final act as ataman. "Who would be the ataman of this kuren?" he shouted. Every man in the thick crowd below had to hear him. Oleg, Andriy, Joseph, Albin, and Noman walked out of the crowd.

Chern stepped back; they began to discuss, argue, and remember. Who gave out the best ale? Who was the best fighter? Who wouldn't command like a noble?

Marko stared as the chern shoved and shouted, hands on weapons. He was shocked that fighting hadn't ignited among the Cossacks; elections brought out passions. The crowd fractioned. "Who do you choose?"

"We want Firqa!" the largest group cried, and distress briefly panged the former ataman.

"Very well! Noman Firqa, you are ataman of the kuren until my return. If I perish you shall govern for a year if those here will it. All agreed?"

A resounding, "Aye!"

Marko descended, and walked to the porch. He retrieved the mace from his belt, and handed it to Noman. "Your mace Ataman!"

"My thanks Cossack," Noman responded, concentrating on keeping his face stone blank. What of Marko's conduct in the church?

"Huzzah," Albin yelled. Was he disappointed or relieved? Chern began to cheer; elections were a source of pride, noble boots did not trample their soil! The night would be one of feasting, drink, and dance! Perhaps they would even travel to towns under Zaporozhian guard for women!

Marko faced Bohun and Aleksandr. "Pack. We leave in the morning."

"*They broke into two groups and formed two circles. One consisted of the officers and the other of rank-and-file whom they call chern. After a lengthy discussion the chern in their traditional sign of consent threw their caps into the air. Then the mob rushed over to the other circle that of the officers, and threatened to throw into the river and drown anyone who disagreed with them.*"

-Erich Lassota, Witness of a Cossack election.

CHAPTER 11

Afternoon, Cherkassy

To any city dweller, Cherkassy's church was a plain example of Novgorodian architecture. To the Zaporozhians it was an unparalleled marvel! So straight and even! Kureni, while sturdy homes, looked like large playhouses constructed by drunken children. Sich craftsmanship had little place for art.

Aleksandr, Marko, and Bohun waited on pews. Dudek had left for food, papers, water. The priest returned, chewing pastry with scrolls stuck through his belt and books under his arm. Dudek was younger than Ostap, he had full brown hair, a thin mustache, and a wide smile; at the moment he wore simple clothes. "This was all I could find," he said swallowing; the dessert was far too doughy.

Marko said, "You would have records of confessions?"

"Certainly, one of our local customs."

Marko paled. "Oh."

Dudek's thick laughed filled church space. "Don't worry; it's not exactly credible evidence in courts."

Aleksandr made an effort to laugh as well, then spoke. "Thank you for your help."

"My pleasure," said Dudek, taking a seat next to Aleksandr. A priest and a sorcerer side by side! Only in Ruthenian lands.

The priest leafed through scrolls, "These are the confessions I could find relating to 'demons' and this," he held up the book, "is a catalogue of Cherkassy addresses."

"Thank you!" Marko blurted, overcome with gratitude.

"Not at all," Dudek replied, leaning back. "I have copies."

❀ ❀ ❀

"I found a webbed arm in a fisherman's net; it only could have come from a rusalka."

Aleskandr sighed, nothing so far.

Marko sat up; the inn offered few chairs, all uncomfortable. "Obviously a mother threw a deformed whelp to the waves, its limb washed up."

Aleksandr dropped the page. "Agreed. Oh, here's one," he cleared his throat then said, "Upon falling asleep I saw a living wall of human skin speaking Latin."

Bohun laughed. "A bad dream?"

"Could be, although it is common for magi to give victims dreams of terror to rob them of rest; a frequent sorcerous assault," said Aleksandr, scanning Cyrillic.

"Such a curse can be cured with a potion sold at every tavern," Marko joked.

Bohun added, "That's not a bad idea."

"Listen to this! 'I have lain with my aunt.'" The inn room shifted to silence.

"The man deserves congratulations for keeping his hands off his daughter," said Bohun, trying to smother laughter.

Marko remarked, "Dudek must be a very wealthy man."

"What else is in there?" asked Bohun. "Did a dirt worker claim that a Domovik impregnated his supposedly pure daughter?"

Aleksandr flipped pages, "No."

"No peasant would have such imagination," Marko interjected, "I think Dudek included that by error or just to entertain us; hard to top a talking skin wall," replied the sorcerer.

"Read on," Marko ordered.

"Someone's whelp claims to have spied a Lisovyk while picking berries; that's useless."

Bohun spoke. "What about a Domovik?"

"Good idea," Aleksandr's eyes danced. "All confined to houses, something so small would be easily questioned."

"Don't be so sure," replied Marko. "An ataman told me about how a Domovik defied God's laws of nature."

"Was he speaking truthfully?" Aleksandr waved pages, "people love shaping facts."

Marko answered, "I wouldn't take his word for gospel but it isn't wise to assume that Domoviks are weak. We have no evidence, only stories our mothers whispered as they nursed us."

"Domoviks, gods of hearth and home?" Bohun added.

Ignoring the question Aleksandr raced through pages, "The Domovik in my home is like a parent and a pet; he cooks and comes whenever I call."

"Read on," Marko ordered.

"What's the address?"

Aleksandr tore paper from Dudek's book, "Karas Vedmid, he lodges near the marketplace."

Pain rippled through Bohun's stomach. Would he be recognized?

"Is it far?"

Marko said, "Not at all."

Cossacks left the inn, carefully avoiding inn staff. The sun was hidden by clouds and roofs: as if it was twilight. The streets were filled with Armenian merchants, occasional carriages, and guards. City dwellers stared at the unique clothing the Zaporozhians wore.

Children mobbed around the puppet theatre; it was a vertepy. Marko was suddenly flooded by childhood memories; vertep performances were the highlight of every boy's Easter. The puppets were controlled by elaborate matrixes of wires and strings that resembled vast spider webs. If he had talent, a single puppeteer could manipulate up to forty puppets.

Marko tried to follow the story. Mamay, the Cossack ideal, was fighting his way out of hell. The puppeteer was a smooth faced lad in Cossack garments with sandy hair. He jerked a string; Mamay's blade struck a red horned devil.

"Daemons look nothing like that." Aleksandr's voice almost made Marko jump. "Adorable theatre though."

Marko sighed; it was if he could taste sweets from his boyhood, "I once loved vertep plays." Sinners writhed in hell flames.

"I could never sit still for puppets," said Aleksandr with a shrug. "As a boy, sledding was the highlight of Christmas."

"Hills or roofs?" Mamay leaped up from hell.

Aleksandr answered "Both. Bohun is waiting."

"Aye." Mamay rode away.

Aleksandr and his companions took a shortcut through an alley. The three men had to balance on a plank over a swamp of feces and mud. Marko thought he saw something swimming beneath the board.

The trio reached the end without falling into muck. The alley's end revealed a sloping street with fragmented cobblestone, homes built from scrap lumber, a view of a tower. As they walked past a house that looked as if it was constructed from a wrecked ship, Bohun admired the tower; a five story spire resembling a minaret, built from the finest stone. They took a left turn, came to a large street with empty vending stands; Bohun recognized it from the previous night. "Which way?" he asked.

"Follow," said Marko, turning right.

The Cossacks entered the abandoned marketplace. Aleksandr sighed, "A pity; I'll have to wait to see Cherkassy's foreign whores."

With Aleksandr in the lead, they made their way to homes at the market's edge. Marko stared at houses; ropes hung on the edge from man sized holes and residents had to scale the walls to reach second and third stories since the stairs had rotted away.

He knocked. A raven-haired beauty answered, her eyes grew wide at the sight of the strangers' weapons. "Yes?"

Marko removed his hat and lowered his eyes. "We're looking for Karas Vedmid."

"Who wants to speak with Mr. Vedmid?" She adjusted her humble gray dress.

Marko displayed his mace.

The girl's eyes widened more. "Wait a moment!" She seemed to be short of breath. Cossack heroes at her humble door!

The girl paced outside, yelled, "Vedmid!"

"Quiet!" An elder shouted, "They can no doubt hear you in chelm-land." His beard gave him a gnomish appearance.

"Three Zaporozhian wish to speak with you," the girl replied in a hushed tone.

Knotted hemp ropes fell to the chinked pavement. "Climb!"

Gripping the rope, the Zaporozhians obeyed. Aleksandr climbed, boots against the wall, often stopping to check the surface. Marko advanced up the rope by gripping it with both hands while his feet rested on knots. Bohun went up the rope using only his arms. Cossacks often practiced rope climbing to prepare for siege warfare.

As they finally reached the top Karas spoke. "Impressive!"

The Cossacks sat on the roof floor, panting. Marko spoke. "Couldn't you have come down to meet us?"

"And climb that distance?" Karas replied, pointing at curving stairs behind him.

"You old buzzard!" exclaimed Bohun. "You didn't tell us…"

"Because I wanted to see if Sich life had become soft since I was young," Karas said, cutting off the gunman.

Aleksandr asked, "You once lived in a kuren?"

"Aye." thoughts of Zaporozhian life brought light to the old fool's eyes. "Do you still hold annual chaika races?"

Marko answered, "Of course."

Karas smiled. "Good, good. Without tradition we have nothing."

"Too true."

Karas asked, "What did you want to speak to me about?"

"Actually we want to speak to someone else," replied Marko "the Domovik of your home."

"It's for the Sich," Aleksandr added.

Karas' eyes dimmed. "Oh."

"Do you know *his* name?" asked Aleksandr.

"Aye."

Aleksandr was shocked, he might be able to command the Domovik with *Its* name! "What else?"

Karas started to walks toward stairs. "He will tell you."

Cossacks followed Karas down twisting stairs. Aleksandr almost wished he had jumped off the roof; the stair had dangerously slender boards, and little light; it was a tight space. With each step he felt as if he were climbing trees, balancing on limbs. The four men reached Karas' quarters unscathed. Aleksandr glanced around, it had a small woodstove, a bunk, a few books, and no windows; it would be flattering to call this dwelling humble.

Karas spoke. "Forgive me if I do not offer food or drink; I have very little."

Marko smiled, "I can give you some of my provisions. Do you have a taste for wolf flesh?"

"I was raised on it!"

Bohun broke his silence. "Could you light candles?"

Karas turned. "One will have to do.

"Yes," replied Marko, opening a container of coals.

"You'd like to speak with *It* now?"

"If you don't mind," replied Marko.

Karas took a small cake out of a box. "Ekatrina made these, you spoke to her earlier."

"Lovely girl."

"Like my daughter," Karas grinned. "Nay better; my actual daughter can't keep her legs closed."

The Cossacks became quiet: it was foolish to comment on such matters.

Karas placed the cake on the cleanest space he could find. He spoke, "Come friend of this home, eat the cake made for thee; talk to me."

For minutes, nothing happened. Just as Aleksandr was beginning to call the trip a waste, *It* appeared from behind a cupboard. The hair-covered Domovik crawled; it had a dangling beard, large eyes of every color, bald scalp, and tiny fingers. It danced, and every time the little feet touched the ground, the walls boomed.

"What is it, friend?"

"Men from the Sich wish to talk to you, would you honor their request?"

"Hmmm," the Domovik's eyes shifted shades, "Sure!"

Marko approached, "I wish to establish a deep friendship between your people and Cossackdom."

The Domovik played with its beard, "Oh?"

Marko asked, "Will you introduce me to your rulers?"

The Domovik began to laugh, a sound not unlike falcon screeching. "Do you know why my kind chooses to live in peasant hovels or slum wrecks? We flee to those homes, an existence preferable to our old lives!"

"You can't lead us to your court?" Aleksandr asked.

"Courts?" Inhuman laughter rang out. "We have no courts! Isn't that just like your race to assume my kind live under the same systems that you do!"

"What of your rules, contracts?"

The Domovik's eyes danced with color, "Oh that! Very well but I'll only tell this to him," it said, stabbing a finger, thick with hair, at Aleksandr. "Everyone else must leave."

"Yes, master," Karas said, bowing.

The four men left, leaving Aleksandr behind. The Domovik began to speak as soon as he heard the door slam. Aleksandr learned of customs far more draconian, alien than even the Goetia. The Domovik spoke of his kind's way of making and breaking contracts.

It felt unreal even to Aleksandr, as if he was floating through dream realms after invoking Morpheus. He had viewed spirits countless time, but all in visions or through scrying mediums; never in the 'flesh' or whatever the Domovik's body was made of.

"How can I gain an audience with your kind? I have something to bargain with."

"I'll tell you who to see, then leave," it hissed, uninterested in the human's plan. "In this home, I am more than God."

Outside, Bohun looked away from Ekatrina hanging laundry to see Aleksandr, slack jawed, emerging from the darkened home.

"What now?

Aleksandr answered, "Back to the lodge."

"Why?"

"I need to write down everything that *Thing* told me," said Aleksandr, staring at rooftops, "And to explain our next move."

"And Vladimir began his reign in Kiev alone and erected idols on the hill outside his palace with a porch: Perun of wood with a head of silver and mustache of gold and Dazbog and Stribog and Simargl and Mokosh."

-The Primary Chronicle.

CHAPTER 12

"He spoke of ancient eldritch contracts. He explained alien customs. He whispered of the power held by their potential allies." Aleksandr inhaled deeply as he reached for a tankard of ale on the table next to one of the inn's beds.

Bohun stared at ceiling beams, hands clasped in mock prayer. "If only they were demons!"

Marko laughed, set his face still. "We could conquer all empires without losing a single Zaporozhian!"

"Tempting," replied Aleksandr, throat burning, "But the creatures would demand a terrible price for such a request. Tyranny is not a Sich custom, don't think like a Liakh."

Marko asked, "Why should they even ally with us? There are far more powerful armies."

"Most do not even think of us as an army," Bohun added.

The sorcerer yawned. "I have something to trade."

"What?"

"He'll tell us when it's time," said Bohun, a Cossack with great respect for secrets.

"The *imp* told me of a local Vodianyk."

"Oh?"

"The Domovik described It as a…" Aleksandr, craving alcohol, paused, "…lazy slug who would sell anything for the slightest favor."

"Did the house lord give the water spirit's location?" asked Marko.

"He gave me a good start; but first we have to go to prison."

❧ ❧ ❧

Cherkassy's jail was a frightful place, a tower of holding pens. For a fee, a well-to-do prisoner would be placed in a small, somewhat dry room. Prisoners lacking ducats were thrown into a pit to wallow in filth from fellow inmates.

The Cossacks currently sat in a small cabin inches away from the jail, an office for Dimitri Petro, the prison head. Dimitri was an obese man nearing middle age wearing a tunic, Turkish trousers, and boots, which was a laughable effort to appear as a true Cossack. "You want a prisoner?"

"A real scrap of slime, someone no citizen would mourn," said Aleksandr.

Dimitri stroked his thin mustache. "Come this way."

As the four men left the box and approached the tower, Aleksandr was surprised; there was no overpowering smell of shit. A guard saluted, opened the door to the main room overlooking the pit. The Zaporozhians stood before a mass of iron bars, separating them from a mucky pit full of half naked prisoners crusted with all manner of filth. Prisoners crouched on their toes, a feeble attempt to keep most of their flesh clean.

"He raped five women," said Dimitri, pointing at a gray-bearded man hunched against the granite wall. "Granted they were whores from Constantinople."

Marko laughed. "Is it even possible to rape whores?"

"All too easy," replied Bohun with a knowing smile.

Aleksandr said, "We'll take him." Dimitri gestured for guards, who plodded through waves of muck, to seize the rapist. Within minutes the Cossacks were out of the tower, accompanied by a chained serial rapist.

❧ ❧ ❧

Cherkassy was located near rivers, much like the Sich. A thick marsh lay outside the waters. Aleksandr and his fellow Zaporozhians walked on dry land, a clear path past muck, mire, and thin woods. Marko sighted quicksand, thought of childhood memories of men draining a similar hole only to find the corpse of a missing girl. Most people in his settled Cossack village thought the girl had been taken to serve Tatar or Vodianoi desire.

They were said to be vile amphibian creatures driven by lust, hunger, or boredom.

An average Vodianyk is possessed of a froglike face, a mustache, webbed 'hands', a fishtail, and scaly skin coated with the most foul algae. The Cossacks were on their way to where locals made simple rituals to call on the Vodianyk's favors. Belief, as Aleksandr explained, augments sorcerous workings.

❧ ❧ ❧

Bohun walked slowly; hand on purse, pushing their new prisoner along. The ritual site entered Cossack vision; stone piles, scorched earth. "It looks like a campsite," he remarked.

"True," said Marko, almost tripping over a stave covered with arcane characters.

Aleksandr dug a small hole, wiped mud off fingertips. He placed a small box into the hole, and covered it. He began to speak, "Creature of the deep, friend of fish, immortal lord of waves; accept the gift I lay at your shore." He turned to his friends, "No matter what, do not interrupt me."

"Aye," said Marko.

Aleksandr inhaled, and began the hymn.

"Hear, Neptune, ruler of the sea profound,
Whose liquid grasp begirts the solid ground;
Who, at the bottom of the stormy main,
Dark and deep-bosomed, holds thy watery reign;
Thy awful hand the brazen trident bears,
And ocean's utmost bound, thy will reveres:
Thee I invoke, whose steeds the foam divides…"

He paused for breath, and continued, "In the name of the contract made with the Domovik who rules the home of Karas, I charge the Vodianyk of Cherkassy to appear," bubbles began to churn. "In the name of Veles appear!"

Water formed a whirlpool that looked like a portal to a realm neither of heaven or hell. A massive head slowly rose from swirling current. Cossacks couldn't look away from the blood colored eye stalks. Bohun couldn't decide which animal it most resembled, a slug, frog or a sturgeon? The sea beast lifted a meaty paw.

"You're no mere fisherman; speak so I can return to the pleasures of a Rusalka."

"I demand an audience with your leader, the Domovik told me of your ways…"

"And the contract we made?" The Vodianyk's eyes flared. "I never should have worked with that tiny slime," snapped the creature.

Aleksandr diverted his eyes from the Vodianyk's flaming stare, "I have something your kind want."

Laughter. "Free labor?"

"It's for your leadership to learn of."

"You think I care? You flatter yourself, child!"

Aleksandr smirked, "I know your true name."

"Lies."

"Can you risk your name becoming as common as a song from the Cherkassy folk to Azovites?"

The sea being's eyes began to dim, "I'll grant your request for something in return."

Aleksandr turned to Marko, "Bring our gift forward."

"Aye," said Marko as he kicked the rapist at the sorcerer.

Aleksandr gripped a grimy chain, "He's healthy, fit, nowhere to go."

Stalk eyes began to glow. "Perfect! I have so much work in my palace!"

"So we are agreed? You introduce me to your leader in exchange for a new servant," he paused. "On the condition that I am not harmed or imprisoned and that you take me to your leader through the subtle planes."

The Vodianyk almost spat bile, the child had skill! "We are agreed."

"Do you swear upon your one true name!"

"I swear upon my one true name," *It* said, eye light fading.

Aleksandr pushed the fear petrified prisoner into his new life of slavery. The rapist fell under the surface, dirt washing off. A webbed paw grabbed manacles pulling him beneath, the rapist thrashed as he drowned in silt water. The Vodianyk rotated his fleshy head,

"Your hand, child."

Hesitatingly, Aleksandr reached at the sea lord who seized his hand, it felt like gripping a fish fresh from the Dnieper. Slowly the world slipped away. The Vodianyk sank beneath the surface, leaving the inmate's body drifting. Aleksandr's body became heavy, weight he was about to be free of, his eyes fell shut revealing a golden pillars in his mind's eye.

Marko saw Aleksandr collapse. He rushed to his friend's side to find sorcerous eyes empty.

"Get the blankets."

Bohun obeyed. "When will he return?"

"You remember what he explained to us," said Marko, rolling up blankets to cushion Aleksandr's vacant body, "Aleksandr will return to his flesh once he has struck a deal with those *Things*."

❦ ❦ ❦

Twisting water, titanic sea plants. Aleksandr's body lay on land while his spirit form traveled a subtle realm modeled after sea kingdoms of legend. He floated below a mass of weed or tentacles; his sight was obscured by whirling green light above. It was not the same as a mere swim; there was no sensation of cold, current, or wetness, only the void of the deep.

Out of coral blue light the Vodianyk appeared with his servant tethered on a chain of scarlet force.

"On to see my leader?"

"Yes," he replied, it was not the speech of the world he left behind; 'words' penetrated his mind.

A mocking tone rang through his being, "You know you haven't called me by my real name."

His thoughts were racing. "Names have power, they are not to spoken lightly," replied Aleksandr.

"You are wise beyond your years." Each 'word' rippled through Aleksandr's spirit form.

"Thank you," said Aleksandr.

"Did that house pet tell you what *We* are?"

Aleksandr stared at writhing tentacles changing colors. "No."

"Not even I have all the answers, let me tell you of the *Inspired*."

What separates a spirit from a mass of force? Self, identity; the source of which is ideas. The Vodianyk explained how members of his 'race' are formed around ideas without such archetypes or concepts 'They' would be nothing. A member of the Inspired can alter its form but it must adhere to its Idea or risk Death. The Inspired have no kings; they cluster into groups of those who share similar Ideas led by those who most embody the Concepts that give the Inspired life known as the First. The closet thing to law is a vague set of rules regarding contracts and protocols.

"I'll take you to market," the Vodianyk said, tugging his servant's energy chain, "To witness our society in action."

"That's kind of you."

"Not quite," the Inspired replied, smirking. "I can't have a male servant, I'm defined by lecherous lust for female flesh, although he will fetch a fine favor or contract. Do you have a favorite song?" he asked Aleksandr.

"Reapers on the Hill," replied the sorcerer.

"Good choice." The Inspired picked up a flute; if it weren't for the fact that they were in the subtle realms Aleksandr would have sworn that it was carved out of human bone. Arcane music began to play.

"Oh, this loving
Is worse than sickness!
Sickness I can live through.
And grow well again;
But my faithful loving
I cannot part in it while I live."

Such a common song! Instantly a whirling coral pink portal materialized. Abandoning survival instincts, he followed his tour guide into the vortex. The two beings rushed through coursing passages made of every shade of color. This was the first time he had experienced such speeds, as if he were Zmey Gorynych soaring above ruined cities.

In the physical plane Bohun watched Aleksandr's body twitch, turn.

Aleksandr took in the environment of The Market: a vast jewel plane surrounded by inverted mountains. He willed himself to fly. An ocean of structures greeted him, leviathan skin tents, huts made out of giant shells; imagination has no limit in the subtle realms. The Vodianyk appeared beside him. "A splendid sight! Follow me."

They soared past stands displaying crowns of pearl, the jewel floor shifted color. Others venders sold sculptures that sang in Angelic tongues and signs in alien script.

"We're not in the subtle realms?"

The Vodianyk smiled, "The Inspired," it said, jerking the servant's leash.

A dancing Rusalka caught Aleksandr's eye; she had small breasts, he thought of his first. Her skin was crystalline while her hair was the hue of pure gold.

"Concepts of lust, femininity gives them form," the Vodianyk's voice tore him away from her burning green eyes devoid of pupils. "Their behavior encompasses the full scope of human womanhood; the whore, the hag, the young mother drowning an unwanted newborn in river water or her own milk."

The Rusalka spun higher, moving like vertep puppet as her dove-light carried her towards mountains. Aleksandr realized this was a blend of every lustful dance, whether cordax, the raqs sharqi, or tsifteteli.

"If she wasn't so far away I could act out one of my central themes: The Lech."

Saying nothing, Aleksandr tore his gaze away from her eyes; emerald abysses, and followed the Vodianyk past tents. "Come buy a soul," the living canvas sang.

"Not today," the Vodianyk snarled, "You just bottle aethyric energy and sell it to gullible Domoviks." Skin tents fell silent. "As you know, there isn't any other kind of house imp."

"Haahahaha, so true," replied Aleksandr.

"We have no 'money' here," the Inspired explained as they passed a display of giant translucent fruit. "You 'pay' for what you want through contracts or promises for favors." Rusalka dancers approached, flying together like a pest swarm.

"You can't break contracts or promises?"

"Impossible under The Conditions," he grimly replied, groping a Rusalka whose eyes turned blank at the touch of slime upon her breast.

"Conditions?" Aleksandr gaped; the mountains began to rotate around each other like falcons circling carrion.

"We swear upon our true names. If an Inspired breaks a contract or an oath, *Its* name becomes common and the violator can be commanded by almost anyone." Mountains began to settle at different angles as the floor turned green.

"Understood," said Aleksandr as they left the tent sections, entered a narrow canyon of grey stone and pink ground. The Cossack-Sorcerer stared skyward. Homes of a crystal diamond bubbles were built into the canyon's wall. The sea-Inspired scanned the homes; Aleksandr hoped it wouldn't take very long. He liked to think time was the same in the Inspired's realm as it was in the earthly and subtle realms. It was a comforting fantasy.

The Vodianyk finally spoke. "Follow," he said, climbing high into air as if Metatron had laid out a stair invisible to mortal eyes or sorcery.

"I'll be right up!" Aleksandr soared; flight in the Inspired reality was just as easy as it was in the subtle realms. He savored flight; an impossibility on earth!

As he approached the diamond homes he studied their intricacy; they were not mere chunks but a series of tiny honeycomb-shaped fragments, millions of pieces interlocking to form an alien structure. Aleksandr could see no one inside or any simple affects. Obviously the Inspired had few needs.

"Prepare for a 'tingle' through your subtle body," the Inspired explained as he flew through glass. "All things have life here."

"Aye," Aleksandr said as he slowly thought himself through crystal. A razor shock of pain hit his consciousness; instinctively he rushed through the crystal. Pain is possible in subtle realms or wherever he was. The subtle body is never separated from the meat mind, a skilled attacker can 'loop' memories of pain through the meat mind into the subtle body; a favorite cacodaemon tactic.

As pain began to retreat he took in an Inspired home. From the outside it seemed tiny, little more than a settled Cossack's hut. Inside it was as large as a Liakh palace! His host had few things: tiny suns, stars, moons floating on stands, statues that conformed to thoughts; Inspired art.

The Vodianyk chuckled as a statue blurred, shifted into a Turkish whore. "Carnal even outside your own flesh," It joked

Aleksandr ignored the creature. "Why the glass shield?" Surely an Inspired wasn't crippled by a need for shelter? Did they take on the mortal love for comfort?"

It smiled. "That isn't a simple roof; through our Magics, that crystal network allows an Inspired to create any type of home. This is actually small by our standards."

"What's large?"

"One of these across the canyon is the size of a galaxy inside. The law generally penalizes luxury like that but there are always exceptions."

The pair continued to walk through the titanic room. Aleksandr thought of massive caverns near seas. The Vodianyk entered a gaping pit; and Aleksandr followed, expecting to fly downwards as in the subtle realms. He was shocked to find himself walking down the wall like an insect; the unique laws of Inspired reality.

"Come down!" A voice roared, making canon fire seem delicate.

"Our host awaits," the sea-lord explained, bouncing wall to wall.

"I'm thrilled," replied Aleksandr, leaping down into inky space.

Aleksandr and the Vodianyk reached the pit's floor, a narrow green space with a large portal dead ahead. As he slowly flew forward, Aleksandr spoke.

"What lies ahead?"

"Nothing of danger to you, an old friend," It said with a smooth smile. Aleksandr counted fangs.

Aleksandr was inches from the door, which vanished all at once like mist under desert sun. A room filled with hovering jars lay in front of the Cossack-Sorcerer; certain containers were filled with energy leaping about like a captured toad while other held body parts; human, some species not of earth. The walls reflected a view of the world outside; one second a sight of the canyon, the next an overview of mountains. It moved like a rapid puppet show. The voice, soft this time, spoke.

"Forgive this cramped small room." Small! The room was the size of a cathedral, it dwarfed the Hetman's quarters.

A young man emerged from behind shelves; he had neatly trimmed blond hair along with a matching beard. He wore a Novgorodian tunic, boots, and a flowing cloak fastened with a Varangian brooch. "I am Sadko," he said, voice booming with pride.

On earth Bohun looked away from sword practice on the prisoner's carcass to watch Aleksandr's meat body for a few seconds.

"By the names of God!" Aleksandr exclaimed as he paced back to a wall displaying mountain scenery.

"You think there is only one?" replied Sadko with a wise wink.

"You could be a Rusalka in the form of Sadko!"

Sadko glanced down, "I don't have the chest for that! No sorcery can hide a Rusalka's shapely form!"

"That would be a deviation from their founding concepts," the Vodianyk explained as it examined an organ jar.

Sadko stared at the wall: mountains aimlessly flew around one another. "Would you like to hear my tale?"

Aleksandr answered, "I know them all."

Sadko chuckled, a grandfatherly laugh, "Good, your boyhood wasn't wasted. I meant the Sadko tale that was never told: how I came to be here."

"Yes."

"Understand that the stories you heard about are distorted. True, I had adventures that would rob an average man of sanity but those tales are little more than anecdotes passed down through generations."

"Did you visit the sea tsar?" Aleksandr asked.

"No, a member of the First." He motioned at the Vodianyk. "They have no tsars."

⚜ ⚜ ⚜

Centuries ago Sadko was abducted in front of a crowd; his talent on a gusli had captured inhuman ears. Sadko's kidnapping inspired an entire order of occult boyans dedicated to the power of music. Taken to an underwater palace beneath earthly waves, he was given a Magical method of breathing while submerged. The condition: If he failed to entertain his employer, the Magics would be revoked, leaving him to drown as slowly as possible.

Sadko didn't even try to measure time spent in the coral pink kingdom. He was treated pleasantly with food, Rusalkas, impossibly good wine. He wasn't abused; the threat of a slow death on the ocean floor, with lungs flaming, removed any need for force. The Novgorodian combated fear by focusing on the challenge along with his beautiful new gusli made out of whale bone by Inspired limbs.

Planning provided another outlet, he observed the Inspired to learn their customs. One day he was playing for his employer in a magnificent room of pearl, green coral, and leviathan teeth. "I have a challenge for you," declared Sadko.

"Should I be insulted or amused?" an alien roared in reply, the words seemed to tear through him like fangs.

"No, curious."

That *Inspired* became silent as a wraith. "Very well then, your challenge?"

"Do you swear to truth?"

"On my true name," replied the First, "until you leave this room. State your challenge."

Sadko smiled, it was cowardly for any Inspired to refuse a challenge, to fear one from a mortal would be an act of utmost cowardice. "I am about to play a song, if you do not love it; you shall reward me with immortality."

"Agreed."

"On your true name?"

"Aye."

Sadko began to play. If he failed at music he was not worthy of life.

He ceased; his dry throated burned, fingertips throbbed, a death at the hands of an alien ruler almost seemed desirable, a fitting end for the great Sadko. The music echoed through the chamber; Inspired Magic infected the very air.

❦ ❦ ❦

"So you won!" Aleksandr exclaimed.

Sadko smiled; his gift for tale and song had not fled him. "No. In my contract I did not define 'immortality." He picked up a gusli, "thanks to this cursed thing, the First ripped my being out of my flesh; I became a phantasm bound by inhuman rules."

"Oh," said Aleksandr. Sadko was trapped, unable to move on. A sorcerous prison.

"I briefly returned to the surface, to tell my wife. She passed my words on. I became fiction; no more than words to whisper to a bawling a child."

The Vodianyk turned his mucus coated back to pictures of a Domovik brawling over hearts. "Time to conclude our contract," he said, slackening the aethyric rope that constrained the former inmate.

"Mmmm, sufficient." Centuries ago Sadko would have connected to the wretch; he had left emotion with flesh.

Aleksandr couldn't feel anything for the prisoner who belonged to no host; a rapist was a fair price for guarding the Sich.

Sadko snatched the leash. "Our contract is over." His words caused the sea-Inspired's worm-like lips to mesh into a smile.

Aleksandr spoke. "Will you bottle him?"

"Oh please don't insult me," Sadko exclaimed, grimacing. "All of this is mere décor," he said, sweeping a hand over decanters. "This present goes into my private room." With that, he disappeared through a red wall.

"Come," said the Vodianyk, "the First await."

"Sadko entered the white-stone palace.
The Sea Tsar was sitting in the palace,
The Tsar's head looked like a haystack.
The Tsar then spoke these words:
"Hail to you, Sadko the merchant, the rich guest!
Sadko, you've sailed upon the sea for a long time,
You haven't paid me, the Tsar, any tribute,
But today you've come to me yourself as a gift.
They say you're a master at playing the maple gusli.
Play your maple gusli awhile for me."
Then Sadko played his maple gusli,
Then the Sea Tsar danced in the blue sea,
Then the Sea Tsar was carried away with dancing."
-The Bylina of Sadko.

CHAPTER 13

Aleksandr had expected a space nearly identical to a Liakh throne room or a hall as large as the Sejm. Instead he stood before a solid liquid barrier. To mere sight the fluid was simple water; in reality it was very much alive. A type of servant? Dark walls boxed him in. Objects undulated like a wounded man sucking in final breaths.

"How would we profit from this alliance?"

Finally. A reply! "Because you need humans, we provide you with your lifeblood: ideas."

"Any mortal can do that!" Shrill voice speaking as one, flawless harmony. They sounded not unlike howling babes.

"We Cossacks have unique ideas; our lives become legend before we die. The Sich and the Inspired have much in common."

No reply.

Time did not exist. Aleksandr kept that in mind while he waited, hours, minutes, seconds; simple words. Finally the voices began to speak,

"What can you offer?"

"Mecys Sapieha."

"How?"

"I worked for him; the Liakh seems to trust me."

The aquatic veil parted, the walls began to move back. Aleksandr found himself facing a small council of horrors. To the left was Koshchiy in his preferred form, a medium-sized human elder, a moss-like beard concealed genitals. In the centre: a member of the Gamuyun people; beings with human heads, bird bodies. To the right: a naked man with a trio of heads, Triglav.

"You protected him?" All six spoke at once.

"Yes; it was a simple task, I meant no harm or offense to any of you, my deepest apologies."

"Accepted."

"Thank you," the room had increased to the size of a kuren, a large inky room. Aleksandr felt as if he was floating in a moonlit lake.

"We Cossacks shall deliver Mecys Sapieha to you in exchange for an alliance: your aid, for your warriors to fight alongside men of the Sich. Do we have a contract?"

"Aye." Koshchiy scratched his sores a lot.

"Upon your true names?"

Water fell down, barricading the Inspired from the Cossack-Sorcerer. Fear began to erode his mind, would he return to an elderly body? Had he been left for dead by fellow Zaporozhians?

"What is your interest in the Liakh?" asked Aleksandr. The six Inspired predictably ignored him.

"We want the boy delivered in a certain manner," one of the divine heads explained. Aleksandr listened to Triglav's instructions.

❀ ❀ ❀

Blood flow. He lifted an arm to shield his eyes from glaring sunlight; it was as if his limbs were frozen in rigor mortis.

"Welcome back," said Marko, sheathing a sabre.

Aleksandr ignored his ataman, "I'll explain on the way back to the inn." He required rest; his limbs were like meat on a slab.

❀ ❀ ❀

Aleksandr's hand darted across the table, quill carving words into parchment. He had to record his findings: no rest, no time. "Can we snatch the Liakh without the Hetman's approval?"

"It falls under my authority," replied Marko, recently informed of the situation.

"That's a relief," Aleksandr returned to scribe-craft.

"We could spark war," said Bohun, mildly disgusted that the Cossack-Sorcerer had worked for a Szlachic.

Aleksandr smirked, "not a concern; the Liakh dwells in Kryvyi Rih. Why would a member of one of the mightiest Commonwealth families live at the edge of the map if he wasn't a nuisance to be kept away from the Sejm?"

Marko spoke, "Knowing Liakhs, they might even welcome their son's death."

"I doubt our possible allies merely want to kill him; too unimaginative." He paused, reached into his bag, began to remove tools.

"Should I leave?" asked Bohun, as Aleksandr donned a lamen.

"You're welcome to observe," he replied, placing a scrying medium upon the table of his practice. "Please remain silent."

The words of the first incantation echoed through the room.

"Aleksander listened to Triglav's instructions."

"In the name of the blessed Trinity, I consecrate this piece of ground for our defense; so that no evil spirit may have power to break these bounds prescribed here, through Jesus Christ our Lord." He spoke as he traced a sphere with his sabre.

He slowly continued to speak.

"Lord, thy will be done on earth, as it is in heaven; make clean our hearts within us, and take not thy Holy Spirit from us."

"O Lord, by thy name, we have called him, suffer him to administer unto us. And that all things may work together for thy honor and glory, to whom with thee, the Son, and blessed Spirit, be ascribed all might, majesty and dominion. Amen."

A force flooded the room; it was as if all of Ruthenia had been set afire. Bohun became exhausted; it was an act of endurance to stand before an Angel. Color filled Aleksandr's mind; he opened his eyes to enjoy the sensation of divine, invisible energy. Marko felt ill, the Angelic presence was intensely powerful. Michael began to take a shape within the crystal; a figure clad in ancient armor, hand clasping a sword.

"Michael in the name of God the Father, the Son, the Holy Ghost and the Tetragrammaton, I request that you no longer protect Mecys Sapieha." Force surged, Marko smothered the urge to vomit; it wasn't a toxic presence, it was simply too much for a mere ataman to feel.

Aleksandr finished by giving the Angel license to depart.

❦ ❦ ❦

Aleksandr began to copy his original work onto hide; delicate parchment could rot in the steppe. This version would be in Latin as opposed to the Ruthenian Cyrillic of the original. He looked up from his work, "You should hide the rapist."

"Aye," Marko said, leaving for the door followed by Bohun. The innkeeper was away, the pair quickly moved down oak stairs for the massive door, practically a gate.

Crowds of merchants, women, occasional coaches filled cobbled streets; everyone hurrying home, the sun was about to fall. Marko felt pangs of anxiety; to him cities were alien lands. He was disappointed: no vertep theater in sight. They darted past wagons, begging children; the mob's roar seemed to deaden their senses. Fingers brushed Bohun's thigh. He ignored the grope: His money was secure in the inn. The Cossacks left the city and began to walk down a twisting trail.

"Do you have the dagger?"

"Right here," replied Bohun, holding up a bollock dagger.

They continued in silence until they reached water, the inmate was still bobbing on the surface. Bohun pulled the body in, his ataman did not have to issue orders for this task. Once the corpse was land bound, Marko took the blade, set to work.

He punctured the chest, deflating the lungs. After checking the skin for tattoos, he carved up the rapist's face, leaving only flaps hanging. Bohun lashed stones to the body, filled the chest cavities with rocks. They heaved the weight into the muddy depths, to disappear like its former inhabitant. Marko coughed vomit, tasted stag.

"Do we leave tomorrow?"

"Yes." Aleksandr stooped to rinse off blood, his hands gave him the look of a fish monger. "A ride from dawn to nightfall."

Bohun smiled. "The steppes are our true home."

"The Zaporozhians spent most of the year seeking adventure on the Dnieper River and Black Sea, on the notorious ' Wild Plains' or sometimes even further afield, but returning to the sich in winter."
-Richard Brzezinski

CHAPTER 14

DAYS LATER

"None of our women have ever serviced a Szlachic," the owner: an obese man with thick red hair; average height,

"You're certain?" he asked, leaning against a garish wall with peeling red paint.

Aleksandr took in the brothel: one of many destinations for runaway serf girls from the Commonwealth, women taken in raids, wives who preferred whoring to their husbands. Girls sprawled on pillows, ignoring muffled noise of male pleasure, female pain.

"Oh yes, no mere disguise can masque manners."

"True, thanks for your time."

"What's all this about?"

He turned his back and smirked. "A man who spoke poorly about my mother," as if he had any family. Aleksandr left the brothel, feeling pity for a brown haired girl clad in a ragged dress who appeared thirteen at most. He entered peaceful streets; at this hour the whore's lane had few if any customers.

Marko said, "Report?"

Aleksandr faced his friends, who were seated on a rotting bench apparently made out of wood pulled from a shipwreck. "No Szlachta clients."

Bohun spat ale at a shit pile. "Exactly the same as the last few whore houses."

"Yeah," replied Aleksandr, standing behind Marko. The streets were narrow, no room for three men to stand shoulder to shoulder.

"What now?" asked Bohun, slapping wood chips off his garments.

"The market," said Marko, "we need to find out where Mecys prefers to eat and yes, you all get meat there."

Bohun faced Aleksandr. "Could you purchase some cheap mutton for me? I have few ducats."

"Of course," replied the Cossack-Sorcerer, smiling.

The trio turned left and the street became bizarrely narrow. Buildings seemed to bleed into each other. Bohun thought of running across roofs. Arching gangways bridged gaps between buildings. Marko realized the risk of being knocked unconscious by plummeting wood. The airtight road opened to an empty square.

"Where is everyone?" asked Aleksandr.

"Unfamiliar with city life?"

The Cossack-Sorcerer ignored the sarcastic question.

They walked through the square, Marko admired the precise brick roadwork and the fountain; an imitation of Byzantine art. They left the square, timber towers faded behind their shoulders. A row of buildings, Venetian architecture, stood before them; grey stone, sharp scarlet tiled roofs. Was the square a line between rich and poor?

"Could he live here?" asked Marko.

"Possibly," replied Aleksandr, as he thought back to past information.

One day after arriving, Cossacks took a coach to Mecys' home, to find it deserted. Guesswork said the Inspired snatched Mecys, leaving a trap for the Cossacks. Or, after viewing an Angel, Mecys could have become paranoid about the idea of a Sorcerer having his address. House Sapieha, long tired of the boy, could have slain him. The options were to search bars, brothels, or restaurants that Mecys frequented.

Carriage clatter destroyed Aleksandr's thoughts. He looked up from pavement to see the market. A much more conservative fair than Cherkassy; food carts, trinket mongers, all well organized. Worst of all, no dancers.

Aleksandr browsed meat; salesmen feasted their eyes on what they assumed was another mere peasant. Finally he chose two pieces of pork; a common meat. Tatar raiders wouldn't touch pigs. "Five ducats," he said, starting low.

"Seven." The pig flesh seller was abnormally skinny, with blond hair, a thin mustache, and western clothing.

"Done," Aleksandr replied as he reached for food.

As if on cue Bohun approached, Aleksandr handed him his slab of meat. "Thank you!" Bohun exclaimed.

Aleksandr shrugged.

"I'll repay you."

Aleksandr said, "No need, seven ducats is a boy's wage."

Bohun hesitated, "Is this mutton?"

"Nay, pig, why?"

"Ostap told me city folk carve slabs off corpses to sell at market," he said sinking his teeth into overdone flesh.

Aleksandr spat gristle, "If that was true it would taste far better."

Marko approached. "We need to find Szlachta."

Aleksandr pointed with pig flesh. There was a large crowd due south, a few feet away. As Cossacks advanced they saw what was in the heart of the crowd; a fighting ring. Two men clad in trousers, boots, and executioner masks were walled off by a blood lusting throng.

Nobles approached a tavern, would they drink until dawn? Aleksandr smiled in relief; they passed the tavern to continue into a narrow and shockingly clean street. Marko glanced at a girl sitting on a ledge of one of the three story buildings with faded paint and chipped stone. He feared that the structures would cave in on the six of them. Giggling, the girl threw clumps of waste, causing nobles and Cossacks to run.

"You'll hang for that, whelp!" screamed a noble.

Bohun didn't think the man was joking as he scraped shit off his shirt with a dagger.

The group stood on a dirt road, flanked by homes built in the Ottoman style. That child had ruined the original plan, and Marko realized it was time to improvise. He paced forward.

"Do anyone of you fine gentlemen know of anyone who is hiring?"

A young man turned, he had a mustache like that of the janissaries, a small župan hat; he was the only noble without a sabre. "Hiring?"

"Sellsword work," replied Marko.

"We have no need for that vile trade," the Pole snarled.

Bohun spoke, "Do you know anyone who does?"

"The Sapieha whelp," replied a Szlachic at the back, hand on rapier. "He's hiring sellsword scum."

Aleksandr smiled. "His address?"

❦ ❦ ❦

They wore Western clothing, masks, and rapiers strapped across their backs. They stood on a ledge overlooking Mecys' new apartment and stared at the two story building. The first floor was fully lit; the second floor was dark.

Time to strike!

Cossacks leapt down from the church onto their target's roof with a slight impact. They parted silently. Aleksandr went left to plant objects so suspicion could not fall on Zaporozhians. Bohun and Marko entered windows. There was no glass as the building had been constructed in Andalucían fashion.

Aleksandr threw around a chapka hat, jeweled pin, and silk glove. Those were not possessions of common Ruthenians. He took thick hemp rope from his pack, lashed it tightly around a beam, then lowered himself to the dirt. He tied the rope to a pillar. By the moonlight Aleksandr drew weapons and waited guard next to their transport.

It was a narrow hall. Two guards, backs to Mecys' bedroom. Cossacks, masks off, approached. "We're here to relieve you."

"My thanks," groaned a young man in a capeline helmet, leather armor, and knee boots.

"You're welcome, friend." With that the two Cossacks drew daggers, and stabbed the young sellswords in the throat. "It's our pleasure." Marko flicked veins off his blade, continued to stab, vocal cords spilled out of necks.

"That's enough," said Bohun. His blood drenched shirt clung to him like a lake leech.

Marko made no reply; he opened the door inch by inch. Bohun took a torch from over the corpses to illuminate the pitch dark bedroom. Dim torchlight shone on an unconscious Mecys, unshaven, stinking of a smell Bohun couldn't place. He strode over to the bed, shook him like a cripple having a fit.

"He's not waking up!"

"Opiates," Marko said, "courtesy of Tsargrad; it seems the Sapieha clan's stance on peace with infidels is not purely for pacifism."

Bohun hauled the young man to the oak floor as if Mecys was but a barrel of rifle powder. "Hurry; the next sellsword shift could be in minutes," he said, depositing a false ransom note on a lice ridden pillow.

Armed with a dagger, Marko opened a window next to the door. The torch revealed a ledge, more than enough space for three men to stand. The two Zaporozhians carried Mecys toward the rope prepared by him. One hand on the body, another on beams, finally they reached it. Bohun held the line between Mecys' arms, and locked manacles around captive wrists. Steel cut into flesh, drawing blood. One push sent the unconscious Mecys speeding down the rope.

Within minutes Aleksandr stood beside their prize. The Sorcerer cut the rope. Marko gripped hemp, began his descent, and soon Bohun followed. The two reached dirt without accident.

Aleksandr smiled; somehow even in darkness Bohun could make out his stained, fragmented teeth.

"My compliments!" He kicked Mecys, but there was no response, "The point was to take him alive. The Inspired have little use for carrion."

"He lives. Thanks to opiates, we have no need for this," he explained, brandishing a blunt piece of firewood.

Cossacks moved swiftly dressing Mecys is Ruthenian clothing, tying him to a horse, dousing him in ale. The once great noble was now a simple Ruthenian drunk. The three adventurers spurred their horses as they heard their captive's former home come alive. A pursuit was unlikely, no one left to pay sellswords. They disappeared into back streets.

Finally, the Cossacks reached the meeting point; a half-demolished barracks, on the edge of town. The shell of a structure looked as if it had been struck by Greek fire, only a small room remained intact. After tying their horses behind a wall, the Cossacks entered with Mecys slung over Bohun's broad shoulders. Marko rested against a wall, stars shone through cracks in the fragile ceiling. Bohun placed Mecys upon a floor of broken glass, animal waste, and rubble. Aleksandr crouched, drew a knife, and thrust; piercing Mecys' ear.

"Haaaaaaaaaaaaa!" Mecys came to screaming, gripping his disfigured ear.

Bohun kicked the captive's jaw; teeth clattered to the floor. "Quiet."

The captive used his to linen to stop the blood flow. He tried to speak. "Whaaaa?" Aleksandr entered his line of vision, "You!"

"You heard my fellow Cossack; quiet." He ripped linen out of Mecys' smooth hand. Blood pooled; it was the signal.

Bohun felt sick again, the same feeling from the inn. Blue light spilled into the room, dancing on the walls as if they were in a sea cave. The light slowly took form: Koshchiy, suspended in mid-air. Marko and Bohun didn't possess the strength to move. A storybook villain hovered above ground, mere feet away from shock enthralled Cossacks.

He turned to Aleksandr. "You like secrets; that's why your kind takes to sorcery. Want to learn more?"

Conquering fear, Aleksandr said, "Yes."

❀ ❀ ❀

Centuries ago, when Yaroslav the Wise drew breath; the founder of house Sapieha made a contract with Koshchiy; a son from every generation in exchange for the ascendance of his house. Koshchiy accepted, from then on he had reliable source of human minds, their ideas to rely on. Then disaster struck: Mecys father foolishly refused, preferring to send his third son to Ruthenia where the patriarch thought his offspring would live in peace. Koshchiy was enraged. He could never take tangible form and he had no contract with any other Inspired to snatch Mecys for him. The old beast became patient and studied Mecys' routine.

Then inspiration struck! He would merely use superstitious Tatars, who lived on the borders of Ruthenian lands, to take the boy. He entered the dreams of beys; sometimes as djinn, other times as Eje, ordering them to take Mecys. Koshchiy used his sorcerous might to influence Mecys' judgment, sending him into a Crimean trap! Mecys was now a captive of Tatars, within Koshchiy's grasp. Then disaster: the Poles offered a ransom for the boy. The Khan took the ransom, ordering his beys to release Mecys. Desperate, the withered Inspired took the form of a Lisovyk, and attacked Aleksandr's fellow Zaporozhians at the exchange point.

⚜ ⚜ ⚜

"You tried to kill us!" Marko shouted, stabbing a finger at the ancient wraith.

"Would you have done anything differently in my place?" His sharp voice seemed to cut through the very air, the Inspired's smoke-like form twisted as he spoke.

Marko had no reply.

Koshchiy bent down to face Mecys. "Now my new allies, in the corner you will find a pair of manacles, bring it."

Aleksandr suddenly noticed bejeweled shackles to the left, as if they had been there all along. Requiring no further orders, he snapped them around Mecys' wrists. Instantly a beam of light snaked out from the chains, entering a phantasmic palm. Green light spilled into the room, filling the air like fog.

Exhaustion struck Marko, he tried to stand, tried to move. He thought of rejecting Christ; hell flames were a fair price for being able to move. Aleksandr struck the floor; anything outside his mind melted into night.

⚜ ⚜ ⚜

Aleksandr awoke to a welcome sound: flowing water. Perhaps he lay mere feet from his beloved Dnieper. The Cossack stood. He was in a Varangian ship, fellow Cossacks sprawled at his feet, Koshchiy at the helm. "Where?"

"You're on The River to the lower realms." As Koshchiy spoke Aleksandr noticed that the oars moved independently; as if the Norse ship was crewed by the dead.

"Come again?"

Koshchiy traced diagrams into the air. "There are a trio of worlds; your kind live in the middle world. You're currently on the river to the lower world, and my race live in the high world."

Aleksandr craned his neck. Walls of aquatic blue force flowed; encasing the ship like a casket. One simple question entered his mind.

"How?"

"The ship allows those from the middle realms to survive in The River," Koshchiy replied.

Aleksandr thought of childhood swims in the sea, below waves with only a reed to draw breath through. He sat next to an oar, half expecting to bump into an invisible galley slave. He looked at his friends. The two Zaporozhians did not have the appearance of men enjoying deep slumber; it was as if they were completely crippled. Where was Mecys?

"My property is already taken care of," replied the wizened Inspired. "If you wish to contact us, sing 'the enchantress'. It is a ballad of your lands."

"Understood," he said, trying to stop hand spasms.

Great, vibrant light exploded into Aleksandr's eyes, was he blind? Relief came with sight. This did not seem to be the painful rays of the middle realms. A distorted image formed above The River; a giant being sitting atop a throne with a silver head and a golden moustache.

"Hail Perun!" shouted Koshchiy.

No response.

"I beg admittance into the middle realms."

No response.

Finally the god spoke. "GRANTED." One simple word came out like roaring fire from the mouth of Zmey Gorynych. The light grew in intensity; Aleksandr felt the same ill sensation that touched Bohun. Aleksandr fell to the deck, into darkness.

Marko awoke, feeling not unlike Lazarus. He was filled with joy; his friends were safe. Bohun lay sprawled on the ground, Aleksandr sat staring at clouds. The vast plains of Zaporozhia greeted Marko. Home.

"In Zaporozhian Cossack country women are excluded from the clan; those who serve-for propagational purposes are relegated to islands, and when in need men go thither to use them.."
-Donatien Alphonse François, Marquis de Sade.

CHAPTER 15

Little had changed. Marko resumed his post without conflict. Bohun used his new wealth to purchase a yurt, relief from the noise of a kuren. Aleksandr's time was spent for educating the Hetman in the customs of the Inspired, preparing him for the Contract.

Aleksandr let memories fade as he entered the officer rada hall. The Hetman stood in the center wearing hussar boots, military trousers, a župan; he looked like a regal lord standing for a portrait. "Welcome Aleksandr," the Hetman smiled as he gestured with his bulava. "Is this garb suitable?"

Aleksandr seated himself. "Most do not even wear clothes."

"What ritual will you perform?"

"Singing, so no need for any infant sacrifices."

Aleksandr inhaled, this was no mere chapel hymn. There would be no time to cease to draw breath. He stared at paper in his hand, and then began:

"MY girl tricked me…
But she's so nice why should I mind?
Mother! Could'st thou a nicer find
To be the wife of this thy son?"

Samiylo began to sense vibrations in the air, as if the song had pierced the sky.

"As minnows in the water play
So would you slip and slide and turn
The while my heart must glow and burn.
My heart has reached its utmost bounds,
Yet still that fire gnaws, surrounds."

The vibrations began to grow; the space in front of the two Zaporozhians hummed with what both men knew to be life.

"Then, if you love me, plague me not.
You will not lose. See what you've got.
But, if you love me not, my own,
Charm me until I too am stone.
You'll lose if you don't love, I swear,
But, charm me, maybe I won't care!"

Piercing sound filled their heads; Samiylo clutched his ears, had a cannon gone off? The vibrations became waves; visible to untrained sight they flowed through the hall like smoke from an English witch burning. Suddenly there was a flash not unlike muzzle flare. Samiylo fell to floor planks. Aleksandr reeled back rubbing his eyes.

Sadko stood on air before them; not quite solid, but no mere wraith. "The Inspired have appointed me as an envoy."

Samiylo stepped forward, bewitched by the sight of a folk hero in a humble rada hall. "Oh hero of Novgorod, you honor the Sich with your presence."

Sadko ignored the compliment. "We offer complete support against any invasion and partial support for campaigns."

"I want full support against invasion for the next five centuries," replied Samiylo.

"Done. We have a contract."

"What now?" queried Aleksandr.

"Kaffa."

Aleksandr left to sound the chapel bell to summon the Sich.

❀ ❀ ❀

AN HOUR LATER

Kaffa, the hated capital of the Crimean khanate; the nexus of the Tatar slave trade.

"Fellow Zaporozhians," Samiylo began to address the general rada of Cossacks; chern, Atamans, "since the years of Yaroslav the Wise, our people have been preyed upon by Tatar infidels like beasts on the steppes. We shall take Kaffa! Plant a dagger into the Khanate's heart!"

Ostap stepped forward out of the crowd in front of the rada hall. "Why should we approve our own suicides?"

"What Cossack mistakes courage for madness?" A short distance, in the crowd, Marko smiled at his hetman's wit. "Come out!" emerged from the rada hall, "the spirits and races not of woman born stand with us against any enemy of Ruthenia! Cossacks, do you approve my plan?"

Sabres filled the air. Chern howled then threw their caps to the sky;

atamans fired pistols in unanimous support for an invasion of Kaffa. Men scattered into artels to begin work at preparing falconets, rationing food, sending riders out to settled villages.

Samiylo returned to the rada hall, followed by Sadko, who informed him, "We cannot transport your men to Kaffa, but thanks to spirits of the waters you will arrive at that cursed city in a fraction of the normal time."

"My thanks," the hetman said, turning his head from maps, charts.

Finally Baranko spoke. "Do you really expect me to approve of this hell-born alliance with demons?"

Samiylo kicked the old priest, who fell to the ground, and his klobuk rolled on the floor. The hetman lifted the old fool by his stained robes, hissing. "Listen to me! I let you live off the Sich in exchange for nothing. You support my decisions or fend for yourself in the steppes!"

"Cossacks are of the Greek religion, which they call Rus in their language. They hold feast days in great respect, as well as days of fasting, which they define as refraining from the eating of meat, and to which they devote eight or nine months of the year. They are so fastidious about this practice that they believe their salvation to depend upon distinctions among different sorts of food........ Beyond that, they are a faithless people, treacherous, perfidious, and to be trusted only in circumspection."

- Sieur de Beuplan

CHAPTER 16

THE NEXT DAY

Father Baranko stood on a hill over looking the Dnieper's bank, moving his anointing brush over the Cossacks below him.

"…Surround us with your holy angels that, guarded and guided by their host, we may arrive at the unity of faith and the understanding of your ineffable glory. For you are blessed to the ages of ages. Amen."

Baranko felt like a whore.

"Finally," Marko muttered. He wore a linen shirt, chain mail, a vest made from wolf skin, English trousers, and boots. He took his place at the chaika's helm, no one rowed; the current was enough to propel the four ships away from Ruthenia.

Since it was a Tuesday, Aleksandr uttered an invocation from the Heptameron as he donned a capeline helmet.

"I CONJURE and call upon you, ye strong and good angels, in the names Ya, Ya, Ya; He, He, He; Va, Hy, Hy, Ha, Ha, Ha; Va, Va, Va; An, An, An; Aia, Aia, Aia; El, Ay, Elibra, Elohim, Elohim…"

In the Hetman's chaika directly ahead, Noman sat, enjoying a laborless voyage. The Sich had already melted into the distance. The ships were surprisingly stable, not unlike walking across the floor of a kuren. Noman was comfortable in his costume. A kuczma fur cap kept his ears warm, a cloak was draped over his wool shirt, shovary pants ended at his postoly shoes. Unlike the other chern clustered about the chaika, wearing boots, tunics, western pants, Noman carried a recurve bow compete with an ornate yet small quiver case on his left hip while his sabre hung on his right side.

In the third chaika, Bohun sat next to Ostap; the old goat was asleep with a lap full of playing cards, and he smelled of decaying meat, beer, and vomit. Bohun took a kalkan shield off his back. It was light for a shield, made of iron-bound cane. He placed it next to his Hungarian sabre, musket and porochivnycia gunpowder flask. A northern squall swept through the ship. While it failed to wake Ostap, it chilled Bohun, who pulled a cloak tight around his chain mail; his lower half was warm due to shovary pants and postoly shoes.

The Cossacks were electrified because no Zaporozhian had ever before experienced such speed! Thanks to unseen Inspired power, chaiki raced by the caves, stones, and mudflats of the Dnieper. Hetman Samiylo swallowed when a bend lay ahead. Suddenly the chern began to shout in surprise, the ships were turning. It was if Triglav steered every vessel!

In the fourth vessel Oleg checked his paper and wadding. Chainmail covered the young Cossack's chest, his pistol was thrust into a sash, and his English trousers were dotted with holes unlike his shoes. Oleg pulled a chunk of stag out of his sack, he tested his berdish axe's sharpness; the moon blade easily sliced off corrupted flesh. He swept his eyes over the chaika as he ate. The other Cossacks checked weapons; few trusted their new inhuman allies.

Joseph stood at the helm in a command; a strictly ceremonial post. Joseph shivered, the squalls chilled him; even with his kalpak, cloak, wool trousers, and boots. He slung his rifle over his shoulder and tightened his sabre as he stared at the approaching view of the sea.

In the leading ship Marko waved at a passing Cossack patrol as the chaika passed the vine covered lookout point. Bohun smiled at the sight of darkened caverns at the Dnieper's edge; as a whelp he would dare other boys to enter the caves which were believed by all children to be lair of Zmey Gorynych. The Zaporozhians had no need to sneak past any galleots; they easily drifted through channels, passing artificial barriers. Before long the flotilla entered sea waters. Ferocious waves rocked chaiki, shocking Marko out of his thoughts and onto the deck. Aimed at Kaffa, the ships cut through the waves like kraken; no need to hug the coast.

Joseph could feel Crimea approaching, the land of his birth. He was the product of rape, his mother sometimes said his father was a soldier in the elite sekbans other times her rapist was an outlaw. While the Cossack never knew his father he knew he resembled him, mother beat him constantly, taking her vengeance out on the son of her rapist who had ruined her life. Joseph's childhood was spent friendless on the streets or inside his mother's huts receiving abuse: as a fatherless child he was a whoreson, lower than any Christian's pig. Hatred of his mother and Crimea grew in his breast. He heard of the Cossacks as he left childhood. Just as every

Tatar hated and feared them, he came to love the wild men who lived the life he had dreamed of. Finally as a young man he stabbed his mother to death and left Crimea for the Sich where he was accepted after converting to the Greek faith and taking the name 'Joseph'. That day his life truly began.

Marko asked, "Tell me; why is it that only I can see you?"

Sadko's form shifted to a smile. "The sea-Inspired taught me *True Arte*; which no man or woman can use."

"Your speech baffles me, Novgorodian."

Sadko's form shook as if he were laughing.

The chaiki spread out across the sea, forming a position to receive enemy ships; a testament to the Hetman's mastery of tactics. The small fleet passed boulders that looked like the finger bones of the giant Svyatogor. It was only due to Inspired guidance that the chaiki escaped the fate of being smashed on stones. Wind had died but the ships sailed on at high speed for Kaffa like a hawk diving for prey.

❦ ❦ ❦

MUCH LATER

"Kelmek!" Noman shouted, pointing an engraved pistol at a terrified Tatar in a small boat; from what Noman could make out he was a small turbaned man wearing the robes of a devout Mussulman.

Quickly the Tatar obeyed Noman's order to approach and rowed toward the chaiki; all of which had stopped on Sadko's command. The ships terrified the Tatar; the infidel vessels did not look like boats dead in the water, it was as if some force was holding them back like bulls on a leash. Finally the Tatar climbed into the hetman's chaika, immediately kneeling down; arms outstretched to show his new captors that he had no weapons. Noman barked questions at the man who promptly replied, the alien language sounded like the grinding of a carriage to Cossack ears.

"He's a fisherman with a house nearby," explained Noman. "No family."

"Has he seen any Mussulman warships?"

Noman obeyed the hetman's order, then replied, "No; the khans prefer cavalry to navy."

Samiylo's eyes went still for moments, and then he asked, "Who will take this Tatar and scout the land ahead?"

The quartet of ships became quiet; there would be no accusations of cowardice for staying behind, volunteering for this campaign was proof enough of bravery. Finally Bohun stepped forward. "I will."

"He's not going alone," replied Noman, stepping out of the throne of his chaika.

"I would be honored to be one of the first to set foot on land that will be ours!" Joseph exclaimed as he walked forward.

"You'll have assistance," said Samiylo with his back to Sadko.

At flintlock point, Noman forced the Tatar into his meager boat, Joseph and Bohun joined them. Bohun took in the boat as Cossack ships drifted away. It was a moderately sized rowboat; he was shocked that it didn't collapse under the waves under the weight of four men. The Tatar was small in stature, he had a gentle face and a trimmed beard; not youthful but far from grandfatherly.

Finally after a boring trip, their boat ran aground; Bohun half expected to hear the muezzin's screech the moment he stepped onto the yellow beach. The beach was narrow and resembled a pebble path. After tying a rope around the prisoner's neck, the Cossacks began to climb the hill that began where the slim beach came to an end. They soon reached the hill's summit, to be greeted by a view of a valley. A cottage was at the bottom of the valley and rolling gray hills dotted with trees and brush. The fisherman's cottage was worse than a serf's hut. Clothing and trash covered the floor while fish stink hung over the home like a vultures over war dead.

Noman said something to the fishermen, who whimpered a reply. "He has a horse in the back."

"Good," said Oleg, chewing salted sturgeon.

"Baqalamaq!" barked Noman; the fisherman obeyed the order to crawl. Bohun watched as Noman sheathed his sabre in neck, bone blocked his blade so Noman had to finish him by opening his neck. Once the fisherman was dead, Noman stripped the body, and used his blade to open the floor. He deposited his victim under the hut, then put the boards back in place.

Bohun suddenly felt ill; it wasn't the execution either, a presence far more potent than sturgeon rot enshrouded the hut. He stared at what looked like heat waves flowing over blood coated boards, sudden pain made all three Cossacks shut their eyes. Seconds later they stood facing Sadko.

"Oh don't look so surprised," snapped Sadko. "What did you think your leader meant by assistance?"

"Couldn't you have done all this?" whined Bohun.

"I'm your ally, not your serf; we aid you but we won't do every task for you."

Noman asked, "Did you propel our ships?"

"Must I explain it all to you?"

Noman's eyes dropped, he became sheepishly silent.

"I'll lead you to the farm,"

The small company left the hut. Noman mounted the dead fisherman's mangy horse and rode at a slow pace beside fellow Cossacks. "How many people live at the farm?" asked Bohun.

"A small family of five."

"Kill none," ordered Bohun.

"You do not sit at ataman radas!" growled Joseph, drawing his pistol.

Bohun gave the young chern a sharp glare. Joseph understood who held authority as he put away his pistol.

The land ahead was alien to Bohun. It was as if Zmey Gorynych had burned away all trees with his three mouths, leaving nothing but gray hills that looked like witch mounds, or piles of dust kicked up by a giant's horse. Joseph admired the magnificent view of the sea; it was said that great treasures from the eras of Athens and the Byzantium lay at the bottom of its depths.

Somehow the company made it to the top of the next hill. They lay on the summit staring at a farmhouse the size of a wealthy peasant home with horses grazing in pasture behind the house. "Take this," Noman handed a Tatar knife to Bohun, "Leave it on the ground."

Bohun only nodded as he and Joseph began walk down the hill. It had a steep slope that made Bohun recall memories from his time among artel expeditions to the Urals. The hill faced the windowless rear of the farmhouse; it was unlikely that they would be detected; however both men remained on alert. At last they walked on a level ground. Bohun and Joseph spread out. The farm was on a total plain; no place to hide. If spotted they would have to flee in opposite directions.

Joseph slowly approached a horse with a brown spotted coat; he let the horse smell his scent and finally mounted without trouble. The beast received worse treatment from Tatar whelps. He gently directed it towards the hills; a Cossack like any true steppe warrior has no need for saddles. He turned to see Bohun mounted on a gray horse full of life, unlike Noman's beast. They ascended the hill and rejoined Noman. The pair had barely reached the peak when ordered, "Follow."

Bohun mumbled a haunting tune as they wandered deeper into mountain foothills.

"God, lead us forth, poor captives.

From heavy bonds.

From infidel faith,

To the bright dawn,

To quiet waters,
To a gladsome laud,
To a Christian world.
Hear, God, our prayers,
The prayers of the hapless.
The prayers of poor captives."

❦ ❦ ❦

"Finished loading?"

"Aye; a canon ready to slaughter Tatars," Andriy replied as he wiped old powder and rust off his hands with sail canvas.

"A fine job," said Marko with a smile.

"I'll say one thing for Turks; they make good cannons," Andriy said laughing, tapping a falconet taken from the Ottoman galleot, whose crew paid the price for trying to invade Zaporozhia.

Marko laughed in agreement.

He gripped his sabre, "We'll find out soon." Andriy's head was enturbaned, he wore a tightly fitting shirt, leather armor, breeches, and hessian boots, a kalkan shield lay against his bench.

The ships had moved closer to the coast. Cossacks now had clear sight of cliffs, the color of dried wolf bone. Rocks the size of guard towers littered the beach of shells, the stones were the color of rain clouds and resembled fangs pulled from a sea serpent's jaws.

❦ ❦ ❦

Horsemen followed a trail that twisted through foothills, a short distance away from a road, to avoid any patrols. Sparse trees made Noman feel at home, so much of the Crimea was naked. He diverted his eyes from the sight ahead; a child could easily mistake the moss carpeted mountains for castle walls. He felt like a Circassian chief in his mountain home. The riders made no sound save for the noise of sabres, arrows, and compound bows as the horses plodded over stones and thick roots.

Joseph finished loading his flintlock. He tried not to stare at the Sirin; her breasts above plumage were small, while her voice sounded similar to flowing Dnieper water. He tucked his pistol away in his sash, and then gripped his wrist tight. Lust for inhuman females was a grave sin. He lightly gripped his mount's mane to slow the beast's pace, if his horse fell down the steep foothill ledge, Joseph's skull would shatter on granite.

Bohun resisted the urge to light his pipe. Smoke could alert nearby infidels, thus he put away his pipe, which was nearly the size of a kard dagger. The weight of his kalkan shield was an unpleasant distraction from his burning urge to sip the leather flask of ale in his bag. He was thinking of women from settled towns when he saw it: smoke. "Do you see that?" He said quietly to Joseph.

"Aye."

The two men dismounted. They left their horses with Noman. Followed by the Sirin, they approached the end of the tree line. Bohun peered out from behind a lichen-encrusted boulder. Plumes of smoke rose into the sky from a town.

"It's only a short distance from Kaffa," said the Sirin

Joseph asked, "Certain of that?"

The Sirin ignored him.

On instinct, Bohun's hand darted for his sabre. "Can you get this back to the hetman?"

"Of course," the Sirin said, tonguing her feathers.

"Then why did we go?"

The Sirin answered, "No benefit in that for *Us*."

"What?"

"That doesn't matter now," the Sirin cut off Bohun. "A patrol is on its way."

"Help us!" Joseph begged.

That smile again.

❧ ❧ ❧

The hetman held a rope as the chaika bucked on the waves, then turned to Sadko to ask, "This village, is it close?"

Sadko's form shifted to that of a priest, "Yes."

The hetman raised his bulava mace. "We will be on land soon!"

❧ ❧ ❧

Five warriors, they wore plate armor and spiked helmets with chain mail veils that masked their faces; the Tatars looked like daemonic high-waymen. As he watched them approach, one detail struck Noman; the cavalrymen had no rifles! "Snap their bow strings," he said to the Sirin.

"Done," replied the winged Inspired.

The five Tatars came within range. Bohun gave the order to, "Go! No guns, we can't draw others here." Joseph pressured the lever, a piece of pine, causing the boulder to fall. The stone crashed into the road, achieving the objective of trapping the Tatars. Too much risk in trying to crush them, the boulder could have missed.

Tatar mounts went wild! Hoofs flew, and riders pulled reins strangle-noose tight.

Cossacks ran down just as Tatars drew blades. Joseph fired an arrow but it only bounced off a ghazi's helmet. Joseph's target went for a bow. It was useless so he charged at Bohun. Noman blocked a slash from a Tatar. Sunlight beamed off Quranic inscriptions on armor. Infidel steel cut through Bohun's leg; ignoring blood flow, Bohun stabbed at the Tatar, who easily blocked the attack. Joseph fired another arrow; a direct hit in the jugular; armor has limits.

Noman's foe dodged a lunge then counterattacked, cutting Christian flesh. Bohun's shield blocked a thrust; he swung the kalkan wildly causing his enemy to leap back. With falcon speed Bohun gutted the Tatar. With his spine facing the boulder, Joseph parried an attack. The Ghazi stabbed high, then low. He narrowly blocked a thrust for his kneecaps. Noman's sword cut into Crimean armor. Torso exposed, the Tatar slashed, clumsy and desperate; easily parried by Noman, who thrust half his blade into enemy heart. Sabre arm searing, Joseph blocked another slash. He kicked the Tatar, swung his blade down. Joseph sidestepped as he thrust his sword into neck, a weak armor point.

Christian eyes turned to the surviving Muslim who ran for the horses, leaving his sword behind. Joseph nocked a shaft and aimed, ignoring all else but his enemy's neck. His fingers released the dart; a miss. The Tatar began to mount his horse. Joseph took another arrow and aimed while his target was struggling with high stirrups. He loosed the dart and the arrow impaled the Ghazi's neck. It snapped when the body hit dust.

"In the early sixteenth century many Tatars became Cossacks; even later in the century runaway or kidnapped galley-slaves from Turkish ships sometimes joined the Zaporozhians. In 1570 Sultan Suleiman complained that the Cossacks had been stealing whole Tatar families and bringing them to Kievan towns where women and children were settled, the men employed by Cossacks."
-Linda Gordon

"Cossacks ran down as Tartars drew blades."

CHAPTER 16

Boşboğaz was a fishing village without a garrison. After all, why would Kaffa's closest neighbor require a defense force? Cossacks ran through surf a short distance from the targeted town. With his back to the chaiki sailing for Kaffa, Ostap barked orders.

"Hide the boats, load guns." The ataman had volunteered to lead the capture of Boşboğaz. Chern obeyed and began to ditch small boats and fumble with wadding and powder.

Zaporozhians spread out through the country. It was a sun drenched land with more boulders than trees. The men climbed the hill in waves; if attacked the gunners would fire, then men armed with swords or berdish axes would counterattack. To Oleg the land of Tatary seemed alien compared to Zaporozhia; no golden grass twisting under the sky and he would have to march into mountains to enter a forest. The hilltop provided the warriors with a clear view of Boşboğaz's red tiled homes, mosque, and minarets on the sea's edge.

There was a crash! Ostap turned left to see a helmet rolling and three riders yards away. "Hold your fire!" he ordered. "It's Bohun, Joseph, and Noman!"

Soon the three Cossacks rejoined the war band. After customary greetings Bohun began to discuss tactics with Ostap, who told the gunner what he planned to, "Fire a falconet at their square."

"And alert all of Kaffa?" asked Bohun.

"What do you suggest?"

Bohun walked back to horses. "Disguise ourselves; we ride in wearing Khanate armor."

"Strip them," ordered Ostap, who pointed at the Tatar bodies, tied to the three mounts.

Noman stepped over a Ghazi's body, "Who else speaks Tatar?"

❧ ❧ ❧

Joseph felt entombed in the dead man's armor. He could barely breathe through the mail, which left hardly enough eye room to aim his new bow.

He rode beside Noman and Bohun on a dusty road to Boşboğaz.

Bohun was pleased to see so much dust. They could take Boşboğaz without blood simply by using one of the Golden horde's favorite tactics: tying weights to horse tails to kick up a cloud of dusk and make it appear as if an entire empire was about to take the Crimea.

Noman draped a horse blanket over the pistols in his belt. No true Tatar cavalryman would carry modern weapons. All three kept their bows and sabres close. Guns would be a last resort in the conquest of Boşboğaz.

As the horses raced toward the targeted village, Oleg realized how far he had come. He was the fourth child of a burgher family. The peasants owned more than his father, who took out his anger on his fourth boy. Oleg's childhood was patchwork of beatings and deprivation. On his fifteenth birthday Oleg was sent to Krakow for education. He thought he had found relief from abuse, but the beatings he received from other children for being Ruthenian, and the canings from teachers for his lack of discipline, proved him wrong. Three years later he was sent back to a home, threatened by creditors. With money stolen from a fellow student he bought a war flail and a horse then fled to the Sich where his education truly began.

"Remember the words?" asked Noman.

"Aye," he replied, thinking of the basic Tatar phrases that Joseph had taught him. Oleg tensed; they were yards away from entering the town. No military in sight, only peasants.

An elderly man greeted the disguised Cossacks as they reached the village's edge.

"Räxmät," Joseph thanked the old fool.

Boşboğaz drew closer, the road conscripted like snake skin under Crimean summer sun. Oleg stared at houses constructed of marble hued plaster or tile; they were so small it was like staring at a toy house in a vertep play. The Cossacks entered the town. The Mosque dominated the town square; a humble plaster structure with a domed rooftop and a minaret next to it.

An Imam greeted Noman who asked in Tartar, "We have ridden many miles and we need to rejoin our unit, are there any soldiers here?"

The Imam shook his head. "Nay."

Joseph directed his horse toward the holy man. "I have a message for your town's leaders."

"The council is almost about to start," the Imam replied. "Join us, friend."

Ostap placed his palm on Bohun's shoulder. "Wait for the signal."

"Yes, honored ataman," Bohun moved his hand away from the falconet cannon.

❀ ❀ ❀

Noman entered the Mosque, leaving his fellow Zaporozhians outside. A group of no more than ten men of varying ages sat cross legged in a circle. "We are honored to have a Ghazi with us this day," the Imam announced as he shut the pine door.

Noman removed his helmet then took his kalkan off his back slowly. He swung the shield at the cleric who went down gasping with the kalkan digging into ribs. Noman drew two pistols, "Lie down, arms spread!"

Shocked and helpless men stumbled down to their bellies and outstretched their arms. Noman walked to the Imam, sheathed a pistol then placed a cold blade on the elder's quivering throat. "Tell them to obey me!"

The Imam did as he was told.

Noman knocked three times on the door. Outside, Oleg told Joseph that he had heard.

"The signal!"

Joseph coolly walked behind the Mosque, drenched an arrow in oil, and set the dart alight. He fired it at clouds; a clear sign for the ataman, but far from a feat: a steppe archer can propel arrow miles away.

❀ ❀ ❀

"We shall take Boşboğaz!" Ostap ordered, seconds after sighting the flame arrow.

The hetman mounted one of five horses taken from fallen infidel warriors. He led chern downhill to take the helpless town, which he now knew to be defenseless. Half remained on the hillside with cannon, muskets, and bows ready to execute the ataman's alternate orders if events turned chaotic. Cossacks swarmed toward Boşboğaz like a Dnieper wave over dust. Chern marched forward, their osedlets twisting in the sea wind like banners. The hair lock was a tradition dating back to the Huns; to infidels the Cossacks truly were the scourge of god.

"Remember your orders," Ostap cried with his mace in the air "a show of force but no civilian deaths and no rapes."

Zaporozhians thronged into Boşboğaz. Ostap lowered his mace; it was permission to sack the village. Bohun stumbled off his mount and into the nearest home to find a father and son cowering in dirt. He battered the thin bearded man with a pistol butt, as the Mohammedan crumpled down Bohun grabbed the boy. "Where's your mother? Out with her legs spread for a low ranking bey?" He punched the whelp who sobbed and crawled to join his father.

No wine! No beer! Oleg took out his rage on a sheep, allowing blood to coat dirt.

Bohun left the house with a full purse; it took moments to find their money. The father's sole weapon was an old wheel lock rifle. He returned to the ataman. "Where do we place captured weapons?"

"In the mosque," ordered Ostap, pointing his mace at the place of worship, now ringed by chern guards. "Then find Oleg, Noman, and Joseph."

Bohun walked by Ruthenian men looting homes, beating people of any sex, burning homes. He passed burning homes, heat rolled through the air making him feel as if he was under the waves with Sadko on a journey through to the sea king's palace. He coughed up soot as he ran by chern butchering lambs. Boşboğaz would soon be like a slaughter field, without innocent deaths, a sight to terrorize patrols. Chern let him into the Mosque where he dumped weapons on a pile of guns and swords.

Bohun left the holy ground and immediately sighted Oleg and the two Tuma Zaporozhians. "The ataman wants to see you three."

They made their way across town square to Ostap who was still mounted, staring off like a head on a stake. "What are your orders, honored commander?"

"You'll find Tatar clothing in the house over there," Ostap said, pointing at a home in front of them. "After you've changed take the four horses," he took parchment out of his coat. "Follow this map; we need men watching the roads to Kaffa."

"Yes ataman," replied Bohun, taking the map.

"Who will lead?" Ostap asked.

A ternion of voices announced, "Bohun."

Soon the four scouts were wearing Crimean garb, riding to tie off Kaffa's veins. Oleg thought back to boyhood hunting, how his father taught him to surround the territory of prey.

❦ ❦ ❦

Fog waves. Samiylo could make out that the coast had changed from boulders and cliffs to smooth beaches and caverns.

"Have we reached Kaffa?"

Sadko said, "Nay."

"What about your kind's soldiers?"

"It is too soon for that."

Samiylo felt shame; a Cossack hetman mocked by a dead folktale character.

Sick with terror, Aleksandr reread grimoires to mask his fear in front of other Cossacks. He tested his knowledge of Goetic hierarchy and invocations; the sight of Angelic seals relieved fear. Maybe he would learn Mohammedan sorcery from whatever scrolls or tomes lay entombed in Kaffa's depths.

Marko tended to coals that would soon be used to set torches alight to fire cannons at Kaffa. As evidence of Inspired aid, another ship carrying so much shot would have sunk to join Greek vessels at the bottom. Like any experienced ataman, he knew how to judge morale. Tension cowled the chaika; men found comfort by checking weapons, examining useless sail canvas, playing dice games. Other chern stared off into fog occupying themselves with memories of family, women, and raids.

❀ ❀ ❀

Bohun steadied his horse, and then placed one hand against stone for balance. Each Cossack scout waited behind boulders, staring at the roads ahead. Oleg was so bored he felt like rock, though he understood why they had to watch the highways. Once Kaffa was under attack, riders would be sent to the forts, and any messenger would have to be slaughtered like a stag.

While his kalpak shielded his face from blaring sunrays, gnats mobbed around Noman as if trying to choke him. Joseph inspected his bow; the string made from bovine intestine did not seem to be at risk of snapping. Decades ago his uncle demonstrated the art of crafting a steppe bow: how bone and sinew were steamed and bound onto a wood frame to make one of the deadliest tools a warrior could possess.

"When you hear cannon fire, prepare to attack any messengers."

"The Cossack destroy, rob, burn, lead off into slavery, kill; often they besiege fortified cities, take them by storm, devastate, and burn them down."
-Portelli D'ascoli, 17th century Italian missionary.

CHAPTER 17

Boulders blanketed the steppe like a wreath. Ostap feared that every stone hid a Ghazi, thirsting for Christian blood. He led most of his men toward Kaffa while a small unit remained behind to control Bosbogaz. Mussulman villagers marched in front; enemy arrows would only pierce infidel flesh. A young mother, whose children remained in Bosbogaz, looked back at the ataman to ask, "How much further?"

Ostap knew Tatar language well from years of ransoming captives, so he was able to reply that it was, "Not far."

"Will I see my Tima again?"

"Never."

"Now!"

Sadko's form altered. The fog slowly dispersed, exposing two galleots, the same ships used by the corsairs from Salé, Bou Regreg, and other pirate republics. Marko stared at alien crafts that had no more than four pyramid shaped sails. Their make reminded him of a kilij blade, though one thing remained familiar, gun ports. Each galleot flew the Khanate's bayrak flag: a Tamga on a green background.

Samiylo watched chern who passed out grappling hooks, checked rifles, or sat in prayer.

"Where do you want me, honored Hetman?"

Samiylo turned to Aleksandr. "At my side."

Andriy's hand jerked toward his sabre, the galleots resembled bat winged beasts. He half expected the ships to soar into clouds to join the wild hunt. He stood by the falconet waiting for to hear the rih horn; the signal to fire.

"I shall aim your cannons," Sadko's form shifted as he 'spoke.'

Marko watched Tatar corsairs scramble about their ships loading rifles and cannon, all desperate actions. Orders echoed across the waves. Christian and Muslim ships continued to drift closer together. It reminded Aleksandr of hawks, seconds away from sparring, circling each other.

Hetman Samiylo sounded his horn and falconets fired. The roar attacked Marko, who fell down gripping his ears. Gunners commonly bleed from the ears. Shots de-masted the closest ship and demolished the second galleot's bow. Galleots returned fire. Only Samiylo saw Sadko wave a crystalline clear hand, which caused enemy fire to miss the chaiki. Chern rowed furiously for the galleots, eager to board while other Cossacks fired at the galleots, decimating bows.

❧ ❧ ❧

Zaporozhians had advanced; Marko could now see men littering the enemy's deck. Body parts drifted past, the ataman reached down to grab a hand but threw the meat hunk back. No jewelry. He ignited an arrow with a torch, then fired the dart. It punctured sail, which exploded into flame. As Corsairs rushed to suffocate the fire, Marko pointed his sabre at burning canvas and said, "Fire!" No need for Inspired aid, for the shot destroyed the cabin.

Aleksandr stared at chern with drooping oseledecs, wearing blends of Muslim and Christian clothing at war. If he had the courage to speak, he would praise God in all his names for the fact that not one Cossack was lost. The sorcerer traced a finger over his amulets. It felt like lies, since there is no greater test of belief than cannon fire. "I've an urge to join the boarding party, most serene Hetman."

Samiylo extended his bulava. "Granted."

❧ ❧ ❧

"Who are they?"

"I need time," replied Noman, focusing his scope on dusty riders. The Sich flag came into view. "Ostap and his men."

"Praise to Saint Achaicus."

❧ ❧ ❧

"...defend us in battle, be our protection against the wickedness..."

Aleksandr ignored mumbled prayers while he slid back trigger hammers, inches away from enemy guns. Would the subtle realms become his new home if he fell? Along with other gunners, he climbed onto the ship until he saw Tatars on the deck. Rifles and pistols cracked, killing Tatars and giving Cossacks time to board. Ears booming with pain, he jumped on deck.

The sight of throngs hacking at each other made him drop pistols, his muscles felt like frost. Rapidly he drew steel as a Tatar in Ottoman clothing rushed at the new foe. The sorcerer landed a kick onto a robed thigh and the Ghazi stumbled back. Aleksandr thrust his sabre into heart flesh.

He picked the body clean, sawing off fingers for rings, pocketing a money purse, taking and holstering a small pistol.

An arrow landed in his armor. Aleksandr had no idea if it was a fatal hit because he was in shock. Aleksandr spied a Tatar archer a short distance away. Quickly thinking, he dragged the dead Ghazi up against his chest for a carrion shield. Arrows struck dead flesh, driving Aleksandr closer to the edge. Tatar archers can fire volleys in seconds, making his sword useless. He had to save the pistol for…

He felt iron; a solution. Dropping his sabre, Aleksandr gripped rope and began to swing the grappling hook. Soon the hook blurred into gray air mass. Ever the gambler, he dropped the corpse and then let go. The hook cut towards the archer, landing in his flesh. Aleksandr wrenched the rope. Hook barbs skewered the archer's throat, exposing bone. Another tug and a Tatar jawbone broke off.

The sorcerer explored his chest. His armor had stopped the shaft from doing more than cutting his skin. He pocketed the arrowhead.

The flood of men hacking at each other with swords began to ebb. Cannon smoke clouded vision, he couldn't tell if he was on the winning side. Safely behind chern, Aleksandr sheathed his sabre, balanced on rails, then leaped into the remaining mast's rigging. In boyhood he had fantasized about exploring ships, now as he stared down on a deck filled with archers, he ached for childhood comforts. Arms throbbing, he continued to climb until he could see the entire Tatar side.

He hooked his limbs through ropes, secured for a nearly impossible shot. Aleksandr drew the pistol and inserted it through a loop. The flintlock was now level with his eye. Weight from the sword on his back kept the gun steady. He swept the deck for officers. His eyes passed over men clad in ragged garments with kalpaks, finally settling on an older bearded man in robes, boots of the finest leather, and a turban. Narrowing his breathing, the sorcerer turned sniper concentrated on the officer, waiting for him to stand still. The man kept pacing around the Tatar held deck portion. Finally he paused. Aleksandr pressed the trigger and the Tatar officer crumpled.

Shocked at the assassination, Crimeans halted, allowing the Cossacks to swarm the deck.

❧ ❧ ❧

Noman snapped his scope shut. "They're Tatar messengers, Ataman."

Ostap stared: distant dust clouds. "How many in number?"

"Five."

Ostap smiled. Citadel sized stones hid more than twenty chern; he turned to the captive mother who was leaning against rock. "You've a daughter?"

"Yes sir."

"I trade with Circassians, every tribe has men who would pay greatly for a virgin girl."

"I beg you! Spare my child!"

Ostap tugged at his mustache, "I will free you and your family without ransom," he paused, trying to remember words, "if you obey me."

❦ ❦ ❦

Aleksandr watched Andriy split a Tatar's skull open with an axe. Marko gutted a boy; the captain must have been a catamite in life. He climbed down, drawing his sabre to join the killing floor. He slashed a wounded man's arm, exposing soft pink muscle. His sabre flayed the Corsair; it was far easier than skinning a stag.

Cannon fire rocked the deck. Chern were using the galleot's guns to smash the remaining ship. He fell back as the partly skinned Corsair rushed toward the sorcerer, peeled skin flying like a flag. Instinctively Aleksandr raised his sabre, impaling the sailor, showering him in gore.

❦ ❦ ❦

The ataman had given one order: Do not kill the woman. Chern were insulted as if they needed to be told to avoid slaying a source of ransom or pleasure! The woman ran out to greet messengers, almost tripping over rocks, hiking up her skirts. Ostap heard her call out, "My husband! You must…" Wind drowned out her voice.

Bohun calmed his mount as he watched her lead Tatars. There were four men in armor identical to the cavalrymen he had fought, they carried spears, bows, and kiliji swords. He curled fingers around a nock; unlike Noman, Joseph, or Ostap, Bohun had never learned the Mongol draw.

Joseph drew his pistol. Enemies were nearly within the circle formed by concealed chern, was that the Sirin? He craned his neck; it was a humble bird, not even a hawk that could be taken as a messenger from Tengri.

Oleg watched Crimean horsemen, drawing close to the road, boulders on either side.

Noman locked eyes on Ostap, who would give his signal to attack.

❦ ❦ ❦

Aleksandr stripped clothing off a corpse. As a sorcerer he had little respect for the dead. Exhausted, he stumbled across the deck, past Cossacks looting bodies. The guns had gone silent. Marko perched in the rigging shouting in Tatar; was it surrender negotiations?

Aleksandr entered and admired the cabin. In life the captain must have had great taste; the walls were covered with Turkish tapestries. He peeled off his leather armor to find that the arrow cut was no longer bleeding, while bruises dotted his chest.

❀ ❀ ❀

"Isänme!"

The bey looked over the shoulders of warriors at a young Tatar. "Kaffa is under attack!"

"Oh?" Joseph directed his horse forward, "who is that beauty?" he asked pointing at Ostap's captive.

"A pilgrim whose husband is trapped under rock," replied the bey.

Joseph almost snorted. He tried to select an officer. All of them wore identical plate armor, mail over much of their faces, and spiked helmets. He drew a flintlock, his arm rushed out in a blur. Gunfire roared and a Ghazi collapsed with his heart blown into pieces. Before the Tatars could react, Joseph kicked his mount then drew another pistol, the fire missing the bey as his horse carried him into boulders. Ostap's captive ran.

The bey nocked and loosed an arrow at their attacker's direction. Joseph saw an arrow sailing over a rock and he raised his shield. It bounced off cane.

Ostap raised his bulava high and four Cossacks poured from the vast stretch of boulders.

Noman rode out shooting arrows, all missed save one that struck a Tatar's thigh; few men rode with leg armor. Oleg fired at the Ghazi to the bey's left; a miss. The Tatar shouted in broken Latin, "You should have thrown pebbles instead!"

A Tatar charged at Bohun swinging a kilij, prompting Bohun to draw his sabre and ride out to meet the challenge. Joseph released arrows, which only bounced off shining Mussulman armor.

"Ataman, let us fight!" a chern begged.

"That would be unwise," replied Ostap, putting his Bulava away in a sash.

Bohun blocked an attack. A clash of sword steel rang out the Cossack thrust. The Tatar warrior raced at Joseph, who loosed an arrow at the Crimean's horse. It speared the beast's eyes, causing it to buck wildly.

The bey began to retreat; his men were nothing compared to the message. His duty as a believer was to his Khan. Oleg's command to "surrender" only made him laugh.

Driven mad by vision loss, horse hoofs flew, scraping stone. Joseph focused his bow on Tatar mail, and let fly. Bohun jerked the reins; his horse darted right, carrying his rider away from the Tatar's attack. He kicked, causing his mount to turn left. Bohun slashed out with sabre. Joseph's arrow had skewered his enemy's neck. The tuma dismounted slowly, approaching his fallen enemy.

Gunfire shattered rock and Joseph ran through rock dust. Bohun drove steel through mail, gore spilled out of armor, just like cracking open clams on the Dnieper's shore. Joseph's boot landed on his enemy's bare left arm just inches away from a second pistol. An arrow shaft stuck out of his side. Joseph finished him with a blade.

Chern surrounded the enemy bey, who called out in Latin, "I challenge you!"

Ostap smiled, "Anyone for it?"

Oleg raised his hand.

❁ ❁ ❁

Rubbing his eyes, Aleksandr buckled on his armor. Now that he had worn it during killings, it felt comfortable, like a kuren bunk. The sorcerer ignored the captain's luggage, which could be protected by bound spirits; he would plunder the Khan's chambers.

He opened the door: Marko stood in the deck's center.

"Any captive Christians in the galley?"

"None," replied Marko, sweeping his arms over Mohammedan bodies. Galley service was an effective prison sentence for Khanate Tatars.

"Your orders ataman?"

"Kaffa is close. Let me explain my plan..."

❁ ❁ ❁

Oleg felt as if his chest had been branded. He gripped his lance. Horsetail hung near the blade, the young chern locked his legs around the horse's torso.

A few yards away was their bey, mounted on his war horse without armor. "Come on boy," he taunted in mangled Latin. Zaporozhians surrounded them so the bey wouldn't escape.

He took in the Tatar; the man wore simple clothes, a well trimmed beard that highlighted his gentle Mongolian features, and hair the length of a woman's dangled around his ears.

Oleg held firm, waiting for his enemy to make the opening move. The bey spurred his horse on; Oleg kicked his horse; two warriors speeding at each other with lances. He thought about boyhood tales of Turks impaling righteous Christians. Less than a yard away, Oleg tightened his legs. He hurled his lance, at the same time drawing his sabre. The bey easily dodged the missile, but Oleg slashed, shattering bey's lance.

The Tatar yanked the reins, causing his horse to wildly turn left, away from Oleg. He unsheathed his kilij and charged at Oleg, who rode out to meet the attack. The bey thrust low, slicing Oleg's thigh and horse flesh. Shocked at the pain, the Cossack's mount darted right.

Horses undulated, making swordplay similar to trying to hit a stag while balancing on rolling barrel. Oleg slashed; the bey easily blocked his clumsy stroke.

Joseph kept his hand on his pistol, despite the ataman's orders that if the Mohammedan won, he would save Oleg's life.

Thinking of the Parthian shot and his aching arm, Oleg kicked his horse, which carried him away. The bey raced after what seemed to be a retreat. When the Tatar was only feet away, Oleg swiveled, swinging his sabre, which cut through the bey's flesh. The Cossack chopped down, slicing his mount's head.

Ostap stared on; would he drape red cloth over such a young face?

Oleg beat the blunt sword edge into his horse and the beast carried him away. He tugged the reins and the horse turned around. A gash long as a kilij blade covered the bey's chest but somehow he and his mount lived.

The Tatar's face remained still as Tengri's sky, but he muttered in his own language and then galloped on, waving his sword. He embraced pain just as he had accepted the true faith. He came on Oleg, wildly stabbing in every direction, penetrating only air.

Oleg continued to block and counterattack. He wanted to tear this proud Ghazi down and see his pride die before his life was extinguished; to know that he, a proud member of the Khan's elite, had been defeated by a mere youth from the wild fields.

Bohun strained eyesight watching the duel. He admired Oleg's fencing skill, how he could block attacks with split second reaction. The bey's strokes began to slow; he lurched forward in his saddle like a scarecrow.

Oleg attacked, thrusting his sabre into the other man's chest, perforating a lung but missing the heart. The bey coughed blood. He tried, and failed, to talk. The Zaporozhian corrected, wrenching his blade around in a half-circle, grinding marrow and organs until his sabre reached Tatar heart. A corpse fell.

Oleg stumbled off his horse. His arms felt dead. He began to clean his sabre when he heard the chants from the throng.

"Oleg!"
"Oleg!"
"Oleg!"

Cossacks erupted into a celebration, crying his name! Only Ostap remained silent.

"Cossack saykas are ravaging the coast and have set fire to...villages! Oh my sultan come to the rescue!"
-*Evliya Celebi*

CHAPTER 18

"You killed everyone?"

"Aye."

"A fine job!"

"The second ship is useless."

"I can see that, Marko," said Samiylo. The second galleot was already beginning to sink.

"The one in our control has no remaining cannon shot."

Samiylo spotted Sadko at the bow of his chaika. "What do you suggest?"

❦ ❦ ❦

Aleksandr leaned against mast timber. His cross had fallen from his neck during the battle; farewell to a trinket. He removed his helmet and tried to recall silence. The deck screamed with chern boasting of kills, trading trophies.

"Wine?" He turned to see Andriy who repeated the question. "Wine?"

The sorcerer's throat burned. "No."

Andriy shrugged. He drank the corsair captain's wine. Men who lived in the Khanate had a loose understanding of Islam.

❦ ❦ ❦

"Kaffa is only a few miles away," Sadko said to the hetman with a voice comparable to steppe winds.

"I need a volunteer," Samiylo shouted at the men in his chaika. "I can't promise survival; you chose me to lead, not to lie!"

Andriy approached and knelt. "Allow me, most serene Hetman."

"Granted." The hetman turned to Marko. "Your ataman will explain."

❦ ❦ ❦

Ostap craned his neck; the men he left behind to guard roads had faded into distance as though they had sunk into the waves. He knew Crimean roads well. Kaffa was not far. Soon he would see those hated gray walls, those guard towers spiking toward heaven.

The Sich needed treasures in lowly aristocrats. Ostap's first ransom freed a family taken from a village miles outside Kiev. When they embraced him he felt worthy of God's love for the first time.

Chern behind mounted Cossacks marched in square formation, the best structure to receive cavalry. Zaporozhians who owned guns were on the outside. In the event of battle, gunmen would fire, then other Cossacks armed with blades would attack, then they would retreat under cover provided by archers.

Oleg stared at his bow case hanging on his horse's side, how many empires had steppe archery founded? Bohun rode besides him. "If Marko dies in battle, you could become the kuren's next ataman."

"I'm chern, an infant."

"No Cossack forgets heroism."

❀ ❀ ❀

Andriy hauled a small row boat onto the Corsair craft's deck. His ataman only had to explain the orders once; only a catamite could forget such simple commands. He fell back onto oars as the galleot began to tear through the water, propelled by some unseen power. Every fear about demons his mother taught him in their humble settled Cossack home came to mind. Excitement replaced terror; he was in command of his own ship! At least until Kaffa harbor. He looked down-sea at automated chaiki moving off like toy birds in a vertep play. Once the ship was stable, Andriy went to work unloading supplies.

❀ ❀ ❀

Samiylo gazed at beryl-hued water like a sorcerer watching an Angel appear in a scrying medium.

"There are Athenian ships at bottom of this sea," Sadko informed his ally.

"Did you know the crew?" Samiylo asked with a chortle.

"The ships sailed long before I left my mother's womb." It was strange to speak of flesh. "I've traveled the sea's floor and seen much treasure."

Samiylo said, "Any remaining scrap counts as treasure."

"Aye."

The second galleot dipped underwater. Fowl dove from shale cliffs to snatch up meat chunks from dead Tatars bobbing on waves, massed together like a dam. As Aleksandr watched a heron swallow entrails, he thought back to Marko's account of his battle with the Kerkes. He climbed up from his seat, pleased that he could stand without his knees trembling.

He walked past a dice game. A chern with a dark beard said, "Come! Gamble!"

"Nay," said a Cossack in worn capeline helmet. "He'll possess the die like a demon, and win every ducat!"

Aleksandr smiled, he couldn't do such a thing as control dice. "I'll play fairly, my word as a son of Zaporozhia."

The bearded Cossack grinned. "Your bet?"

He dipped into pockets and found few coins. "Two ducats?"

❧ ❧ ❧

Marko examined his firearm; no damage from battle. He attached a damp cloth to a stick, rammed it through the barrel, cleaning away corruption. With dry swabs he removed water traces. He began to wipe his sabre of blood, a pointless task yet an effective display of his abilities to men from his kuren, without boasting like a boy.

❧ ❧ ❧

"Oh!" Aleksandr cried in mock outrage.

The bearded chern pocketed ducats. Aleksandr had learned that his name was Yaure.

❧ ❧ ❧

The distant sight of Kaffa made Bohun's chest as weak as if he had been shot with a falconet. He directed his horse downhill, staring at the well formed Cossack company. No general would have thought that 'bandits' could become elite combatants.

He waved hands as he rode down in a signal: No troops. "Peaceful as a newborn's crib," he reported to the ataman.

"You've never known fatherhood," muttered the old man.

"Orders?"

"We wait, as the hetman commanded."

"Aye most serene Ataman."

❧ ❧ ❧

Andriy left captain's quarters, the only space apart from the deck that wasn't loaded with Tatar bodies. He watched the chaiki halt at land. Innumerable men poured from ships fully armed to take Kaffa, leaving enough men in each vessel to fire cannon. Forming his hand into three fingers, Andriy crossed himself then began to whisper a prayer to the few saints that came to his memory.

"Military experts claim that this rabble, because of its bravery and skill, is unmatched in sea-warfare by anyone in the world."
-Ottoman historian Naima

CHAPTER 19

The Hetman watched Kaffa return fire. From the hilltop he could barely make out men scrambling along ramparts.

"Your ships will be untouched."

Samiylo turned to Sadko, "You have my trust."

Yards away, Marko addressed men under his command, "You all know that the Tatar favors the bow over the gun, yet Kaffa has Shiqtare riflemen, even Christian snipers recruited from Wallachia."

Bohun fitted an arrow. The Hetman's forces were split half on the south side of Kaffa while Marko's men stared at the Western part of Kaffa from behind boulders. "Most serene hetman, I would like to volunteer as one of the riders."

❧ ❧ ❧

Aleksandr finished loading a falconet; he drew back, allowing Yaure to touch a torch to its fuse. The sorcerer turned away, his head in pain. He removed his capeline helmet then asked, "A direct hit?"

Yaure squinted. "A main wall, near the shop camps."

Aleksandr ignored Yaure as he discharged a pistol, the signal.

❧ ❧ ❧

As the shot echoed over waves, the hetman turned away from Ostap to Sadko, aloft over cliff rocks. "Now."

Andriy tumbled toward the stern, scurrying to his feet he peered over the side. The galleot was beginning to enter Kaffa harbor. He rushed into the captain's quarters, grabbed an oil jar and a box of coals. Sitting on the bed, he inserted a touch wrapped in dry grass into the glowing coffer, igniting wood. He fanned the flames, and then touched the stave to blankets. He dragged furniture to the bed, now covered by fire. He exited the cabin leaving an oil trail.

Andriy worked quickly. He now had an excellent view of minarets, towering walls, and vendor camps. Inching past oil as he made his way into

"...soaked canvas that instantly exploded..."

rigging, he balanced on a beam carrying a torch and an almost empty jar, which he splashed on a sail. He held his torch on soaked canvas that instantly exploded into dancing flame.

"Bless your courage Andriy," the Hetman mumbled. Putting away his scope, he turned to Sadko. "Increase speed."

Andriy threw wood and fire ignited, blanketing the deck. He lowered his boat over the side, jumped to find the water was almost warm, unlike the frigid Dnieper rapids. He was about to swim for the boat when a blow struck him, and some force began to drag him under. The young Zaporozhian writhed like an impaled woman, as he fought for the surface's sweet air.

❦ ❦ ❦

Aleksandr focused his scope on a galleot afire, and cutting through waters directly for Kaffa's entire fleet, an empty rowboat, "I don't see Andriy."

"We cannot risk the chaika to save him."

❦ ❦ ❦

Andriy had not been claimed by ancient krakens or sea serpents. Mundane wreckage from rigging clung around his leg, pulling him down to sea rocks. His lungs seared with pain, he swallowed water. He drew a kard dagger, blindly trying to cut ropes in shadowy water only to find them too thick. Only pistol shot would cut them off. Andriy began to slice away footwear, blood soon colored seawater: sloppy work of a half drowned man. He ignored pain, and continued cutting. As ropes fell away, he darted up toward air.

❦ ❦ ❦

Oleg stared at Kaffa. To his untrained vision, the walls seemed to be mountain thick. He watched camps of vendors fleeing for what safety that proud, evil city offered.

Joseph envied the men Ataman Ostap left at roads; oh to be tasked with cutting messenger flesh instead of conquest!

Noman proudly wore Ghazi armor. Any Crimean would see that he had already slaughtered warriors of the Khanate, a devastating insult.

Marko watched lines of Cossacks under his command, an almost innumerable horde. He examined armor for flaws, sharpened blades, and loaded firearms.

❦ ❦ ❦

Andriy surfaced to the sound of artillery; the khanate returning fire. Desperate to slow the burning ship, he took many breaths, then dove, putting his weary lungs to a test. He clung to galleot ropes watching cannon shot sink all around him like fallen angels crashing down to dust. He now understood the general range of Crimean cannon.

Just as he was about to swim off, he saw oak fragments. What was once his boat now littered the waves. No matter; he had swum greater distances as a young chern. He pushed off against ship wood and a few cannon balls fell near. Andriy began to swim for his life.

❧ ❧ ❧

"Stupid," Yaure said staring at cannon bursts from Kaffa. "They've given away their exact artillery range."

Aleksandr kept silent, scanning the harbor: Andriy entered his scope, a ragged soaked man swimming through cannon fire, a man worthy of being elected as ataman. "Prepare to return fire," he ordered.

"We've little shot," Yaure said, pointing at a small pile of cannon balls next to Cossack seamen.

"Do you value the life of a fellow Zaporozhian, a Christian?" The sorcerer gave his scope to Yaure. "Turn that glass toward the flaming ship."

❧ ❧ ❧

Vomiting water, Andriy swam for land. His chest ached as if cannon shot had landed on his ribs. He half expected to choke up bone fragments. The Cossack-pirate halted, allowing the current to carry him for his arms' sake. Now out of cannon range, he could afford rest. He almost hoped that he would swim into colder water to numb the relentless pain from his foot wounds.

Yards away was coastland. He rotated in the water toward a fragmented view of the fiery ship, now a short distance from Kaffa's entire fleet.

❧ ❧ ❧

Infantry mounted and afoot, spilled out of Kaffa. They wore civilian clothes and unmatched armor. Either the Khan thought very poorly of Cossacks or his most important troops were at the docks.

Oleg stood in a line of archers hidden behind a hill, below a unit of warriors. He tried to get an exact count but failed, was it 15 or 20? He watched Marko wave his mace. Joseph and Bohun obeyed the signal to attack.

Two horsemen rode out from the north, releasing shafts. Tatar infantry reacted like a peasant mob, discharging guns and loosing arrows without aiming. Only a few arrows hit Cossack shields. Noman and the other mounted archers screamed insults in Tatar as they shot at infantry. Oleg counted at least five men down, but he couldn't be sure of his count. Combat was a quick blur; it was as though he was watching an ancient chariot race.

"Prepare yourselves!" he heard his ataman cry as infantry chased the three men directly toward Marko's forces.

"No time to pray," he heard Noman mumble as infantry advanced into their trap. One lone petty officer stood yards away, screaming in Tatar from his horse.

"What is he saying?" Oleg asked Noman.

"Orders for them to stop," replied the Tatar.

❦ ❦ ❦

Yaure hauled Andriy aboard. Aleksandr was shocked that he was still alive. Ragged clothes hung from his pale body, blood trickled from wounded feet. "Bring alcohol and cloth!" he ordered chern.

"Hurry," groaned Andriy, choking up water, "We need to finish the harbor." The fired ship had set the entire fleet aflame, and warships burned like faggots. Tatar efforts to choke off the fires were hopeless as the blaze consumed vessels.

❦ ❦ ❦

Tatar infantry came into range while the two Cossacks turned left, safely out of range. Marko ordered men, "Shoot!"

Oleg and his fellow marksmen obeyed, releasing an arrow swarm. He strained his eyes, trying to distinguish Christian from Mussulman. A Tatar rider fell and a rock drove the arrow bulging out of his eye socket into brain flesh. A Muslim rolled, spasming, arrows jutted from his torso and groin. A Ghazi pulled shafts from leather armor that saved him from death wounds. Oleg nocked a shaft and aimed. He loosed but the arrow missed and soared off. He fitted a second shaft, sighted his target, and then let fly. That arrow flew toward sea waters.

❦ ❦ ❦

"I could do something for your wounds," offered Aleksandr, as he watched Andriy tie blanket strips around his feet.

"Perhaps later," he smiled. The cuts were not so deep; he had survived worse as a boy.

Aleksandr left Andriy lying on a bunk with Zaporozhian remedies: a wide alcohol selection from past raids. Years at a rada, men openly contemplated going to war with Venetians merely for their spirits. He passed chern loadings guns and took his place at the bow, which gave him an excellent view of the other chaiki, now fanned out across the harbor.

Yaure waved the Sich flag, an angel standing over a slain serpent, and ships began to fire on Crimean targets that now lay within range.

Aleksandr welcomed the cannonade, the explosions. It was victory's symphony. Unlike fellow Cossack-pirates, he could develop new senses.

❀ ❀ ❀

Oleg fumbled for a dropped arrow. His fingers felt like ice and he saw the bey's eyes falling into darkness. Finally he scooped one up, nocked and then launched it only to watch it fly over men.

He remained on the sidelines instead of joining others rushing into combat. Below, men fought, giving the Khan and his beys entertainment. Oleg watched Noman fire a pistol that killed an armored Tatar, a foolish waste given the close range. He could see that Bohun was winning a duel with a Tatar armed only with a dull axe. Cheers of admiration filled his ears as Marko defended Joseph from the Muslim that wounded him. Oleg chose to keep an arrow fitted to his sinew bowstring to appear as if he was still trying to snipe at enemy troops.

❀ ❀ ❀

Yaure fired the falconet from the bow as he wiped blood from his ears with a swab rag. The shot exploded forward, destroying dock sections and massacring troops. He squinted but it was too far way to get a body count. It was possible to see Tatars futilely discharging rifles at chaiki which were easily out of range from Kaffa's cannons.

Aleksandr smiled. The entire Crimean fleet was degraded to driftwood, which combined with the chaiki, effectively locked Kaffa off from the sea. Cossacks gunners avoided firing on Kaffa proper because any shot would likely fall short thanks to the city's mountainous height, Yaure feared killed Christian captives, though a quick death from a falconet was a mercy as opposed to life as property in Tatary. The Zaporozhians opted to fire on and destroy troops sent to the docks, which had little cover. It was as effortless as shooting at a livestock herd.

❀ ❀ ❀

Five surviving Tatars raised arms, stepping over at least fifteen Tatar dead to surrender. While some chern had been wounded, no Cossack had been killed. Oleg turned to Marko, who stood on a hill, cliffs to his back. "Tend to wounds, strip bodies of armor, weapons, and anything useful."

Oleg walked downhill, putting his bow away in the ornate case swinging at his hip and covered in ornate Turkish calligraphy. He saw Joseph bury a berdish axe in a half dead man's neck. Bohun searched pockets. Chern worked fast; crows would soon descend.

Oleg paused at a Ghazi in full armor. He removed the spiked helmet to find a young face coated in wounds and bruises. As he began to remove plates he found a purse filled with coins.

"I'll take that," Oleg looked up to see Bohun standing over him with a Tatar sabre on his shoulder.

"It's mine," he meekly replied.

"My kill."

Seeing disaster ahead, Marko yelled, "All money will be turned into the Hetman, who will fairly divide it." He paused. "You can keep armor and weapons which will sell for fortunes."

Noman passed by, carrying an ornate Ottoman rifle. "I'll take that to our most serene hetman."

"I don't stand in the way of your living," Bohun snarled as he handed over plunder.

"Ataman! The hetman demands your presence," shouted a chern in a capeline helmet holding a newly accrued Turkish pistol.

"Thank you."

"Miroslav," said the young unshaven chern. He wore rough cotton shirt under leather armor, gray trousers, and Tatar boots. Marko correctly concluded that Miroslav was not from his kuren.

"Who is your ataman?"

"Ostap, sir."

Marko nodded. He climbed the hill, staring at the cold sight of Kaffa as he walked to the Hetman, who stood admiring the sea while chern stabbed a sapling into soil. "You asked to see me most serene Hetman?"

"Tomorrow you are to wear simple clothes, no different from a chern. We can't have Tatar marksmen picking off commanders."

"And my armor?"

"Keep it, I advise you to wear your armor under your garments."

"Understood, sir."

"I have orders for chern under your command. I need a few items…"

❦ ❦ ❦

Cannon fire had reduced what was once a strip of vendor tents to wreckage. Yaure thought back to ships smashed on rocks as he stared at piles of timber and canvas. He could barely make out body parts thanks to the distance. He pointed a falconet at stairs leading to Kaffa's sanctuary and fired it, producing an explosion that knocked a nearby chern down. He stared through smoke at a new crater in the cliff. A miss.

Aleksandr cleaned his ears. The bleeding had been caused mostly by his helmet. From his view on the bow he could see Yaure loading a falconet, and the sorcerer turned, cringing in anticipation. The cannon discharged and Aleksandr seized lines in fear of capsizing.

Regaining his calm, he opened and focused his scope. A massive fissure lay in the center of the stair. But was it wide enough to justify wasting a previous shot on a gamble of a target?

From the Hetman's position he saw the flag flowing from a newly planted pole, the signal to cease fire.

"Cossacks plundered and ransacked the city, made its families slaves, and then set fire to the buildings. In short, they not only desolated the whole place, but robbed and spoiled every house and family in the neighborhood , and afterwards set off in their boats."
  -Naima

CHAPTER 20

"I will not abandon my people," Mehmed Giray IV said as he left the balcony to catch a distant view of invaders. "What message would that send?"

Canibek nodded at his Khan's wisdom. "Very well." The bey felt imprisoned in the Khan's tiny circular chamber.

"Father!"

Mehmed turned to see his son Kamil running through sekbans, the Khan's personal guard, and past the men of the kurultay assembly. Wearing embroidered robes and slippers, he was a handsome boy with gentle Tatar features who kept his head smooth due to pests. Kamil leaped into the arms of his father, who could see terror in his child's eyes. "Who are these invaders?"

"Pig eaters, savages from Ruthenian plains," Mehmed explained, "who I will defeat." He smiled upon seeing that his child had relaxed. "Would you like to hear poetry?"

"Yes," the little prince exclaimed, clapping his hands.

Mehmed sat with his son on the cushions at their feet. "I wrote this poem last night." The monarch's library was filled with scrolls; mostly his own works.

Kamil lay back on cushions ,tracing designs on the wall with his finger, trying to imagine how such tiny images of tigers and warriors were implanted onto cloth.

Mehmed cleared his throat, and began to recite from memory:
"Why is the soul sobbing, why does it drop into woefulness,
have you decided that it will never get rid of the grief?
On a beautiful day, pain is your happiness,
say, have you decided that justice will never console you?
The soul doesn't fear the loss of the torment,
the pain has set the "check," and now the "mate" is dawning,
like a barge on a wave, and a dark sunset,
have you decided that a mild wind will never start to blow?

What happened, my soul, what is going on with you?
Why are tears of blood filling your eyes?
You have lost the joy that you used to have
have you decided that it will not find (another) stronghold?
Destroyed, deceived in the service to his own kin,
he is burning his soul in a fierce flame
there is a peace in this: grief from day to day,
say, have you decided that life has already passed, and that nothing happens?
Tied with my soul to my black-curled love
my breast burns in flame, it loses its peace,
why do you sob in woe?
why? Have you decided to beweep your desires?
I have recognized the essence and the measure of the world
Thank you, I understand you within myself.
On the gate of enlightenment, I have learned the secret.
The lands of Osman give, they don't take away.
The Almighty turns the wheels of destiny,
those secrets of the course of life that are invisible to the eyes,
and the secrets of meaning not given by the reason
He has built the world out of particles of fog.
Carefree, he awakes and creates from the non-existence,
From earth, water and fire
the Creator has built your soul and floats without faults.
But do not be careless, everything that exists is a gift,
in the hands of Azrael lies the deadly stock,
he sells the soul of the lover as a commodity
the destiny makes things happen for the man and it deceives him.
But come now open your eyes
you have been weakened by your wound, but don't despair
the Creator gives justice, and you should chase away the grief,
his Name may be one, but his grace is many oceans."

Mehmed drew his son close to him; feeling his heartbeat gave him hope and made him remember what he was willing to die for.

※ ※ ※

"While we have the harbor contained, it's not a suitable entry point. Zaporozhians would have to take a long narrow climb while completely exposed to any missiles. There wouldn't be enough survivors to take the city," Andriy explained, admiring the Hetman's tent.

"Thank you," replied Samiylo, turning back to Ostap, Marko.

"Any further questions?"

Ostap said, "Leave."

Andriy obeyed. He felt no rage at Ostap's insult; he could feel nothing but joy at how his feet were fully healed, save for scars. Praise Jesus! Or whoever that sorcerer worshipped.

He passed tents made from patchworks of hide or sail, and walked by men melting down Tatar helmets into bullets.

"Has your health improved?"

Andriy turned to see Aleksandr sitting on a log next to a lean-to shelter. "Yes, thank you."

"Thank Michael."

Andriy stepped closer to the shelter, out of the way of a bare-chested chern with a foot long oseledet carrying a bucket of stag fat which was fuel for fires. "How is that you have not called on Him to aid us in battle?"

"Angels will intervene individually if evoked by those with... skill." He paused searching for metaphor. "Imagine a game keeper helping an injured fawn after hearing its cries of pain; yet that man will not aid one stag herd in a conflict against another."

The comparison made Andriy pale.

☧ ☧ ☧

"It is simple; we wait for Khan Mehmed to make the first move," Samiylo answered Ostap.

"And our allies?"

Ostap faced Marko. "I'd rather understand how we can use them first. When I received my first pistol, I didn't fire in a random direction."

Marko nodded.

"We are agreed?"

"Aye." Marko raised his mace in acknowledgement.

"Ostap, give my orders to the others," Samiylo ordered.

☧ ☧ ☧

Bohun joined chern rushing to the camp's center where Ostap stood on a stone holding his mace. He stood next to the Hetman's tent as the saintly old man explained that they were to prepare for war, but remain hidden from Tatar sight to make the camp appear defenseless. A trap! He lost sight of the ataman as Ostap left to rejoin Marko and Samiylo whose orders resulted in a rush of chern hurrying off, most of whom had little if any work to do.

"Do you have a grindstone?"

Bohun turned south, toward Oleg. "No."

"Oh." The young man began to leave.

"What son of a Turk wouldn't allow a hero like you to sharpen steel?" asked Bohun in mock outrage.

Oleg remained mute.

Bohun went through his pockets. "Here," he said, throwing an object.

A wet stone landed in the young chern's palm.

❦ ❦ ❦

Samiylo smiled, as he ordered gunners. They had concentrated fire on a specific point in the wall; the Khan would believe that his enemies intended that spot to be their breach point. Kaffa was shaped like a square and the northern wall couldn't be attacked since it faced the harbor, the east faced the steppe and couldn't be attacked without riding around the entire city. That left the Western wall, and as the best entry point, the southern wall.

Below the hetman flags, from every kuren whipped in the wind, sweeping across the steppe as Zaporozhians lay in wait, fanned around the city. Kaffa's guns roared back, hitting only dirt and boulders, Marko stood in the open, pointing toward the sea with his mace: an order for men under his kuren's flag to fall back.

Bohun ignored deafening Tatar cannon fire and fired a falconet at the decoy entry point, then enjoyed the sight of shot smashing into the bone white city's western wall. Kaffa's simple yet effective architecture brought thoughts of coffins to his mind. Bohun scanned with a scope finding sniper holes, he aimed and then ignited the falconet, which fired, impacting high wall: a miss.

❦ ❦ ❦

"Report."

Canibek cleared his throat then said, "We now know where the invaders intend to breach."

"And the Akincis?"

"Out of the question; the cannon fire is too heavy."

"Military casualties?"

"Only civilians have been killed by the invaders' guns."

"And our guns?"

"More than adequate."

The Khan struck a tapestry covered wall of the divan chamber. "The forces of this land are serene and holy; the instruments of God! The descendents of Chingis!"

Canibek bowed, as if to display his neck to an executioner. "Of course, my Khan."

Mehmed motioned for the bey to rise. "Continue with the barrage."

"Yes, most serene Khan of Crimea."

"You may leave," Mehmed said, sitting down on a tiger skin to pour tea.

❦ ❦ ❦

Aleksandr used a kard dagger to slice of a joint of stag, fresh off a spit. He bit into overcooked meat and then took a seat next to the cook fire blazing in the middle of camp. The booming firefight in the distance required few men, so most supped or sang songs in a futile effort to overcome the noisy cannon fire. Any military commander, Muslim or Christian, would be shocked at the sight of fighting men with scalp locks like serpents wearing mismatched oriental clothes and acting as they pleased.

He stood up and began to walk back to his quarters, passing men smoking pipes the size of short swords. Others bartered for plunder or prepared weapons. Camp shelters ranged from tents the size of cabins to huts, with some men lying on grass covered in sail canvas. He turned his head to see men from the village and roads returning to camp, maybe his new friends from the chaika were among them.

He entered his tent. Andriy was long gone; either out with the harbor gunners or scouting. The sorcerer prepared himself for the task of leaving his body to gather intelligence. He sat down; the best posture to begin the process of leaving flesh.

❦ ❦ ❦

Canibek preferred to work with his cousin Ismail, a sekban officer who stood at nearly six feet with a thick beard for such a young man of twenty. He preferred to wear his hair long in the style of the golden horde. Canibek spoke to his cousin as he entered the courtyard. "Greetings, kinsman."

Ismail only nodded. He wore the standard dress of sekban units, a sheepskin jacket over leather armor, Turkish salwar trousers with boots made from horse leather. He made a sharp contrast to Canibek who wore the turban, lavish robes, and mintan shoes of a bey.

"Your plans for the invaders?"

"My soldiers are focusing on where they plan to enter," he said pointing jeweled fingers up at troops on the wall. "Your opinion?" Unlike Ismail, Canibek was a man of politics, not war.

"They don't follow standard Western tactics, the invaders are more of a flock than an army," he said, fingering the pistols on his belt. "No uniforms." That was what his fellow officer Hamid had told him.

"Cossacks," Canibek said as a chill raced through him.

The cousins climbed ladders up to the ramparts to be greeted by a vast sight: the sea and sekban members scrambling to come to attention. They wore uniforms similar to Ismail, only they carried rifles instead of pistols. Some carried doglocks instead of muskets. Unlike Turks, Sekbans carried straight Mongol sabres; a symbol of Mehmed's pride in Giray ancestry.

"As you were," Ismail ordered.

"Where are they attacking?"

Ismail pointed down and yards away at a wall that looked as though it had been struck by a Djinn's hammer. He turned to fellow sekbans. "Fire!"

A beardless young sekban saluted and then ignited a cannon which fired at the enemy; for a moment Canibek thought the gun had exploded.

❧ ❧ ❧

In his spirit form Aleksandr watched Tatar cannon fire smash into a boulder; a comical miss. Still adjusting to fleshless life, he allowed himself to drift over the camp watching chern dancing a blend of Turkish, Tatar, and Ruthenian motions while waving nadziak war hammers and sabres in the air. He went high above the shelters like a hawk gliding on thermals, only to find himself staring down.

The Inspired beings ignored him much the way the Crimean Khan would snub a lowly noble. The sorcerer moved toward Kaffa feeling much like a boy who had stumbled into a serpent mating nest, he moved over the firefight between Muslim and Christian gunners. Zaporozhians had damaged the wall, but neither side had claimed lives. He went past Marko staring at maps, Bohun loading cannons, Oleg cleaning guns with his back to moss coated rock. Tatar shot destroyed boulders yards away from Ostap who ran, carrying a falconet in his arms like a pet.

Aleksandr drifted over the steppe, which had been transformed by cannons into a wasteland of stones fragments. The craters lacked Zaporozhian dead only thanks to Inspired aid. He went through walls in a gray blur. Once inside he immediately saw a woman who dragged what remained of her husband away from where a cannon ball had struck. Apart from her and the soldiers, Kaffa's grounds were deserted. The sorcerer instantly began examining the city for weaknesses that could be used against the evil city.

❧ ❧ ❧

"You'll be safe here," Canibek said, sweeping his torch through an underground chamber equipped with food, water, sleeping mats.

"You're certain?" asked Damakan, the bey's pregnant wife.

"Aye, only the Khan and his sekban units know that these rooms lie under the court; no cannon ball could strike this place."

"If only the other women were so lucky…"

Canibek sighed. "They are under protection."

"I und…"

Canibek moved quickly, gently pulling his expectant wife close so he could see her gray eyes and short cropped dark hair by dancing firelight. He kissed her deeply as he stroked her swollen belly; his wife knelt to take him in her mouth. "No need for that," he said, fully ready.

Damakan undressed quickly, even shadows couldn't hide her milk-heavy breasts, and then climbed on top of her husband. "Is this our last union?" she asked, mounting Canibek, who gasped as he entered his wife.

"No, I'm too important to be bait for guns."

"But if you're captured?"

"Alive I'm an invaluable hostage; in death I'm worthless," he said, suckling her breasts.

❦ ❦ ❦

Returning to flesh, he felt pain. Aleksandr stumbled about the tent, trying to reach ink and parchment as his surroundings blurred and spun. He began to speak an ovation for eloquence and stability of mind.

"Oh merciful and Omnipotent God, cleanse my Heart and reins, strengthen my Soul and Senses…."

The tent and his perception returned to normal as the mage chanted. He immediately began to record the weaknesses of Kaffa.

❦ ❦ ❦

Ismail had heard of the wild men beyond the rapids since boyhood. They were said to be evil unwashed beasts that drank the blood of the faithful. They ravaged the steppe like a plague, taking Muslimahs to rape and living parasitically off stolen treasure. He rarely strayed west; any forest could hide bands of them waiting to take travelers hostage for ransom to pay for their debauchery. The Khanate's good people knew the carnal evils of the wild Christians who used each other like boys, and killed children for sport.

"Sir?"

He finished coffee made with the finest Levantine beans then turned to see a young recruit from his unit in the arching doorway. "Yes?"

"The men are awaiting orders."

From the hill Ostap focused his spy glass. The wall was heavily damaged. Tatar guns had not slain any Christians, who darted about the field, constantly changing positions, using the boulders as shields.

"Do you need volunteers?"

Ostap turned to see a young chern. "No. And you are?"

"Yaure Lebedev was the name my parents gave me, most serene Ataman."

"Return to what you were doing, I've no need for volunteers."

✿ ✿ ✿

Bohun's bones seemed to ache from cannon fire. He hefted the falconet and moved behind different rocks, it was a matter of survival to change positions after shots. He moved past boulders, through gun smoke. Just as Tatars began to return fire Bohun dove down as though cowering under the roar of Tugarin Zmeyevich. He gazed out from behind a stone green from moss and the Tatars were focusing on a previous gunner position! He fired the falconet, too tired to try to block out the resulting explosion. The gunner ran to take cover yards away; he would come back for the falconet once it had cooled.

✿ ✿ ✿

"No one has been killed?"

"Aye," Sadko had adopted modern ataman clothing for his form.

"I am indebted to the Inspired," Samiylo informed the Novgorodian, or what remained of him.

"Permission to enter."

"Granted," Samiylo replied to Aleksandr.

Aleksandr walked into the ataman's tent, almost expecting to see that Tatar bitch chained naked to a post by his bedding.

"What is it?"

The wizard placed parchment on his hetman's desk. "The secret weaknesses of the evil city of Kaffa."

✿ ✿ ✿

Aleksandr sketched by candlelight, Kaffa's streets, barracks, and arms depots straining his memory. He began to whisper a hymn to increase memory.

"The Queen of Heaven I invoke, Mother of the Nine Lovely Muses,
　Free from the oblivion of the fallen mind,
　Who joins the soul with intellect and increases reason.
　To You belongs thought,
　All Powerful, Pleasing, Vigilant Goddess,
　Who wakens from apathy all thought residing within, neglecting none.
　From the night of dissolution, You excite the mental eye.

Come, Blessed Power, and waken the memory of Your mystics to the holy rites,

And break the chains of the River Lethe."

Instantly an image of the Jewish Kyrmchak quarter next to a garrison came to his mind.

ᘺ ᘺ ᘺ

"So we are agreed?"

"Yes," Ostap replied.

Marko said, "Yes," also.

"Good." Samiylo smiled, the atamans had approved his tactics for taking the evil city.

ᘺ ᘺ ᘺ

Bohun watched as gunners yards away strung up a flag of their kuren; the signal that they wanted to return to camp. He squinted to make out the sight of men hurrying downhill to replace them, and then returned to work, cleaning and then loading a cannon. He applied a stave to a casket filled with coals, causing wood to ignite. The gunman examined the fuse, hand made by wives of settled men. Finding it sufficient, he fired the cannon triggering a booming roar along with a mass of smoke.

"Unlike its neighbors, the Crimean khanate was not a feudal monarchy, an absolute monarchy, a patrimonial state, or an oriental despotism. It was something quite different perhaps without European parallel."
-Alan W. Fisher

CHAPTER 21

M arko listened to cries of:
        "Five ducats!"
"Six!"
"Eight!"

Before him were Yaure and Oleg, facing each other off in a three feet ring with men thronging around them. They both held dull swords, useless in combat but ideal for practice.

Ostap shouted, "And if Yaure wins?"

"Ten ducats!"

"Eleven!"

From his rock, Ostap listed the names of those who had made bets on hide with a quill dipped in horse blood. "Begin!"

Yaure drew back, bringing his sword into a guard position. He focused on his mock opponent, trying to anticipate how he would attack. Oleg slashed like a serf clearing a field, a clumsy strike easily blocked by Yaure, who counterattacked with a blow to his opponent's kneecap.

Oleg retreated in pain, his weapon in a guard position, causing Bohun to shout, "Don't lose, whoreson! I've six ducats on your hide!"

Marko became bored of the spectacle; entertainment for men requiring distractions from camp hardships. Atamans and chern equally missed Sich comforts. There were no towns to raid, no merchants to extort; cannon fire replaced the Dnieper's purls. Unlike other men, he had escaped dysentery.

۞ ۞ ۞

Canibek lead Ismail through the halls to the divan chamber. "You remember protocol."

"Since boyhood," the tired Ismail replied, annoyed at Canibek.

"That tone is not acceptable in the presence of the Khan and the beys!"

"Understood." Ismail paused to admire a mosaic depicting the pig eater's Jesus. Canibek often boasted that the art had been taken from Constantinople centuries ago; the officer suspected that it was simply taken from raids on Bulgars.

The pair entered the divan chamber occupied by five men wearing the finest clothing imported from Turk lands or the Levantine. After customary greetings, Canibek directed Ismail toward an elderly man who stood at slightly more than five feet, with a neatly trimmed snow-hued beard. Canibek spoke, causing Ismail to look away from the man's gentle eyes. "This is Serdar Bey."

Ismail only bowed.

The officer followed Canibek to a tall brown haired man in his middle years with a shaven face and brown hair. Unlike the other men he wore ceremonial plate armor over robes. "This is Alpay Bey."

As he was about to nod, Alpay gripped Ismail's palm; a Christian greeting, "It is an honor meet a true warrior."

"Thank you, my Bey."

"Your adventure over the walls is the very bravery that will smash the invasion!"

"Thank you, my Bey."

"Reinforcements are not coming."

❧ ❧ ❧

Oleg had won. Bohun walked away counting his ducats.

Yaure limped by, warning Bohun, "You won't live to spend that."

Bohun laughed. "I've survived more than horse theft."

Yaure had no reply.

Bohun approached Oleg. "Well done!"

"Thanks," Oleg replied, nursing a cut on his left arm.

"I'll buy you a drink at a Christian tavern once this all over," he offered, jingling a coin purse.

"When have you ever paid for a drink? You've always raided taverns," Oleg responded with a smile.

"Then I'll teach you how to plunder a tavern," he boasted.

"We've a deal."

The duo walked through camp, passing men sitting on logs shitting, chern loading firearms, and a crowd eating breakfasts of stag and stew. Bohun sighted Aleksandr by a pile of cannonballs then called out, "Aleksandr!"

The sorcerer approached. "You seem well."

Oleg cut in, "My health will improve after a night spent in a bey's palace."

Aleksandr only smiled at Oleg.

Bohun spoke, "As do you."

Oleg added, "But then your kind can heal wounds with words."

Aleksandr laughed. "That simply isn't possible."

§ § §

"That, oh great Khan, means that you will kill every invader!"

"And the stag in my dream?" asked Mehmed.

"A sign of life; meaning that Crimea shall only become healthier under your reign."

"Thank you, Learned One."

Mehmed Giray broke silence to ask Canibek, "What is your plan?"

"We know where the invaders plan to strike; now we simply have to observe their actions and retaliate."

Mehmed sighed, if only he had a Kerkes like those Turkish pigs.

§ § §

Marko admired his new dagger. "How did you acquire this?"

"Years ago," Oleg began, "I participated in my first raid on a distant Muslim outpost. One of them carried that."

"You killed him?"

"No. I was a young recruit, so the others only trusted me to scout. But they allowed me to take a prize." Oleg finished recounting his experience.

Marko drew the weapon, the fully clean blade shone under the sun's rays. While it lacked jewels, the handle was made from the finest oak, the pommel was made from what appeared to be pearl. "Now we know how the Mohammedan butters his loaves," Marko commented with a smirk.

Oleg laughed. Marko sheathed his new weapon next to his flintlock.

Oleg asked, "How did you come to be elected?"

The question almost caused the ataman to become lost in memory. "Years ago I participated in the siege of Azov. Several men were wounded and pinned down under fire. I managed to get them to safety."

"Amazing!" Oleg exclaimed.

"My old ataman had died in the siege so the men elected me as his replacement on the spot. At least I benefited from that siege; we had to give to the Novgorodians."

"They made a good choice."

Mark lifted his shirt to display scar tissue. "A Muslim bullet did this to me; the price to become an ataman."

§ § §

Marko and Oleg parted ways, the young Zaporozhian was eager to sate his thirst with rich alcohol which would provide relief for the long hours filled with cannon fire later in the day. As Marko passed a cart from the captured Tatar village filled with gunpowder, Ostap walked within arm's length.

"Marko sheathed his new weapon..."

"Greetings."

"Hello," replied Marko, curious about his fellow ataman's motives.

"I need you to find Bohun and Yaure. I would go but my bones aren't what they once were."

"What do you need them for?"

"Just tell them to report to my tent."

"Of course," said Marko, slightly annoyed.

"Good." With that Ostap was off to his shelter.

Marko set off to the feasting tables; boards stripped from Tatar houses laid across boulders covered with freshly killed game. After a short walk he found Bohun, sitting and eating a shank. The burly man stopped chewing out of respect for his ataman.

"Greetings my ataman."

"You're to report to Ostap's tent."

"Why?"

Marko exhaled. "I only have his orders, not motives." Then he asked, "Have you seen young Yaure?"

"He's near the end of camp tending horses!" Bohun shouted over the sound of chern arguing.

❦ ❦ ❦

Before her capture by Tatar raiders, Elena had been educated briefly by a kindly priest who had given her the gift of literacy and taught her that life was meant for more than pig farming. The teenager loved to read about the glorious Roman republic. Whenever she had to perform miserable labor she would imagine that was living the life of a Roman Domina in a marble palace eating a dessert of grapes and snow under Greek pillars. Other slave women and guards had told that her education would guarantee that she would be purchased by a wealthy man, possibly even a bey!

The lithe young girl rolled over to her side, like the other captives she lived in a small tall space with large pot to relieve herself in and food supplied by guards who had given her Tatar clothing. The slave women were kept in large buildings that were once prisons or stables surrounded by a three foot wall. Only female guards armed with kilij blades and shields watched over the Christian women, virgins would fetch the highest prices. It was said that Tatar women rode in battles alongside the men with their hair streaming in the wind, eager for blood.

The women were released every afternoon to exercise inside the wall under the control of Muslimah warrior women; fat virgins did not command the highest prices. For hours they had limited freedom, able to congregate with their sisters in slavery. None dared plot escapes, for armed

Tatar women with bows ringed the top of the grey stone wall.

Elena had befriended a little dark blonde child named Mary. Elena had lost her family and so adopted the child, comforting her until the day they would be separated; sold off like used beasts.

Most women had become relaxed about their fate. Many were serfs bound for lives of relative comfort and luxury compared to their former lives of farm toil. After all, few women could choose their husbands, what was the difference between being given to a strange man by infidels or being married off by fathers? Compared to Liakh serfdom, Tatar slavery was gentle. Any children Elena bore her future master would be raised as free Tatars. By contrast, Liakh women had told her that children of serfs were born into the status of their parents and died as bounded laborers.

From his seat on a rock, Noman observed ataman Ostap entering the hetman's tent. A passing chern mounted on a horse temporarily blocked his view. He looked away from the boiling water on his fire, still unfit to drink, and watched Ostap speaking to Samiylo. The tent was yards away so Noman couldn't make out a single word.

Finally Ostap left the hetman's shelter; he walked slowly but with exceptional strength for a man of his advanced years and experience. Noman took the water off flames and began to walk south toward his tent with it, passing men thronged around a grinding stone to have their swords prepared for battle.

"Sharpen your sabre."

Noman turned his head to young Oleg, near the end of the crowd already wearing leather and a Crimean Tatar helmet. "I already have."

"How will we execute the Khan?" shouted Noman.

"Impale him!" came Bohun's reply.

"Flay him alive!" screamed Yaure, near the edge of the mob.

"Hang him by a hook through his throat!" said Marko's voice.

"Saw his head off slowly!" added Andriy.

Noman entered his tent, and then gently placed the pot on a flat rock so as to allow it to cool. His throat was caked by dust and dry with thirst and he couldn't risk drinking alcohol. He poked his chest, finding that his flesh had healed and no longer felt as if he had suffered a kilij slash across his ribs from a Janissary. He gripped armor and began to put it on slowly, reverently, as though he was a priest donning robes before church service.

Aleksandr lay down in his tent and he stared into the gray canvas with the concentration of an astrologer reading his fortune in the stars. He suddenly felt a familiar sickly sensation crawl through his stomach and spread through his nerves; a spirit was in his presence. The sorcerer was not afraid, for he had the Headless One exorcism ritual committed to memory. Slowly, with the reservation of a child sinking into a pool, he shut his eyes to find an image of Koshchiy's smiling image.

"Don't you want to leave your body?"

Why use human speech, Aleksandr thought at the Inspired.

"My existence is derived from the concepts and ideas of your race so I must imitate your primitive communication or become as lifeless as the constellations. Come, leave your body; we're allies."

Very well, the sorcerer agreed, initiating the process of freeing himself from flesh.

Within minutes he was above the camp; a ghost before his time to pass. Koshchiy was nowhere.

"Here I am!" The being appeared in front of Aleksandr in his usual naked, shriveled, bearded form. He opened his palm, and an image of Mecys appeared. "Want to know what his family did to offend me?"

Aleksandr had no reply.

Koshchiy continued, "Centuries ago the founder of his wretched house attempted to find my soul; believing all those tales about it being in eggs or needles. He failed of course."

"But you never forgot the insult."

Koshchiy only smiled. "As my power had made that family mighty, I swore to destroy them." He displayed an image of Mecys screaming somewhere. "A job well done."

❦ ❦ ❦

As Elena tried to sleep in her stall in what was once a stable, she thought of her father. He was a man of peace who hated the Zaporozhians and the Tatars, considering both warring sides to be sinners in the eyes of the Almighty. He moved his family away, deep into the wilderness, convinced that no one would be able to touch his daughter and his wife in the frontier, thanks to God. Elena fell deeply in love with her new freedom from the rules forced upon her sex. There were no sumptuary laws, no gropes from men who respected horses more than women.

Elena had spent nights in bondage wondering why they had come so far; were they gathering intelligence? Was it a feat to impress their evil masters? Now she realized that it had also been intended to destroy their hope and faith by removing the only two people who had raised and cared for her.

From there the slaving party fled for Tatary. The sheer speed of the escape had shocked Elena.

❁ ❁ ❁

"How did life begin?" Aleksandr asked as he struggled to adjust to the subtle realms.

The Inspired had no reply.

"If you're so powerful why not conquer all mankind?" he asked, watching men saddle horses below him.

Koshchiy tried to mime laughter. "You're funny! Slaves can't invent what we need, which requires a wild, free humankind."

Aleksandr realized that human life, for all its sins, in its small span was at least real, unlike whatever existence the so-called Inspired lead. "What are you?"

Koshchiy's reply was another image depicting Mecys in agony.

Aleksandr ignored it. "So you don't know! None of you are aware of what you truly are!"

He expected an angry reaction from the figure that terrified generations through stories, but instead the Inspired in the form of an old man merely smiled, which angered Aleksandr more than any attack could. "We're allies; friends perhaps. I wish to avoid conflict with you," he paused, "Hedge wizard."

The sorcerer almost felt his body twitch as he told the Inspired that he was, "Sorry."

"If you say so." The being opened a thick veined hand and there was an image of Mecys bound in golden chains.

❁ ❁ ❁

Aleksandr returned to the flesh, an action he quickly regretted. As soon as he heard cannon fire, he fell down in shock, landing on a jagged rock. He drew himself to his feet; the pain was dulled since he was still integrating into his body.

The sorcerer focused his eyes on the images ahead. Crowds were running throughout camp, preparing weapons. Feeling as though he was caught in a whirlpool dragging him down to Sadko's home, Aleksandr sat down mentally reciting various rituals to ground himself. Finally the pain in his side became normal and he could feel appendages and hear the cannon roar completely. His muscles began to twitch and throb, a product of inactivity.

Slowly he began to dress. Before entering the subtle realms he had only worn only light clothing. Aleksandr donned leather armor, strapping on his sabre and flintlock.

As he stared at the throngs of chern, he thought back to how he had forsaken order for the Sich.

※ ※ ※

Aleksandr had been born to an urban whore who died whelping him, he was raised by a brothel guard Vlad, who was employed by a vice lord known only as 'The Emperor.' By puberty he was learning the trade of an enforcer so as to expand his employer's control of prostitution. The young man first saw blood at fourteen when he watched Vlad kill one of The Emperor's rivals with a rusty axe. Vlad wasn't a simple thug, he taught his charge how to read and write to complement other skills such as swordplay and marksmanship.

Aleksandr took his name from the great Greek hero. He loved to watch vertep plays about demons, angels, and wizards and learned of the grimoires from other children, even some adults. Years passed and he grew into manhood, continuing to work for the prostitution ring by performing theft, bribing officials, giving beatings and even killings. The young man knew no other life but never forgot the possibilities of grimoires.

Aleksandr continued to hone his criminal skills becoming able to deftly enter any locked door and torture disobedient women or rivals without leaving a single mark. Vlad introduced him to 'The Emperor' a man of a seemingly ordinary appearance with ink black hair, olive skin and a beard; they said he was the son of Byzantine refugees, thus his name.

Then on an unremarkable fall day Aleksandr was ordered to deliver bribe money to an administrative official named Vicotr. The two men conversed after money changed hands, the talk somehow drifted into books. Victor let it slip that he had access to the library, a place under armed guard and reserved for officials, which also held grimoires. Aleksandr continued to probe him for information and facts slipped through. Thanks to complaints about guards and locks, the young man left with details required to commit an audacious robbery.

Years of thieving had supplied Aleksandr with a collection of stolen clothes. He could easily dress as an official even though he would have to shave; a process requiring soap and a dagger.

Late one night he entered the wealthy quarter of town dressed as a beggar; making him effectively invisible. Once he reached the area of the library he changed into garments he carried in a sack. He approached the guards, only two men suffering from sleep deprivation, who allowed him to enter though they had to accompany the 'official' through the library. Once inside the darkened room, Aleksandr attacked them, killing the men with the speed of an Alamut assassin. He wasted no time gathering every book of sorcery and fleeing in.

He spent what remained of that night in his room committing sorcery to memory. He learned the hierarchies of both angels and demons, how to craft talismans, invocations, and planetary secrets. The ambitious young criminal had a plan: kill 'The Emperor' with an evoked demon, then conquer his web of brothels and gambling places like Mehmed II, bringing down Tsargrad.

He studied for days in preparation. 'The Emperor' was too well guarded for a conventional assassination but Aleksandr had learned his true name. He continued his foul tasks while monitoring city gossip on the library heist. One day he received an order to beat a child prostitute into submission. Thanks to an angel he could no longer remember her face, but like any hound he followed the order. After washing blood off his knuckles, the fledgling sorcerer decided it was time to act.

That night he summoned an entity; a minor figure in the demonic hierarchy. Aleksandr's first evocation succeeded beyond his expectations. The spirit appeared as a large shadowy mass and he was very careful to make his very specific request using a sample of his target's handwriting as a link. The ancient being responded by making him feel as though his request would be granted. When the demon left Aleksandr performed exorcism rituals out of fear.

'The Emperor' caught a plague; the exact disease was never identified. Aleksandr was certain he would be able to step in without incident, but the demon betrayed him. 'The Emperor became insane and vented his rage through random killing. Somehow Aleksandr became known as the criminal responsible for the library theft and slaughter. He barely evaded capture. He began stalking his former employer while hiding in beggar quarters and alleyways; finally he ended The Emperor's reign of terror with a bullet from a doglock. He fled into the wild, which carried the risk of encounters with roving Tatar slaver bands and finally joined the only place where he could possibly have a home, the Zaporozhian Sich.

❦ ❦ ❦

Noman lowered his rifle. The Khanate gunners were wisely staying out of musket range, and had wooden barriers to protect against arrows, leaving his marksmanship useless. He stood the rifle against a nearby rock slab that resembled a pillar, being careful to angle the weapon so that if it discharged it would only hit clouds; the camp was in no state to handle accidental gunshot wounds. Even from a distance he could see that his falconet, taken from a galleot, was still cooling. To his left were men firing cannons and then quickly changing positions. Cannon fire began as apocalyptic explosions then became dull thuds; just as the fear of death became a small afterthought, a simple possibility. He watched Andriy assist Bohun with loading cannons; the pair ignored steps like cleaning, a small rebellion that would have secured floggings for them in any normal army.

Marko fired a large cannon, then shouted as smoke began to clear, "Who shall dig?"

Noman, Andriy, and Yaure stepped forward to the spades; the Zaporozhians would have to dig trenches to cement the illusion that they intended to attack from this point.

In conventional siege warfare, trenches became more than simple protection, they allowed an army without occult allies to advance through enemy territory with far fewer casualties. Sadko watched as the three men left the safety offered by boulders to begin digging into the weak soil of the Crimean seaside. Through methods taught to him by those who stole his humanity, Sadko gave them the strength for the task: he had already protected them from missiles, an easy thing to accomplish. Yaure hurled himself into the labor with the fanaticism of a Ghazi; Tatar observers were shocked at how quickly the trenches snaked through the soil.

❀ ❀ ❀

An arrow landed a few feet away from Noman. At that distance the shaft had to have been launched by a Turkish menzil; an expensive long range bow. He continued to chop through soil, the job was shockingly easy, as though Noman was simply scooping flower out of a sack and into another. From a distance came Tatar cries of frustration from their inability to hit a single target with muskets or bows. Finally Marko waved a kuren flag: the signal to retreat. Like the other two, Noman obeyed orders and fled back to the boulders.

Marko gave the signal to immediately resume cannon fire by discharging his pistol at Kaffa. "Do you think the lines will convince the Tatar animals?"

"What wouldn't?" asked Andriy with a chortle.

Marko gave him a blood chilling stare.

Yaure spoke. "I think so; they'll definitely concentrate more of their fire on this area from now on."

"I second that," Noman said in between pants as he rested against a moss blanketed stone.

Marko only smiled as cannon discharge filled every ear; all four had adapted to gunfire to the extent where the men didn't even bother to clutch their ears in pain.

Marko told them, "You can rest here for as long as you want."

"Thank you, Most Serene Ataman," replied Yaure.

Marko only nodded and then walked back to his cannon, shouting, "I need cleaning water! Now!"

❦ ❦ ❦

Oleg rushed to the meeting, struggling through masses circling around old ataman Ostap, who began to speak.

"We need a volunteer; a man willing to risk his life in a grave task," he screamed over cannon fire.

A voice that Oleg couldn't place shouted out, "Tell us more!"

"The details must remain with the hetman, atamans, and whoever takes the burden of this assignment. Whoever takes it will be advancing liberty for those deprived of it."

Aleksandr stepped forward to the ataman's rock. "Your volunteer stands before you, awaiting orders."

Ostap's face did not display his joy. "Report to the hetman's tent."

"Aye, Most Serene Ataman."

The crowd parted for Aleksandr as he began his way to Samiylo's quarters. Soon he stood at the entrance of the hetman's massive tent. "Permission to enter, Most Serene Hetman."

"Granted."

The sorcerer entered. His elected leader sat at a desk. A dark sheet veiled half of his tent.

"Remember how you identified the location of the Kaffa's slave pens?"

"Yes."

Samiylo stooped down to pick up arrows resting on grass. "I would like you to fire these shafts into the pens. It's a request that you are free to refuse; not an order."

"Understood." Aleksandr stared at parchment wrapped around arrow wood.

❦ ❦ ❦

Unlike other great cities, Kaffa lacked an underground; the Khanate's capital did not have the catacomb labyrinths of Paris or Tsargrad's tunnel network. Instead, Kaffa's noble population built countless hidden chambers throughout the city to hide great treasures and other valuables. As a child Ahmad dreamed of finding a secret cache filled with jewels from Rumelia. It became common for nobles to kill builders due to the fear that they would reveal secrets; the murders reached a point that Mehmed Giray had to pass a law that would revoke the lands of any bey who slew workers.

After working his way from boy to boy, he found a street child who told him about a convoy of solders carrying grain sacks, casks, and barrels that went into a house near the sekban barracks. Ahmad traveled to the barracks to find the thatched house next to the building exactly as described. The boy had earned his two bottles of Venetian wine, for the seemingly humble house obviously concealed a trapdoor or maybe a hidden room behind a shelf.

❧ ❧ ❧

Sadko moved his form's 'fingers' as though he was playing a gusli; the instrument that made him famous throughout the Christian world. He watched as Aleksandr made his way toward Kaffa in a small rowboat. It was a vessel too small to spot from the city; the only way to reach a point where he would be able to launch messages into the slave pen window. The former human thought it was a poor plan. In all fairness Samiylo only devised the task after Sadko rejected his request for an Inspired to appear in the slave pens in the form of an angel to encourage revolt. Sadko felt the sensation of humor through his being, an odd fragment from his flesh life. The hetman probably thought that Aleksandr could turn himself invisible while calling down thunder from the sky realms; impossible feats for any simple human sorcerer!

Through his senses he detected that a cannonball had struck a city wall, Sadko hoped his allies were conserving ammunition and didn't expect his adopted kind to fight their battles for them.

The Inspired were wise to reject the request to conquer the Turks; their new allies lacked the required numbers to control a nation and the Inspired had no desire to battle the Ottoman collection of Kerkes. Turks acquired Kerkes through a pact with beings labeled as 'demons' by followers of Abrahamic lies. The Ottomans received a Kerkes every year in exchange for children, easily acquired from Christian populations through the devsirme system. The Sultan was unaware that the 'demons' ripped the essence out of the child; the raw material required to created a Kerkes; a method comparable to the process of training Janissaries. Not even the Inspired knew how to make Kerkes! Unlike the Inspired, the 'demons' had need for humans and certainly wouldn't ally with some of them, while 'angels' were merely content to observe and intervene in insignificant situations.

❧ ❧ ❧

Ahmad finished drawing his map. "It's next to the barracks."

The map was crude but it was impressive enough for Ahmad to be able to read. "You have done well," replied the bey.

"Thank you!" Ahmad beamed.

Canibek paced back his room's window, "Name what you would have as your reward."

"Serving your House is all the reward I require, O' Great Bey."

❀ ❀ ❀

Aleksandr left his boat at the bank then made his way toward rocks. He stared at the bone smooth gray wall of Kaffa. There were no sentries; every soldier was at the point where the officers expected the invaders to breech. Scaling the wall wasn't a possibility; only the window of the slave pit could support a grappling hook and it was stories above the rock covered ground. A thief would need a tower sized ladder to get close to the window.

He began an invocation from the Key of Solomon and nocked an arrow.

❀ ❀ ❀

Slaves drew back like frightened shrews as the arrow soared over the wall, while the guards ran around the wall's peak searching for the archer. Women cease exercising, talking or prayer and swarmed toward the projectile; their guards drew back in shock. Hands grabbed at it.

Elena turned to see that the other captives were moving about. The girl knew very few of them; forging bonds of friendship would only sharpen the pain of separation.

"What is it?" asked one girl,

"Find it!" Mary begged.

"A sign from Christ?" came a female voice.

A red haired girl from Minsk tore the note from the shaft. It was the same message in Ruthenian then in Latin.

"Fellow Christians," she read, "The army of Zaporozhia is at Kaffa's gates to liberate you; rise in revolt against your heathen captors!"

The Minsk girl crumbled the note as Tatar women guards raced forward screaming orders.

❀ ❀ ❀

Canibek lifted his practice 'sword' into a defensive position. "You block attacks like this."

"Understood, O' Bey," Ahmad replied as he imitated the technique, trying not to stumble in the courtyard.

"Pardon me O' Bey."

The noble and his servant looked up. It was Eeraj, who spoke, "Could I train the lad for you?"

Canibek dropped the 'sword' on the ground. "Why not?"

"You are most gracious," replied Eeraj as the bey walked toward his home. "You know the basics, yes?"

Ahmad nodded.

Eeraj's response was a swift attack which Ahmad barely blocked. The sorcerer easily parried the servant's counterattack.

"Where did you learn to fight like that?"

"In the Maghreb," Eeraj said, thinking back years.

🪷 🪷 🪷

When he grew into manhood Eeraj had immediately fled the poverty he had known in the Khanate. First he spent time among the Naqshbandi mystics, and then he left for the Barbary corsair republic of Sale where he found employment in a crew. He found happiness climbing the riggings of polacca ships and exploring the winding streets of Sale, a city that dated back to the Almohad Dynasty. Even as a new member he enjoyed a life spent in coffee shops, using captured women for pleasure and raiding any ship, Christian or even Muslim, from nations that were unfriendly to the republic.

Eeraj was able to rise through the ranks thanks to his education. His captain was a renegade convert to Islam from Ireland, and made him the navigator. He soon had more money than he had ever seen, and women from Christian settlements and Arab tribes who refused to pay tribute to the republic. It seemed his dream of becoming a member of the elected divan that ruled Sale could become a reality.

Then one day his crew raided a ship en route to Damascus. His fellow corsairs were able to take the vessel with no casualties. At first he was disappointed there were no women, for only men who could be sold to Turkish galleys. Then he found a prize locked away in a box. There were magic books: the Gayat Al-Hakim and the Shams al-Ma'arif. He quickly hid them in his robes, for devout corsairs would have burned the as-Sihr books on site.

Eeraj already could read Arabic thanks to his training and lessons from one of his Arab slave girls, yet even he had trouble understanding the texts, which he studied for months. He began to avoid participating in raids; no thrill from battle could match the excitement received from slowly learning as-Sihr secrets. The youth had lead charges onto enemy ships, scaled masts to save fellow Sale rovers, and fought the finest Christian swordsmen to the death, but he could not evoke the courage to attempt a ritual from the sacred pages of his treasured books.

Through sailors he gained news from the Khanate; details about the liberal minded young Khan Mehmed who tolerated various sins, even such as-Sihr; a good monarch with bad advisors. Finally after countless hours spent studying secrets men were not meant to know he decided to work his first ritual. The fledging sorcerer chose an isolated building on Sale's edge. After making his way through the narrow streets he prepared to work as-Sihr; a practice the corsair had heard used only as epithet, a gateway to Jahannam.

In the weeks that followed, Eeraj learned how to evoke spirits, divination methods, and other sorceries. Sale became unbearable, he felt imprisoned like a Christian slave awaiting a turn on the auction block. He banished his fear of dying in battle with the Knights of Malta. Slowly he begun to prepare for his return home, selling objects too clumsy to take along, charting a course to Kaffa. Eeraj avoided selling his slave girls though; he would unload them in his last days as a corsair.

Finally he left in a small craft, alone with a personal fortune, some weapons, supplies, and his precious books of as-Sihr. He had no success in his attempts to control weather. At one point Eeraj spied a Christian warship; he only escaped capture by disguising himself as a lowly fisherman by flying proper colors. He was delayed for days due to damage to his vessel during a vicious storm, but he finally reached the capital of the Giray Khanate; splendid Kaffa.

The sorcerer avoided a grand entrance into the city; he allowed rumors about a wealthy yet mysterious young man in the finest Maghrebi clothing to flood the noble quarter. Eventually he met Canibek Bey, who managed to get him an audience with the great Khan. Mehmed was unable to find a proper teacher for his son Kamil and Eeraj volunteered for the position, a convenient way to his mask his role as the Khan's sorcerer.

⚜ ⚜ ⚜

Aleksandr entered camp. Ignoring the water in his footwear, he stood in front of chern mobbed around a sharpening stone clutching weapons varying from berdish axes to sabres.

"Who will barter for this bow?" he asked, holding the weapon over his sun-burned head.

"How far does it fire?" asked someone from the back.

"It's a Turkish menzil bow," he replied, "It could tear the heart out of a hawk miles away in the sky."

"Give us proof!"

Aleksandr fitted a shaft onto the sinew bowstring, worked his fingers into the Mongol draw then turned towards the waves. He drew back and loosed the arrow, which soared into the sky until it was out of sight. He returned to the crowd. "Well?"

Yaure stepped out from behind a nearby tent with a purse in hand. "What about this?"

"Silver?" asked Aleksandr.

"Pearls," Yaure replied.

"Done."

After the two men exchanged valuables Aleksandr made his way to Samiylo's tent.

"It's done as you asked."

Samiylo stared up from papers, "Truly?"

The sorcerer nodded, straining his ears to hear the hetman over cannon fire.

"Take this," Samiylo held up a sack. "It's gold."

"I had no reward in mind when I accepted the task," Aleksandr said, taking the purse, "But thank you."

❦ ❦ ❦

Elena cleaned Mary's dress with a damp cloth. Few guards patrolled the grounds, most stood the walls, while others had fled to return home, leaving all fantasies of warrior glory in the dust. The captive women either huddled in their open cells or clustered in groups, chattering nervously. What if their 'liberators' only raped and sold them to brothels? What if the invasion was defeated and the Tatars slaughtered the Christian women as vengeance or a warning? Such questions dominated the minds and ears of slaves.

"I'm ready to tell you…" Mary whispered.

"Tell me what?"

"How I came here," the child replied, scratching an itch.

"Take your time." The girl had avoided answering how she had come to be a slave in Kaffa.

"My mother sold me," Mary's words pierced the air like an arrow through flesh.

Elena cradled her young friend in her arms, "I'm so sorry."

The child continue to speak, "My mother would beat me and tell me I was an accident…" Elena learned that Mary was the offspring of a whore who had sold the angelic child to Tatar traders.

A short distance away one of Nihat's fellow guards asked, "Do you hear that?"

"I hear nothing but invader guns," replied Nihat as she watched some guards flee back to husbands and fathers.

❦ ❦ ❦

Elena rolled the corpse off her body. The armor had prevented blood from pouring out and covering her. As though by instinct, she quickly began to look for weapons on the dead man; quickly finding a pistol along with a Turkish sword, then she put on shoes that had belonged to the slaver. She threw a nearby rock down the steps that lead into the pit, the signal, then returned to frantically stripping the body fearing that an entire Muslim regiment could enter the grounds at any time.

Finally she was dressed in the Tatar's clothing; it was much more comfortable than the shredded dress she had to wear. The young woman raced to the next cage, searching the pockets of her new clothes for a key. She could find none, it must been lost during her struggle with the Tatar. As she was about to strike at the lock with her new blade, Elena noticed an important detail: The cage was unlocked! She entered the next one, then peered down into the pit, crying out, "You're free!"

"Halt!"

Elena looked behind her. Two Tatars were at the stairs, both armed with kilij swords. She couldn't understand their mangled language, so desperately, she waved back. It didn't fool them, since captives were already crawling out of pits.

The two guards raced downstairs, almost falling, preparing to crush the revolt without firearms. It was pointless to kill unarmed property. Elena cocked her new pistol; her mother had trained her in the way of the gun. She aimed at the slaver on the left and fired but she missed her target. The shot struck the Tatar on the right instead.

Dropping the pistol, she drew her sword, an object lighter than she had expected, it was as though she was holding a Roman assassin's dagger. The Tatar rushed at her, the untrained woman met and slashed at the guard, who easily dodged the stroke. Elena had no time to pray as their blades connected. Her soul was unprepared for death, if he slew her would she descend into hell?

❦ ❦ ❦

Aleksandr left flesh behind. He drifted out of his tent then through the camp, past a group of chern hauling shot to the front lines. He went higher and the sorcerer considered leaving the planet to see if Mars, Mercury, and others were truly ruled by the beings he evoked and called angels. Out of fear he decided not to do something so foolish.

He could see that cannon shot from his side had successfully created a gaping hole in Kaffa's wall, yet it was too small and high for a grown man to enter. If Aleksandr still had vocal cords he'd have laughed at his own joke; the officers conscripting children for a tiny horde. He sped past soldiers, enjoying the thrill of being inches away from the enemy. They were sad young men with faces scarred by sleep deprivation and dehydration. Some begged their God, others shook in terror. He went by abandoned buildings ranging from coffee shops to homes and passed a bazaar near a mosque. Next came clustered homes that varied from one to three stories high.

Aleksandr passed by the barracks that guarded the noble quarter before entering the area of palaces and gardens, complete with its own mosque.

As Aleksandr went by two men practicing swordplay, Eeraj felt, through otherworldly senses, the presence of another sorcerer. Aleksandr was unaware of this and continued to march toward the slave pens.

Mary peered out of the pit. The child was terrified due to the brawling taking place in front of her eyes. Elena had almost lost to the other Tatar, who had worn her down to the point where he nearly penetrated her organs with his weapon. The other former slaves attacked, killed him with rock chunks.

"Lay down!" cried a tall man Elena knew only as Basil. He had sandy hair that had grown wild during his time in the pit, yet his face was almost smooth, a fact that complimented his green eyes. Like the others he only wore ragged pants and a shirt, few had on shoes; many feet were covered in filth and bleeding sores.

Elena stood on her feet. "I will live, see if there are any more guards."

Aleksandr slowly stood up in his bedding as he returned to his body, making attempts to focus his blurry vision. It was as though his head was immersed in a deep sea whirlpool. He was sure that wounded Andriy had felt better than this. As Aleksandr stood, groggily he began a ritual:

"O Goddess, Earth, of Gods and men the source,
  Endu'd with fertile, all destroying force…"

"O' Bey!"

Canibek looked away from his garden, vaguely annoyed. "Who are you and how did you get past the barracks?"

"I am Nihat, O' Bey," he paused to breathe. "A friend of mine allowed me to enter."

"Speak your mind," the bey replied as he admired a snowdrop flower and considered strangling the guard among the tulips, like the Sultan's

Bostancı-başi.

"The captives have revolted and seized control of the pens!"

❀ ❀ ❀

Samiylo almost jumped at the news. "They've taken the pens?"

"Yes, Most Serene Hetman," Aleksandr replied, lowering his eyes as he spoke.

"You can leave."

Once Aleksandr had left, Sadko chose to make himself visible. "Just in time. I see you've finished drawing up surrender conditions for the Khan."

"Oh, those." Samiylo took a glance at the papers on his desk. "A simple ceremonial practice."

"Ah," replied Sadko as he stared at a woman, lying bound to Samiylo's bed. She was in shock due to repeated rapes.

"Remember my plan?"

Sadko answered, "Of course; the Inspired will do as you ask, like any good ally."

"That's just what I wanted to know," said Samiylo.

"They will benefit greatly from this campaign," the former human responded.

Samiylo ignored the comment and began to dress in his finest garments. While he couldn't view himself in a mirror the hetman knew he had the appearance of a conqueror; one without a crown.

He left the tent, climbed on top of a boulder, and began to speak; informing the men that they would soon launch the final assault on the evil city. It would put an end to the slave trade of Tatary and erect a bastion against the Turk's sprawling empire.

Sadko grew bored of watching his ally shouting, so he left the tent and ascended high above the camp where others were waiting for him.

They asked, "What do our friends request?"

"Listen closely," replied Sadko, moving his fingers as though he was playing an epic on the gusli.

"O Allah! Help me to stay strong and firm in battle. Give me safety, victory, glory, honor and might. Forgive me my sins and shower me with Your Mercy and Good Pleasure so that if I die I may enter Firdaws as a true martyr."

-Ottoman war prayer.

CHAPTER 22

Sadko watched a gunner collapse. He had used the methods gained by leaving humanity behind to make the young man bleed to death internally. His superiors had taught him much about the biology of the species he once belonged to.

He moved over Kaffa. Men in front of cannons were falling like cattle dying from plague. The Inspired were carrying out the requests of Samiylo, who wasn't foolish enough to ask his new allies to do his entire task for him. He came to a stop in front an older man writhing under power. Sadko attempted empathize with the victim out of curiosity; were the emotions enshrined by his former race more than impulses?

Sirin darted over the dying with the grace of a well trained dancer: Sadko thought back to distant memories about slave girls dancing before golden horde Khans, human erotic concepts fueled Sirin's existence. She easily caused hearts to implode, and Khanate gunners continued to fall. They were dead before their skulls smashed into Kaffa's mortared stone. The city would soon be vulnerable to Zaporozhian assault.

The sight of death stimulated Koshchiy. A being born from human concepts such as war, bravery, and victory; the Cossacks were his natural allies. As he watched a young Tatar in Turkish costume bleed from his mouth, Koshchiy thought back, though time didn't exist for the Inspired as it did for humans, to how he killed Prince Ivan for sport in front of the warrior queen Marya Morevna. Imitating human speech, he screamed a boast, "I am Koshchiy the Deathless!"

ꙮ ꙮ ꙮ

Sadko appeared only to Samiylo who stood in the centre of a rada. "It is done."

The hetman signaled with his mace and he watched as throngs of men swarmed away to their duties, though not their deaths, thanks to their new inhuman allies. It was common to think of the steppe's wild men as undisciplined hordes who rushed about screaming battle cries to gods both ancient and heretical, yet chern carried out tasks as quietly as flies feeding on corpses.

Mounted on a warhorse, Marko oversaw cannons. Their previous attacks had been simple distractions, but now the wall that was Kaffa's true weakness was no longer protected by guns. He watched as chern positioned, cleaned, and loaded the most powerful cannons on a hill near the camp with a clear view of the evil city. These guns, unlike the falconets, had not been fired. Yaure stared up from a loaded gun, and Marko sliced through air with his sword. Permission to fire.

Aleksandr braced himself as the cannons began to roar. He walked toward horses saddled by chern, and was joined by Bohun, Noman, and Andriy. All four men mounted as slowly and reverently as Father Baranko baptizing a newborn in the Dnieper. Other chern ran up holding long spears. Yaure handed Aleksandr his spear, once the sorcerer had settled into his horse, which originally belonged to a Tatar cavalryman. Slowly the four Zaporozhians rode to the end of camp, joined by other horsemen on Crimean mounts wearing combinations of Mussulman and Christian armor, with weapons ranging from guns to steppe bows to blades. Their horses stopped on the edge of camp facing Kaffa, where they waited for the signal as cannon fire began to destroy their real target.

❦ ❦ ❦

Aleksandr finished carving sigils of Mars onto his round shield for protection. Like the other horsemen he had one similar to those carried by Varangian warriors in ancient Rus. He held his spear in place toward the evil city as horsemen continued to join the cavalry line on Tatar mounts.

Andriy stared at the evil city as cannon fire continued to destroy the targeted wall. Slowly an opening began to form in the seemingly impenetrable mass of mortared stone. He mumbled through prayers while trying to become comfortable in his saddle. His new Crimean armor dragged at his body.

High above the Khanate's capital, Koshchiy aided Zaporozhian guns so that every shot smashed through the wall with the highest accuracy and precision. He allowed himself to 'hear' the sounds of cannon fire, and see walls collapsing onto what few soldiers remained at the front. Sirin continued to circle the city, making sure that there were no relief troops coming to assist the Mehmed Giray; someone could have made it out of the city at night to flee to Bahçeseray. She went over the slave pens to see that the former captives were walled in and besieged by their captors, who clearly were trying to starve them into submission.

"Slowly an opening began to form…"

Yaure joined men standing in lines wearing either armor from the Khanate or standard Zaporozhian clothing. Each man had a sabre at his hip and a gun in his hand, while others carried berdish axes, spears, and bows. He stood silently next to Oleg, who held an Ottoman musket covered in engravings across his chest, which was covered by a bronze armor plate stripped from a Khanate cavalryman.

From Samiylo's tent Ostap watched as veterans old enough to have fathered sons loaded weapons beside young recruits. No hands shook as they went through wadding and powder. Ostap emptied tobacco packets into his pipe. As a breeze swept through his tent he half expected to smell blood on the wind.

❦ ❦ ❦

Grigor watched Tatar soldiers run through streets like frightened field mice fleeing an earthquake.

"Look!" Elena cried as she leaned against the wall's edge and pointed at the sight of a collapsing wall.

❦ ❦ ❦

In the noble quarter, Mehmed spoke. "You've positioned archers and riflemen?"

"Of course O' Khan," Canibek replied.

"Are the Akinci prepared?"

❦ ❦ ❦

On a rooftop next to a spiking minaret, Eeraj watched the wall collapse like a mighty a sea cliff finally giving way to the raw, thrashing power of waves. He watched infantry troops construct multiple barriers in front of the noble quarter; the lowest wall was seven feet. Slowly he walked on the narrow roof to a view of the harbor; wreckage from what was once the Crimean Khanate's fleet drifted on the surface alongside body parts.

❦ ❦ ❦

Yaure was surprised by how slowly they marched toward the southern wall. The men at the front pushed captives; frightened villagers and disgraced warriors. No one ran like wild men swinging swords, no one displayed any lack of discipline. He continued to keep up his pace, fearing that if he came to a stop the others would trample him. Each direction held the same sight of men in armor or Zaporozhian clothing carrying muskets, berdish axes, and pikes.

Yaure felt very small. The foot soldiers were entirely silent as they advanced toward the entry point, which grew ever closer. No one even bothered to pray; the only sound came from weeping Tatar women and the occasional cannon from camp fired at the Western wall by the few re-maining men there.

Marko's horse carried him across the steppe to the southern wall. At his distance he could not make out any defenders; the horsemen were in range but no arrows or musket balls had fired at them.

Aleksandr felt an urge to wear the wings featured on the armor of Akincis and Vlach hussars to make their mission of going ahead to clear the path for foot soldiers more enjoyable.

❀ ❀ ❀

The horsemen thundered through wreckage where the southern wall once stood. Andriy was relieved to that there were no Tatars in wait hold-ing the pikes made infamous by the Three Leagues' warriors. The area around the southern wall was deserted.

As they passed titanic hulks of mortar stone and crushed homes, Marko felt as though he was wandering through what remained of ancient temple. He dismounted, and after lashing reins to a post, he kicked in the door of a home. No one in there. He took a tip from a coffee jug.

Aleksandr drew his pistol the instant his feet touched the ground. Carefully remaining behind his horse, he scanned the area but it was de-serted.

Bohun jumped off his horse and walked further to scout the land ahead, staying behind his horse with his shield covering his body.

Noman directed his horse into one of the few shops that had not been leveled by wall chunks the size of churches.

"No marksmen?" asked Marko, walking out of the house eating cuts from a cheese block.

"None," replied Andriy.

Marko turned his head to see approaching foot soldiers, then ordered. "Move out; our labor has just begun."

Noman asked, "Where are the slave pens?"

"Far from here," answered Aleksandr as he sipped from a wine hide.

Gunfire tore through a block just feet away from Noman, and the Zaporozhians scrambled indoors.

"The shots came from that direction," Bohun said, pointing left.

Marko said, "The roof should give us a clear view, any volunteers?"

Andriy raised his hand and Marko nodded. Andriy hurried out of the house, dropping his shield slowly. There was no gunfire so he climbed on top of a rubble pile, which allowed him to leap onto the roof. He crouched on the rooftop, and crawled to the edge.

There were three gunmen in standard Tatar costume of fur cloaks, Turkish trousers, and boots. They carried rifles, and one was already reloading. He dropped back down and stumbled through the door to report.

"Three men armed with doglocks, they're out in the open a short distance from this house."

"We all know what to do," Marko stated.

Bohun left the house and drew his blade as he approached a horse; he beat the mount with the blunt of his sabre, sending the beast off running to the left. Noman and Andriy stood with their backs to a wall with weapons in their hands as the horse tore past the Tatars, distracting them. Noman darted out from behind the wall and fired his flintlock, downing the center Tatar before the one to the right returned fire. It was a miss.

Marko loosed an arrow in their direction, missing the Tatar on the right, who began to run. Andriy moved into the open and fired, hitting the Tatar, who collapsed onto a hulk of rock.

The survivor fumbled with his doglock, desperately trying to aim. An arrow from Bohun's bow penetrated his thigh and the Muslim knelt in pain, screaming like a child being boiled alive.

"Keep him alive," ordered Marko, pointing at the wounded Tatar. "Make sure the others are dead. Use only your swords and stay on alert for others."

Bohun and Aleksandr drew their sabres to carry out orders, Marko and Noman approached the Tatar who either wailed or tugged at the shaft jutting out of his thigh.

"Tell him he'll never walk again," said Marko.

Noman obeyed orders, and the Tatar howled in fear at the news.

"But he can live, if he tells us how many lie in wait for us."

Noman obeyed orders, but the Tatar spat curses.

"He's not…"

"I know," Marko snapped. He glanced at Bohun who was about to skewer a Tatar who had only been wounded in the shoulder. "Bring him here and then reload."

Bohun obeyed, dragging the prisoner to his ataman while Aleksandr cut a Tatar's throat with the Muslim's own dagger.

Marko drew his sword then began to slice through the prisoner's cheeks, the Tatar roared from what seemed to be endless pain. Next Marko took off a few fingers. "Tell him that if he doesn't do as we say his clan will find him like that."

Noman obeyed orders. The Tatar began to shriek information. Noman explained that the Tatar had said that most soldiers had been ordered to defend the nobles' quarter. Aleksandr pointed at the area.

"Move these beasts," Bohun shouted, pointing at foot soldiers only yards away.

Aleksandr opened the other Tatar's neck with a nadziak war hammer; it was a swift death. He turned south to see Tatar captives stepping through rubble in front of the foot soldiers. The foot soldiers spilled into Kaffa, encircling their prisoners. One chern asked for, "Orders, ataman."

"Make yourselves comfortable." Marko glanced at the sorcerer. "Use your craft to spy ahead; make sure that Mussulman told no lies."

Aleksandr nodded, and then went inside a house to begin the process of entering the unseen realms.

❁ ❁ ❁

Eeraj listened through walls as Canibek consoled his wife.

"We can hold out for years."

"How?" she asked, caressing her swollen belly.

Eeraj listened as the bey kissed her and then spoke, "We have stores of food, more than enough for us and our child."

Eeraj gnashed his teeth, where was this food? Didn't Canibek trust his own wife? He left the listening point, located next to a tapestry, to pace through empty winding halls. Eeraj paused at a window to stare at sekban soldiers drilling in front of Ismail and other officers. The sorcerer felt his hand move to the pistol on his thigh, an odd impulse since he had no allegiances to gods or men. He turned to stare at a gray hued wall covered by Sufi calligraphy artwork, other paintings depicted exploits of Sufi warriors whose names Eeraj had forgotten.

Suddenly, as if he had been shot, he felt the other sorcerer's presence.

❁ ❁ ❁

Aleksandr stumbled out of the wrecked home, slowly readapting to the flesh realm, He jerked his head away from the stares of the crowd. "There are men on the streets but most are in the noble quarter. I didn't see any marksmen in this area."

"Where are the slave pens?" Marko asked.

Aleksandr pointed.

"Draw maps on the best ways through."

The sorcerer took out hide pieces from his clothing, "I already did so." The maps were so simple that even illiterates would be able understand, they were swiftly passed through the sea of chern.

Marko climbed onto a large stone then held up his mace to call a rada. Silence fell over all. "We shall split our forces so that the Mussulmans do not pick us off easily in these tights streets. Who shall go on the roofs?"

A group including Yaure stepped forward.

"You have your maps?"

"Aye," said Yaure.

"You have my blessing," Marko said as they began to climb onto the roofs from rubble mounds. Kaffa's rooftops practically a second system of highways, the largest gap between buildings was only a few feet.

"Anyone else want to join them?"

Other chern left the rada to join the Zaporozhians on the rooftops.

"I shall lead the first group through the streets, who do you choose to lead the second?"

"Bohun!" came the cry from a majority, though a few had yelled Noman's name.

Marko raised his mace to quiet the chern and began to explain that there were two main routes to the slave pens. One followed a street near the wall and began on a road yards away from the coffee shop. To reach the second route, the other party would have to travel to the mosque, where they would turn down a street to the left next to a minaret.

ٮ۝ۥ ٮ۝ۥ ٮ۝ۥ

Yaure drew his sabre as he approached the chimney, which could easily hide a sniper. He found nothing; the roofs were tomb quiet. The others had spread out across the rooftops so as the cover the most ground. He could make out the distant sight of the Khan's palace, and jumped onto another building. So far he had not spotted any Tatars mainly due to the fact that he was still near the southern wall. Most Muslims had fled to the evil city's safer quarters.

He looked to his left to see that the other chern were entering houses from balconies to search for warriors, food, and money. Yaure carefully balanced on a beam, a fall from either side would be a three story drop onto bone hard pavement. Finally, after fearing that a marksman concealed in a coffee shop would shoot him, Yaure made it across to a building with a flat surface.

He sat down concealed behind a large chimney. The evil city was chillingly silent, like a Persian lion concealed in jungle brush, waiting to strike at innocent prey. He stood up with one hand on the sabre buckled at his hip then began to walk toward the large tower; the slave pens?

Yaure walked past a minaret that stood only a few yards away. He felt shame's touch; he was trespassing on ground that was holy to someone. He jumped down onto a balcony, eager to find something to eat. Like most

Tatar homes, the room was modest, with only a few cushions around a table inches off the ground, while the entry was a Moorish arch without a door. Such an alien place!

There was no food, only the table and half empty coffee. Yaure found musical instruments that he had never seen before next to the cushions, alongside books in a foreign script. Finally he found a slab of lamb. He went back to the window to eat.

That was when he saw the Tatar.

☙ ☙ ☙

Aleksandr rode at the back, behind Tatar captives leashed to his horse. The prisoners were at the front and back, providing shielding from any possible attack with long ranged weapons. The city looked as though its population had been snatched into the unseen realms by gods too evil to name.

He understood just how ancient Kaffa actually was now. Each gray building, with Moorish arches and round windows, looked as though they had stood before Constantine's reign. He spied calligraphy above a doorway leading to darkened rooms; clearly a primitive talisman using names of God or angels. The structures were built so close together that the Zaporozhians and their captives were under a great shadow, as though they were traveling through a mountain pass.

The chern did not march in typical military organization; standard tactics were useless in the evil city. Few spoke. Most carried nadziak war hammers, bows, or swords with their guns holstered. It would be foolish to waste ammunition so early. Aleksandr spied one chern with reins in one hand and a war hammer in another. The sorcerer saw that Marko preferred to walk on foot. He had given his horse to a chern; any Tatar marksmen would assume that the chern was an officer and shoot him instead of Marko. Aleksandr preferred to ride, fully confident that his new Tatar armor would deflect any arrows launched from steppe bows.

The war band turned through streets like sea water flooding through a sinking galley. They passed a structure that Aleksandr had never seen before; it was open without any walls, topped by a dome adorned by calligraphy and supported by pillars so thin that they resembled silk strands.

☙ ☙ ☙

Panic seized Yaure! He didn't have a bow, only a pistol that he had to save for later emergencies. The Tatar on the other hand carried a doglock and a Turkish sword strapped across his back. He slowly moved away from the window; the slightest motion could make him a target.

Yaure walked across the room to the window on the opposite side. There was an empty street and an alley that would take him to the Tatar's location. Slowly he climbed on the window, braced himself, and jumped.

He landed in a crouch and without pain. His fellow Zaporozhians were no where in sight, so it was his kill.

He slid his sword out of its leather scabbard; the Tatar was a yard away. If God was with Yaure, his enemy's gun would be unloaded. Gathering courage, he turned the corner to see that the Tatar's back was to him.

Yaure began to rush forward. The enemy turned at the sound of running, and screamed in terror as his hands fumbled over his rifle. No time to load, so he swung it like a club. Yaure easily dodged the clumsy stroke and thrust at the Tatar, who blocked the attack with his doglock.

Both men could only taste bile as they desperately fought. The Tatar swung his rifle wide as he jumped back and his enemy tried to reach for his sword. Yaure attacked, slicing the Muslim's left hand. As the man retreated in pain he hurled the rifle, striking his Christian foe who recoiled in shock.

Finally the Tatar could draw his kilij, and he lunged with the grace of a Venetian sword master. Yaure barely fended off the skilled attack. The clash of blades rang through the deserted streets, Yaure moved his blade toward the thigh of his enemy, who parried the attack and then stabbed, cutting his unused arm. Acting out of anger, Yaure slashed like an English executioner, hacking at the neck of his enemy, who leaped back with his sword in a guard position, frightened by the display of rage.

Yaure advanced, and he stabbed at his enemy's left shoulder as the Tatar moved his sword to counter the attack. Yaure moved at the speed of an arrow, burying his sword in his enemy's throat. As the Tatar fell dead he heard clapping. Yaure craned his neck to see Noman leaning out of a window.

෴ ෴ ෴

Bohun held his arm up; they had arrived at the mosque. He was surprised by how much it resembled a church or a simple home instead of a foreign monument to evil. The soldiers stood still while the captives sat down moaning in pain, staring off like children whose tongues had been slashed off. One elderly woman fixed her bloodshot eyes on the mosque, a sign from God?

Bohun allowed chern and captives alike to drink and rest while he ordered volunteers to scout the road ahead. Any capable Tatar officer could have realized their destination and then sent men to the ambush Christians. Cowardice was the Muslim's favorite weapon.

"How grateful do you think the slave girls will be?" asked Oleg as he sat on the steps of a coffee shop taking sips from a jug.

"Probably too shocked at the sight of the sky to feel gratitude," replied Andriy, bandaging a cut on his foot received from constant marching.

The scouts returned to inform Bohun that the way ahead away was clear since they had seen fellow Zaporozhians on the rooftops in the distance.

Bohun raised his arm as though to hold up an unseen bulava mace. "Prepare to move out!

Noman smiled. "You have a gift for the sabre."

Still panting, Yaure mumbled his thanks.

Noman began to search the body; he tossed a coin sack at Yaure. "This rightfully belongs to you; by the laws of the steppe."

Too exhausted to count money, he tied the purse to his belt next to his holstered flintlock.

Noman picked up the doglock. "Do you know how to use one of these old guns?"

Yaure shook his head.

"I'll teach you later. Climb, the slave pens are near."

Yaure pointed at the fortress on the northern wall overlooking the harbor. "The slave pens."

The sight chilled Noman's spine. Then he heard a whistle from other chern several yards away. "No Tatars in sight."

"Aye," Yaure said as he gripped his new doglock rifle. Noman had taught him how to load it. First the firearm was turned upside down so that the bolt could be removed, thus allowing powder to be poured in. Second, the ball was to be placed in. Once the bolt was back in, the lock was prepared for priming and eventual discharge.

"Good man," Noman replied, smiling as he patted Yaure's shoulder.

Yaure turned to look at Joseph a few yards away.

That was then the rifle shot destroyed the chimney inches away from him. He drew his pistol and returned fire at the Tatars roofs away.

"The shots came from this direction!" cried Aleksandr, drawing a flintlock.

"Whoever wants to assist them, follow the sorcerer!" yelled Marko. "Anyone who wants to liberate the slave pens, follow me!"

"To the roofs!" Bohun ordered.

Noman finished loading his firearm, and peered out from behind a wall. The Tatars had no uniforms; instead they wore simple clothing like ragged boots, wool pants, fur cloaks, and Kalmyk hats, while they fired doglocks, and of course steppe compound bows. Behind his enemies was the tower over the slave pens, which resembled a large Frankish cathedral in the Western lands.

"We've come to relieve you!"

Yaure stared down at men under Marko's command and chern lead by Bohun! Joseph watched as they hurled grappling hooks onto ledges and balconies and then began to swiftly scale the walls.

"How many?" asked Aleksandr as he rested from the climb.

"No idea," replied Joseph, settling a rifle onto a chimney to aim. "They take cover too quickly."

Noman said, "They're peasants, not military."

"God be praised," quipped Aleksandr as he cocked his gun while Oleg climbed onto the roof with his bow.

Aleksandr spoke. "These Tatars are the only obstacle between our men and the pens." Marko and Bohun's forces had reunited on the ground.

"Oleg, fire arrows there," Joseph said, pointing at the peasants' general direction.

Oleg nocked and then released an arrow, which flew over a chimney. A Tatar rolled out, narrowly evading the missile. Aleksandr aimed, and after muttering sacred words, fired, hitting the Tatar directly in the skull. Oleg released a second arrow and another peasant moved into the open. Noman fired but missed.

As other Zaporozhians joined them on the roof, Oleg nocked and loosed a third shaft, which struck the Tatar in the stomach. The dying Muslim flopped over and then discharged his pistol toward the Christians, hitting only mortar stone. Another peasant darted out to release an arrow, which narrowly missed. Aleksandr fired Yaure's new doglock; his shot hit a building some yards away.

\\\/ \\\/ \\\/

There was a sharp whistle from the scouts; the signal that the street ahead was clear. Marko pointed his bulava mace forward and Bohun and the others advanced toward the slave pens. A row of Muslim captives in front protected the warriors from possible arrows or shot.

The Tatar captives stared around in shock. They felt as though God had cruelly answered their prayers to enter Kaffa. The party slowly turned to enter a wide street. The left side was made up of shops while the right consisted of homes. As they went under a Moorish arch, Bohun noticed that the buildings were entirely deserted. A girl almost slipped on coffee beans that were probably dropped by a shop owner who fled for his life after the southern wall fell.

A shape rushed out from the shadows directly ahead of the war band. It was a Tatar peasant wearing Turkish clothing, waving a kilij blade.

"Don't waste shot!" ordered Marko.

An arrow soared over the party, hitting the Tatar in the chest. The Muslim collapsed, and as his body began to writhe, death slowly claimed another soul.

Did Muslim possess souls? Bohun tore himself out of thought to look to the rear. He spotted Yaure in the distance, who waved like a little boy greeting a friend instead of a warrior who had just achieved a spectacular shot against a Mussulman fanatic.

The party continued through the streets as fear gripped chern; did every alley conceal assassins? How many marksmen were hiding in minarets waiting to open fire on Christians?

❦ ❦ ❦

Yaure aimed his firearm at an escaping peasant and then fired his weapon; the wasted shot struck only stone. The Tatar could inform actual Khanate warriors of what he had learned about the Zaporozhians.

Carefully, Oleg aimed as the Tatar continued to fade into the distance. He squeezed the iron trigger and his gun roared. The Muslim tumbled off a roof; dead before he struck pavement.

"That could be the last one," Aleksandr commented.

"Maybe," said Oleg.

"How were simple townsfolk so well armed?" asked Noman.

"City militias are not uncommon," Yaure replied, thinking of the Three Leagues.

❦ ❦ ❦

"You're certain?" asked Aleksandr.

"Aye, we killed the peasants. No one will be waiting for us."

The sorcerer said nothing. He was frustrated that he couldn't perform the method to leave his flesh body.

❦ ❦ ❦

Marko held up his bulava mace, the chern stopped greeting those who had returned from the rooftops. "Report!"

Aleksandr spoke. "They were only peasants; it was easy to kill them."

Marko, "But you wasted shot."

"True," the sorcerer admitted.

The returning men walked behind the Tatar captives to rejoin the other Zaporozhian warriors.

❦ ❦ ❦

"I am a peaceful Christian woman," the voice called out.

Recognizing the sound of the Ruthenian language, Marko's men lowered their guns.

"Come into the open," the ataman ordered.

Elena dropped onto the street from a fruit market, and the Zaporozhians gasped at the sight of her beauty. Marko explained that she was not safe since combat could erupt at any moment.

Marko raised his mace. "Conceal yourselves."

Then Marko faced Bohun. "How many prisoners could we sacrifice?"

❦ ❦ ❦

Ilmir was finally free! Somehow he and five other fellow Muslims were able to escape the evil Christians. They passed him as they raced through Kaffa, which they could still save. The Tatars turned a corner to find themselves staring at Khanate soldiers, who fired doglocks and flintlocks at them. Women died thinking of children, men thought of battle as they passed.

Andriy was thrilled at how well Marko's plan had worked. The Khanate soldiers had no way of knowing whether or not the Tatars they allowed to 'escape' were their own people. The Crimean soldiers had wasted their ammunition on innocents. From his hiding place in a single room home, he watched the ataman emerge from concealment to stand in the open on top of a nearby building.

Marko dropped his mace.

Elena watched as men of the Sich ran out to greet the Khan's dogs. Joseph approached a Tatar who was frantically trying to reload a flintlock rifle. He ran his sabre through the Muslim's neck, and turned away so he wouldn't have to view blood. Yaure fired his gun, downing a soldier trying to run for safety. He ran up to the man struggling to lift a small pistol which the Christian kicked away before using his blade to chop through skull.

Aleksandr blocked a blow from a soldier's kilij, and retreated with his sword in guard position as his opponent advanced. Noman cut him down with a single stroke.

Years ago she would have vomited. Now after her time in captivity, Elena had no reaction to the sight of her rescuers mutilating and displaying corpses all over the streets. Other men stripped Tatar bodies then loaded the clothing and weapons onto horses.

"I'll lead you to the former slaver fortress," she told Marko.

"Good," the hetman replied, diverting his attention from Joseph, who was suspending a bloodied naked body by the ankles.

Elena had half expected them to lop off and place heads on pikes, but as she had been informed that was too much work; sawing through neck bone could dull a good sword. The street slowly became a nightmare; the dead hung over doorways where children once played, and carrion dangled from stores.

Aleksandr lead a horse to the young woman. "Your mount."

"Thank you." The man only nodded as a reply, and made no effort to help her climb onto the beast.

She nervously sat atop the horse, which she feared would buck her onto the rock pavement. The man that the Christians followed raised his mace, an odd symbol, then rode through the streets, followed by Elena and the rest.

Andriy rode up beside his ataman. "What are your plans?"

"To carry out the hetman's orders and crush Kaffa."

"I meant the girl," said Andriy.

Marko gave him a stare from hell. "Find yourself a Tatar whore instead; countless Mussulman harlots are probably hiding throughout this evil city."

❁ ❁ ❁

Sadko watched the former slaves cheer as his allies entered the fortress that stood over the slave pens; now a stronghold to launch the final attack against the noble quarter. He stared at liberated Christians embracing the wild men from beyond the rapids. Sadko thought of lovers reuniting after years of separation.

"A pleasant sight."

"Aye," Sadko didn't bother to face Sirin.

"Koshchiy demands an audience with you."

"The Deathless One knows where I am," replied Sadko, who focused attention on the Zaporozhians and freed people dancing.

"Koshchiy insisted."

Sadko almost felt anger, a remnant of his former existence. "Very well then. Are we to visit Buyan Island?"

Sirin extended a wind to open a triangular doorway. "Follow."

Sirin moved across the sea, followed by Sadko, who asked, "What if I dive in?"

Sirin ignored him.

Sadko directed himself onto Buyan. He felt cold at the sight of the island's immaculate structures topped with golden domes. Kievan Rus, for all its glory, was never so clean even before the fall of house Rurik.

"Enjoying your stay?" Koshchiy asked as he stepped out behind a replication of a church. He was naked as usual, with his trailing beard covering most of his shriveled form.

"Greatly," replied Sadko.

"You lie." Koshchiy wasn't angry; he had never learned how to imitate that, he was simply stating fact.

"Does this island truly control the winds?"

Koshchiy ignored the question.

"What do you need?" Sadko asked

Koshchiy floated through the illusionary city. "Plans."

"Hmmmm?"

"What are your plans for our new allies?" He opened his palm to show Aleksandr speaking with freed Christians.

"Although gunpowder was produced at Kaffa and firearms manufactured at Bakchisarai they were expensive and....rare so the Tatar cavalry relied primarily on their short reflex bows, easily fired from horseback and having a longer range and much faster rate of fire than muskets."
-Brian L. Davies.

CHAPTER 23

Andriy sat down next to Bohun. "The women ignore us."

Bohun laughed. "They're healing from a hell that few men could survive; go out to search for Mussulmans' wife to satisfy you."

"Don't mock."

I don't," replied Bohun. "Have you seen a Circassian girl?"

Andriy was silent.

Bohun stared up at the towering stone walls under stars. "I traded with the Circassian tribes years ago. They were preparing for wa…–"

"With whom?" Andriy asked.

"Perhaps the Vainakh, maybe the Turks." He shrugged. "I was there to sell arms. I stole from a caravan." Bohun's robbery had left two men dead.

"Did they offer you a bride as payment?"

Bohun's laughter sounded forced this time. "They aren't barbarians; they paid me in Turkish gold and allowed me to stay as their guest."

"They're Mussulmans?"

"Circassians of every tribe are a very noble people, in spite of their vile religion."

Bohun broke from his story as a mounted scout rode past. He continued, "A young girl often cooked for me; her father said he would allow us to marry."

"And?"

"I refused." He paused to drink beer. "After learning I would have to turn Turk." The only way a Christian could legally marry a Muslimah was to convert to Islam.

❧ ❧ ❧

Aleksandr twitched as he approached the strange women in Tatar armor sitting on the steps to the towers. He offered her his food. "I haven't seen you eat, take mine."

"You've been watching me?" Elena asked as she slowly took the wooden bowl of stag and porridge.

He had no reply to her stinging words.

"Sit down."

The sorcerer sat next to Elena on the cold stone step, and they slowly began to talk. It was the first conversation that he'd had with a woman who wasn't married to a settled Zaporozhian or a prostitute selling herself for ducats. He listened as she described her girlhood, and learned about her parents. He told her that keeping their stories alive would heal the wounds inflicted by their deaths.

"Elena!" A cherub of a child ran out of the crowd around cooking fires and landed in Elena's arms.

Aleksandr stroked the child's soft locks. "Your daughter?" The sorcerer had seen younger mothers.

"Oh no," Elena replied, laughing off the thought of motherhood. "Just a friend, though I might as well be her mother."

As Mary ate, Elena spoke of her mother's laugh, her courage, her wisdom… and how she was stolen out of her life. The sorcerer could see that it took great discipline for Elena to fight off tears; he almost reached out to hold her but stopped himself.

"This night we passed along the river Jorugh, and arrived next morning at the castle of Gonia on the Black Sea, which we saw filled with Infidel Cossacks in seventy chaikas, who at the moment they saw us roared out, Jasus! Jasus!"

-Evliya Çelebi.

CHAPTER 24

Aleksandr raced up the steps to find Marko still staring at the nobles' quarters cracking towers like a tracker staring studying a trail on the steppe.

"Yes, Ataman?"

"What do you plan to do after the Khan kneels before our hetman?"

Aleksandr became mute. Life after Kaffa seemed as distant as the Vainakh mountains.

"Will you marry someone and become settled?"

Wind from Thrace rushed through the sorcerer's hair. "No."

"You seemed very comfortable with that girl," replied Marko.

"She just wanted someone to speak with," Aleksandr said with a shrug.

"You can summon angels but fail to grasp what a woman wants," Marko chortled.

Aleksandr once more became mute as a dog.

Marko stared at the mass of people below. Zaporozhians and freed Christians formed a vast throng that didn't even include those exploring the towers' bowels.

"Should she lead the people under our care once we enter battle?"

"Yes," the sorcerer said. Elena did not belong in combat.

"You're glad she'll be safe?"

Aleksandr twitched. "There's no honor in fighting beside a woman."

The sorcerer's use of the word 'honor' nearly made Marko break into laughter.

"I want your opinion on my tactics…"

❦❦❦

Yaure and Joseph walked through a two story building. Yaure judged that by the food and beds that this had been an inn before war descended on Kaffa. Joseph cut a hole in the first story wall and then lay down in a shooting position with his rifle butt tight against his shoulder.

Yaure made his way upstairs. He entered a bedroom that had been stripped of furniture and cloth, leaving only the bed frame. Quickly he used his blade to cut a chink in the wall and lay down with his rifle prepared to fire. He had a full view of the gate in front of the nobles' quarter. As he waited for soldiers to spill out of the gate, he thought of the ataman's strategy: bombard refugee homes, which would either send people pouring into the noble quarter, or it would send soldiers out to rescue them, then the final attack. Mothers, fathers, and children entered Yaure's sights, but no soldiers. He wandered if any of the other marksmen hidden throughout the city were enjoying better sport.

Hidden behind a mosque, Marko stared through a spyglass at the buildings around the nobles' quarter. Innocents were thronging in front of the gate like sinners on judgment day begging to be admitted to heaven. The gunners and their cannons were concealed in the mosque, while Zaporozhian foot soldiers and horsemen were fanned out through the city. That way a Tatar artillery attack would not inflict heavy casualties.

"Orders, Ataman?" Bohun asked, standing in front of a cooling falconet.

"Conserve ammunition," replied Marko. 'It's time for the Tatars to make their move now."

"Do you think this is how Caesar felt?" Andriy asked, as he cleaned a cannon.

Marko had no answer.

ψ ψ ψ

The gates opened, and innocents streamed into the nobles' quarter. Marko closed his spyglass and gave the order.

"Fire!"

Bohun and Andriy fired their cannons. Gun smoke filled the space in front of them as though the Inspired had transported them to a cloud kingdom.

From his post at the inn Joseph stared at the wall through rifle sights. One shot had struck the gates while the other had made an impact to the left. Yaure took aim at a soldier in the standard uniform of boots, Turkish pants, fur coat and Kalmyk hat. Slowly he squeezed the trigger but the shot hit the wall, missing the warrior entirely. Joseph took aim at a well dressed man he presumed to be an officer. He fired, only to miss his target.

Both men saw the officer pointing directly at the inn that concealed them, and they saw a party of soldiers loading a falconet. Yaure and Joseph jumped to their feet to begin the race for their lives. They almost knocked into each other as they met in the hall.

The first shot tore through the roof, hurling both to the rock hard floor. Yaure felt as though he was on a ship being tossed on thrashing waves.

He narrowly evaded a falling beam by rolling right as the wood smashed through the floor. Wordlessly both Zaporozhians ran out of the door just as a second shot leveled half of the roof. The two warriors did not stop running. They turned left to gain cover from a large home to avoid presenting themselves as targets to Tatar gunners.

Finally they reached Christian foot soldiers that almost fired upon them before hearing Ruthenian words. Yaure and Joseph were safe for now.

❦ ❦ ❦

Yaure finished loading his firearm. He would only discharge his rifle in battle if he had no other attack. He tested his blade on his middle finger and found it to be as sharp as a butcher's cleaver. He stood behind a bath house, once a refuge for weary common workers, now a place of cover for Zaporozhians craving thrills that only battle can provide.

Noman tried to count the men he stood shoulder to shoulder with but found it impossible. They seemed to stretch on for miles, every street held crowds of Christian warriors. He stood on the steps of the bath house to stare at horsemen yards away. The beasts did not make a move or any sound as a shot from a Tatar gun impacted a home. It was nowhere close to any Christian warrior. He stared at Marko and the gunners directly ahead behind a mosque; one man was about to fire a falconet.

Sadko guided the falconet's shot toward the wall. He saw the projectile rip through the gate, killing multiple Tatar gunners. He watched the refugees near the gates run deeper into the nobles' quarter toward the glittering spires, which his allies were only a short ride away from. Gunners to the left returned fire with an Ottoman cannon, which Sadko easily directed away from his allies; the shot smashed into an empty inn. He detected Marko firing another falconet. Sadko directed his ally's shot at the gates, which reduced surviving gunners and their cannons into carrion and scrap metal. The nobles' quarter no longer had any artillery defense.

❦ ❦ ❦

The gates were gone; the smoking ruins were wide enough for any horde to ride through.

The Christian guns had become silent.

Inside the nobles' quarter, Menseyit ordered his men. "Hold fast!"

Ears ringing, he craned his neck to see Canibek approaching on horseback from what had been a garden. "Attack!"

Canibek spoke. "They could be waiting with loaded cannons to slaughter any advancing men."

The bey ignored Canibek's plea. "You have your orders, obey them! For the Khan's glory!"

"For the Khan's glory!" shouted the enlisted men.

"Further orders?" Ismail called out to Canibek.

"Nay," he said, steadying his mount. "That is your choice; Khan Giray trusts his officers!"

"Prepare to attack!" shouted Menseyit.

Men rushed at each other, eager for blood.

The two forces moved toward each other on foot like swarms of locusts colliding. Horsemen on both sides remained at the back.

The men at the front ran forward, slamming their shields into Tatars.

Yaure buried his sabre in a young conscript's chest. He blocked a kilij blow with his shield then looked down; the conscript was dead.

Aleksandr swung his shield. Wood knocked into skull, yet the Tatar still stood and counterattacked. The sorcerer dodged a blade stroke, almost falling into another Zaporozhian. Aleksandr slashed enemy throat with sabre steel, killing his foe.

Joseph fell to the pavement. He threw his shield at his attacker, gaining time to stand. He lunged with his sword but the Mussulman struck it, knocking it out of his hand. Joseph drew a nadziak war hammer from his belt and then ran forward in a burst of suicidal rage.

Yaure parried a blow which drove him back. Formal military formation ceased to exist as the two sides blurred into a warring mob. None loosed any arrows for fear of hitting fellow Christians or Muslims.

Somehow Joseph survived without cuts. He was on top of the dazed Tatar and swiftly he used his war hammer to shatter his enemy's head.

Sadko moved over the area in front of the nobles' quarter, now a battle ground, protecting his allies.

Noman used his sabre to knock a pistol out of the hand of a soldier who sprang back to draw kilij steel. The two men attacked each other, their blades clashing like twin thunderbolts in the middle of a wrathful storm. He fended off a slash, and then counterattacked with a direct thrust which his enemy only partly blocked, then retreated.

Noman chased the Muslim past men locked in combat; it was as though the entire area was underwater and caught in a battle between ancient beasts of the deep. His enemy fell, tripped by a chern and the fall knocked the kilij sword out of his hand. Noman raced forward and sank steel into enemy chest. He yanked out his blade and organs spilled out.

"..the Mussulman knocked it out of Joseph's hand..."

War expanded like plague. A small number of the Khan's soldiers were trying to climb for the safety offered by the rooftops. A Christian marksman kicked one to the ground and the wild men cut him to pieces with sword and hammers. The rest were cut down by a thunderous rifle volley.

❦ ❦ ❦

Koshchiy watched with glee as a Tatar recruit, only seventeen if a day, died by a gunshot through his left eye socket.

Oleg smashed his pistol's butt into a Tatar's face. Blood poured into his enemy's eyes and he laughed as his foe slashed wildly while trying to clear his vision. He easily darted behind the Mussulman, and then ran a sword blade through his foe's throat. Oleg watched the infidel die twitching and gurgling as his hands jerked for the blade.

❦ ❦ ❦

A shot cracked past. Aleksandr, saved by his talismanic shield, turned to see a Tatar soldier rushing at him waving his doglock rifle like a scimitar. Aleksandr met his assault with the shield and the rifle narrowly missed his jaw. He slashed at the warrior with his sabre. The dazed Tatar dodged by inches and then lashed out his rifle, striking the sorcerer's shield and sending him back. The Tatar ran forward, exposing his chest for moments, which was all Aleksandr required to stab his foe in the heart, killing the Muslim instantly.

Sirin stared in awe at the sheer mass of men locked in brutal combat. The Zaporozhians were beginning to win, gaining more ground by the moment, drawing them closer to the Khan's palace.

Joseph ran at the Tatar attacking Aleksandr. He brought his war hammer down on the man's head from behind, piercing through skull bone and brain.

❦ ❦ ❦

With his back to wall stone, someone prayed to the ancient gods of the steppe. He finished a prayer to Erlik, who served Tengri as the death god then raced forward. He lashed out with his kilij at Noman, who almost slipped on blood slick pavement as he blocked the attack.

A pistol shot nearly hit Yaure, who almost fell as he stared at a Tatar armed with a flintlock musket a short distance away. Yaure discharged his firearm and the bullet, guided by Sadko, slew the Khanate marksman.

Nihat retrieved a dagger with his free hand and threw it at Noman, who partly dodged the whirling blade which only cut his cheek. He counterattacked with fury greater than any angel summoned by Aleksandr.

From the top of a Dervish lodge, Marko watched with pleasure as the battle raged. The Tatars were concentrated along what remained of the barriers surrounding the nobles' quarter.

Nihat parried Noman's thrust.

Aleksandr shot at a young conscript, who died before his body met the pavement.

Nihat lunged, slicing his enemy's left thigh. He drew back as Noman attempted to counterattack with his sabre.

Yaure dodged an axe attack from soldier then countered with a slash that cut through his enemy's right arm. Blood poured over the Tatar's fur cloak.

As blood streamed out of his leg, Noman drew back, desperately trying to block the Tatar's attacks. Whoever he was, the Mussulman had skill.

Joseph raised his shield to protect himself and a throwing knife impacted the wood.

Noman fell, only a short distance away from Nihat, who was slowly approaching like a beast stalking prey, Noman scrambled over corpses. He could see Nihat's gleaming kilij.

Yaure slashed through an axe wielding Tatar's throat, almost beheading his enemy.

Nihat was only inches away. With the speed of a raptor, Noman's blood soaked hand seized and fired his pistol.

Aleksandr stabbed a soldier in the back who was dueling with a chern.

Nihat collapsed to his knees, his hands trying to plug the wound in his chest. He looked up to see Noman limping forward with his sabre.

"Do it," Nihat said in broken Latin as he closed his eyes. The Christian honored the request. Nihat died thinking of his first love.

Yaure spotted Menseyit, a man whose clothing marked him as a commander. Eager to kill an officer, the young Christian ran through the city center, now turned killing field.

Aleksandr's talismanic shield protected him from kilij attack, he responded with a sabre slash.

Unlike the other sekbans who had chosen to guard Giray, Menseyit had chosen to defend what was left of the Khanate. He sighted a Christian racing forward like a Golden Horde steed and he fired his Venetian pistol at the youth, but missed.

Aleksandr hacked at his enemy's left arm. His foe began to retreat and the sorcerer did not bother to chase him since the Tatar had managed to escape to his fellow Muslims.

Menseyit met the might of Yaure's sabre with a parry from his Turkish sword. For a moment blade ground against blade, and then the duel began.

The youth lunged at Menseyit, who barely fended off the skilled but rushed attempt to gut him.

Joseph rested with his back against a shop. From across the battle ground he saw an elderly Tatar man staring at him through the gates as though trying to decipher ancient text written on Joseph's brow.

Yaure paced back and the officer swiftly moved forward with his blade in defensive position. Both men made eye contact.

Noman stood safely behind fellow Christians. He dropped his sabre; bone had chipped the blade. Quickly he picked up a Tatar sword and then began to prepare himself to re-enter combat by loading a pistol.

Menseyit moved back. The boy had nearly landed a cut on his left arm!

Aleksandr wished he had time to evoke an angel as he defended a chern from a Tatar's axe.

❦ ❦ ❦

Yaure skillfully blocked the officer's strike. Menseyit laughed, and then spoke in Latin. "Some god clearly favors you!"

"No gods, no masters," Yaure spoke as he slashed through his enemy's arm in one motion. Menseyit fell back, allowing Yaure to slice his throat down to the bone.

Koshchiy watched the battle with great pleasure. His allies were clearly winning!

❦ ❦ ❦

Marko closed his spyglass. The Tatars were concentrated along remnants of the gates in a way that made them vulnerable to cavalry. He mounted his loyal steed, which took him to his horse soldiers waiting behind a bath house: Bohun, Andriy, Oleg.

Marko drew his sword with a play actor's flourish. "Time to finish the infidel beasts!"

The horsemen cheered as they drew flashing blades! The riders spread out, taking different streets to the battle field where they reformed and charged at the Tatars from the left flank. Bohun prepared to enter battle with the reverence of a priest inches away from holy ground. Andriy spat bile as the riders rushed upon the enemy like waves crashing onto mud. Marko's first sabre stroke split a conscript's skull wide-open, a sight that caused other Tatars to break rank and flee in primitive terror. Oleg had expected furious conflict, but found that cutting down escaping men with his blade required less skill than a summer boar hunt.

Aleksandr watched with awe as the riders charged through the enemy with greater valor than any ancient hero. The Tatars had prepared for close combat but the soldiers did not have the pikes required to fend off cavalry.

Bohun's horse sped across ground covered by dead bodies. Carrion was torn to pieces under sabre sharp hooves, like grapes in a wine press. A soldier ran toward him, waving a Turk sword like a child playing with a stick; Bohun easily cut him down. Marko galloped after a fleeing officer. The coward dropped his weapons and was attempting to shed clothing to allow him to run faster when Marko's sabre nearly sliced off his jaw; a second attack killed the officer. Gunfire cracked past Marko's head, and he directed his horse at a Tatar gunner who he quickly wounded, before allowing his horse to trample the soldier to death.

Aleksandr approached a dying Tatar and applied his boot to enemy throat. He didn't move his leg until the Muslim had ceased twitching. Joseph finished a dying middle aged soldier with his kilij sword; it felt so light compared to a Zaporozhian sabre. Trying to avoid sullying his blade with Muslim blood, Yaure drove a wooden stake made from a flag shaft through dying soldier's heart; thank God he had not encountered Christians who required the same mercy.

❁ ❁ ❁

Ismail lead the charge toward Christian horsemen. For moments his mount held back with all the desperation of a condemned man sentenced to impalement. He kicked his horse, which sent him into battle, followed by his officers.

Canibek watched as the warriors rode toward the invaders. Retreating soldiers reentered the nobles' quarter, quickly fanning out into the best position to receive cavalry.

Ismail galloped directly at the invaders' leader with his kilij held in position, prepared to kill the evil man who had led the attempt to destroy all he loved. An officer rushed past Bohun, and their swords met in a lightning swift clash, failing to draw blood. Ismail hacked at Marko, who nearly fell from his mount dodging the stroke; he countered with a thrust that his enemy easily blocked. Hamid charged at Oleg, who kicked his beast, sending him forward. The Christian drew and fired his pistol, but the shot only struck stone of a distant minaret. Marko slashed at his enemy's mare, cutting through the horse's thick muscular neck. His foe furiously counterattacked, which the ataman blocked with his shield. Bohun sped toward the officer waving his sword, which slashed through his enemy's left arm.

An arrow from Yaure's recurve bow soared past Hamid's ear. Oleg shouted, "My kill!"

Koshchiy watched cavalrymen pour out of the noble quarter as the foot

soldiers retreated into it. An entire Tatar cavalry unit against a handful of
Zaporozhian riders and infantry.

❀ ❀ ❀

Marko heard distant Dhikr chants. Sufis were depicted as peaceful aes-
thetics when in fact countless mystics were among the fiercest warriors in
Mussulman hordes.

Sirin stared at cavalrymen charging at one another while the Christian
foot soldiers loaded firearms and scattered to marksmen positions.

As they entered a battle, Hamid threw a javelin at Bohun, who barely
blocked the missile with his shield; the impact of the quivering shaft stung
his arm.

Aleksandr aimed his firearm from the window of a shop. Unlike the
first Tatar riders, the faces of the other cavalrymen were covered by metal
face masks; the feared Mirza warriors.

Marko avoided his enemy's kilij attack and directed his horse away
instead of counterattacking. He fired his pistol at a Mirza but missed.
Another Mirza sped past Oleg, who nearly fell off his mount, avoiding his
enemy's blade attack. The Tatar raced away.

Joseph settled onto a roof that gave him a view of the cavalry battle.
Marko and his men had discarded standard tactics, choosing instead to
make quick attacks.

A ghazi charged at Andriy, who used his shield to fend off the enemy's
axe attack. As the Tatar began to ride away, Andriy turned like a centaur,
aimed, and fired his pistol, killing his foe's horse. It fell on the warrior,
pinning him down by the legs.

Aleksandr fired at Ismail only to miss; his shot went through a marble
wall.

Andriy was surprised; the crippled Tatar had made no cries of pain, not
even as Andriy skewered him with his sabre.

Noman took aim at a Tatar foot soldier running at Ataman Marko, and
then fired. The enemy soldier fell dead.

Ismail lowered his lance and then charged at one of the invaders.
Andriy had no time to direct his mount away from the Tatar. Marko finished loading his pistol; in haste he dropped wadding on the sandy gray
pavement. Andriy's sabre stroke shattered Ismail's lance into wood fragments. The attack shocked both horses, sending the two riding past each
other. Oleg used his shield to block an arrow from a Mirza near the gate;
he furiously charged at the man who had tried to kill him.

Now in control of their beasts, Andriy and Ismail extended their shining blades and charged at one another. From a distance Noman watched the two meet in combat. Andriy parried his enemy's blow as he struggled to control his horse. Ismail slashed the Christian's mount.

Sadko used his power to aid the Christian horsemen.

As his horse carried him closer to the Mirza, Oleg tightened his legs around his beast's belly then swooped down and retrieved a lance from the gore-coated pavement. Thanks to Sadko, an arrow missed him by inches.

⚜ ⚜ ⚜

Koshchiy was amazed; the three horsemen were able to hold fast against a superior cavalry unit thanks to support from marksmen and the Inspired. The mass of fighters resembled a snake mating nest.

Marko galloped past Ismail, stabbing his horse. Ismail ignored his mount's pain as he tried to wound his foe's leg. Andriy barely blocked a skilled attack.

With the wind rushing through his dirt-encrusted hair, Oleg hurled the lance. The Mussulman deflected the missile, which gave Oleg time to open with a sabre attack. The Mirza's bow was now useless.

Marko attacked a Mirza from behind with a sword attack to his neck; the Tatar died stunned at the sheer dishonor of the enemy. Oleg's blade slashed across his enemy's thigh, producing no wound due to thick plate armor. The Mirza responded by slashing Oleg's sword arm. Bohun opened fire on a Mirza, wounding him in his left shoulder; the enraged Tatar warrior charged at the invader.

Marko kicked his horse toward Oleg; the young chern was wounded and battling against a skilled, trained elite cavalryman. Oleg clutched his arm as he struggled to parry the masked soldier's thunder swift thrusts.

Bohun evaded the Tatar's lance, which cut into his horse's side as he kicked the beast to silence whines of pain. He aimed then squeezed his pistol's trigger and a roaring shot killed the Ghazi.

Wounded, Oleg retreated, causing the Mirza to laugh at the sight as he gave chase. A dirty little invader fleeing like a street child! Marko threw a lance taken off a Tatar's body just as the Mirza was seconds away from releasing an arrow aimed at Oleg. The shaft's impact caused the bow to fall out of the Mirza's hands. Oleg turned his horse away from Andriy, who had driven Ismail back into the nobles' quarter. Oleg attacked the Mirza whose hand darted to a Turkish pistol concealed in armor and his sabre attack knocked the gun out of his enemy's steel grip.

A shot cracked past Marko's head. He saw smoke from Yaure's position on a roof; the young chern had killed a horsed Ghazi. Oleg dodged a kilij attack, and then countered with a thrust that sent his sword through his enemy's cheek; the Mirza spasmed as a Zaporozhian sabre penetrated his brain.

Aleksandr finished an invocation and fired; the shot tore through a Mirza's skull. Joseph stared in awe at the spectacular shot.

❀ ❀ ❀

Three men dismounted and walked forward with their plated armor raised toward the clear sky. They were the only survivors of the Tatar Mirza unit. One Muslim spoke in Latin. "You must treat us as prisoners."

"Oh?" Marko asked, as he directed his horse toward the survivors.

The Tatar made no response; he merely stood in the wind, struggling to keep his arms raised.

Marko dug a piece of parchment out of his clothing then replied in Latin, "Take this to your Khan."

"What is it?" was the response in broken Latin from an iron masked face.

"The terms of surrender. Lower your arms."

As the Tatar limped away to the noble quarter, Marko gave orders in Ruthenian. "Kill the other two!"

"One finds the Cossack race still   living according to the manners and customs of their ancestors. A savage pride in their complete independence is reflected in their dress and manner   of existence. Each Cossack is the equal of every   other member of the community, whether clad in   simple sheep-skins and dwelling in a cave, or inhabiting a fine well built house and dressed in   velvet covered with gold and silver lace."

-Edward Daniel Clarke.

CHAPTER 25

Eeraj read terms of surrender to his Khan, the text was in Latin. "ONE: No harm will come to any soldier who disarms. Any armed soldier will be killed. TWO: No Muslim civilian will be killed, raped, or harmed in any way. THREE: Giray shall continue to lead the Crimean Tatars as Khan and reside in his palace in comfort and luxury, but without any authority. FOUR: The Giray Prince will go to the hetman as a hostage. FIVE: The Khan will order his subjects not to resist us; for now you know our power."

Giray looked up from his books, not even poetry could comfort him. "Is that all?"

"The parchment says that if we refuse, the invaders will raze our city to the ground and butcher our citizens."

"And?" the Khan asked, staring at the sekbans who formed an armored line around the divan chamber.

"If we accept, we are to fly this." Eeraj handed a Zaporozhian flag to the Khan, who grimaced as he touched the harsh cloth. Had the pig eaters cut their flag from a beggar's robe?

Mehmed stared at Kamil; the pride of his life. "I accept. Have one of the sekbans fly their evil rag."

As they left carrying the stained banner, Mehmed gently touched Kamil, drew the boy to his breast, and wept.

❦ ❦ ❦

Marko handed the pistols to Bohun; he had finished firing the signals that told Ostap and the hetman that Kaffa lay in the palm of Zaporozhia. As he directed his horse to face the broad mass of men; Marko felt as though he was facing an entire nation.

"Listen! Any man who kills, rapes, or harms even a single Tatar will be shot on sight!"

The throng began to move toward the nobles' quarter; like locusts to a fertile field.

"I need volunteers to visit the people we liberated and then to escort the

Hetman and Ataman Ostap!"

A party from Ostap's kuren stepped forward to volunteer.

Samiylo and Ostap rode out of the camp slowly. The hetman had thought he would race downhill with the speed of a man locked in a race with demons, eager to ravage Crimea. Instead he was simply pleased that his work was complete. As they traveled, both men found a unique peace from the sight of smoldering rubble and distant wailing from Kaffa. Ostap could make out the trail left by the Zaporozhian forces; it looked liked the game trail of a vast oxen herd.

The Christians entered the nobles' quarter quietly. Muslim women peering out from their horseshoe shaped windows were surprised; they expected the Zaporozhians to pour in shrieking battle cries in ancient, obscene languages before using any female for their twisted pleasure. Instead the Cossacks were at peace; relieved to have taken Kaffa without losing a single chern, relieved that fellow Christians no longer had to fear Tatar slaver gangs.

Marko lead the forces through the main road. They passed several bathhouses, minarets and a large annular Mosque. Bohun stared at the Khan's palace; he half expected to see the Tatar monarch leap to his death out of shame. Joseph marched past a Tatar boy sitting in a doorway; the child stared at the wild men with the eyes of a dying fawn. Andriy went by what had been a garden, uprooted fruit trees were scattered over soil as if the space had been struck by a storm sent from Buyan Island. Aleksandr walked at the very back of the formation; if the Khan had set a trap or if fighting broke out, the chern would take bullets.

Samiylo's horse almost stumbled on massive boulders as he entered Kaffa. Ostap waved at the Cossack foot soldiers who waited near Tatar bodies.

"Welcome hetman!" Cried one chern with a flowing beard; he wore standard Zaporozhian clothing and his head was adorned by a turban complimented by an ostrich feather.

"Thank you, soldier," Samiylo mumbled; he didn't recognize the young chern.

"The Khan is waiting to surrender all of Crimea to you," said one chern who wore armor stripped from a Tatar cavalryman.

"Follow us," said another who only wore boots and Turkish trousers; his face was smooth while his head was topped by a flowing scalp lock.

Tatar unit after unit passed through the square, dropping their kilij swords, Ottoman guns, and armor. Marko had agreed to let them keep their uniforms; he wouldn't rip off a soldier's second skin. Aleksandr stared into the empty eyes of defeated men, thinking of the sockets in the skeletons he found in graves years ago when he dug for ritual components. Bohun rode out of a bey's palace just as the ataman began to give orders for chern to find carts for the new weapons and to imprison the former soldiers in the stables.

The massive Zaporozhian throng cheered at the news that every man could claim a Tatar horse. As chern swarmed to the stables, filling the streets, Oleg picked up a piece of cavalry armor identical to that worn by the Tatar he had killed in a mounted duel. He thought about his enemy's smile.

Andriy made his way to the front of the men and joined one chern in opening the Moorish doorway to the stables. Chern slowly entered once the doors swung back, revealing an angular gray room filled with horse stalls, the walls featuring miniature paintings of horses, riders, and cavalry battles. Andriy had expected the men to frantically seize and fight over stallions; instead the chern calmly appraised mounts.

"Can anyone read this?" Noman asked, pointing to Arabic script on the stall containing a dark mare. He and Joseph spoke Tatar but could only read Latin characters.

Andriy stood on a crate so he could see over heads and he laughed. "Of course not!"

"Find a Tatar!" a voice shouted, feet away in the crowd.

Joseph left the stables. He spied a Tatar man in boots, cloth trousers, fur cloak, and kalpak near a fruit tree. "Come," he said, grabbing the young man's arm.

The Muslim's hand moved swiftly to his pocket, with thunderous speed Joseph drew his unloaded pistol. "Remove your hand slowly and you live."

The Tatar obeyed, allowing Joseph to search his clothing; he found scraps of bread dotted with pests. The two men walked to the stables passing chern dancing in a circle. A few Tatars had emerged from their homes to stare at the invaders, fascinated by their wild ways and exotic clothing. Joseph and his captive entered the stables. "Read these signs to me."

The Mussulman explained that the horse Noman had asked about was from a Circassian tribe; the fierce and yet noble mountain people were renowned for their horses. Noman entered the stall to claim the beast. Joseph forced the man at gunpoint to read the text on each stall.

❦ ❦ ❦

Elena joined the other captive women in singing as the Zaporozhian Hetman entered the fortress over the pits. Samiylo applauded as they finished. "Thank you!"

Ostap rode forward. "Who will come with us?"

The freed Christians cheered!

Marko watched Zaporozhians in the quarter's square auctioning off horses, standing guard, and celebrating. The Tatars had caged themselves within their homes, too afraid to face their conquerors from beyond the rapids. Bohun rode by on his mount, smoking a long pipe that he had probably taken from a Muslim home.

"Enjoying yourself, Ataman?"

"Aye," replied Marko as he stood up from his seat on marble steps.

"Further orders?"

Marko shook his head. "You and the rest of the men under my command are to wait for the hetman to arrive."

"Yes, Ataman."

"Are the prisoners secure?"

"Some," Bohun said, pointing at the pair of chern guarding the stables, now filled with the soldiers that hadn't been killed in battle or by Zaporozhian cannon fire. "The rest are in a vast cellar that chern found while hunting for supplies."

"You removed the food first?"

"Aye," Bohun replied to the insulting question.

"Enjoying your new horse?"

Bohun nodded, puffing on his new pipe. "When do we take what is now ours?"

The ataman stared at Bohun, who thought of a snake. "Wait for the hetman."

Bohun waved at men going off to patrol the city in search of any surviving soldiers. "We won by the grace of God!"

"By the grace of the Inspired!" Marko snapped, adding, "How else did we fight without losing a single man? How else did this evil city fall before us?"

Aleksandr walked by the Mosque. A mother pulled her son away from the invader, babbling in her alien language like she had rescued her son from the den of a Persian lion. The sorcerer walked past a group of chern then made his way through a garden. Soon he was behind the Khan's palace. He tugged at the shield hanging on his back.

With trembling lips, Eeraj began the last chant. He feared the Djinn.

"Allahumma inna nasta 'inuka wa nastahdika wa nastaghfiruka wa na-tubu ilayka' wa nu'minu bika, wa natawakkalu 'alayka, wa nuthniy 'alayka l-khayr kullah. Nashkuruka, wa la nakfuruka, wa nakhla'u wa natruka man yafjuruka. Allahumma iyyaka na'budu, wa laka nusalli wa nasjudu, wa ilayka nas'a wa nahfidu narju rahmataka, wa naksha 'adhabaka, inna 'adhabaka l-jidda bi l-kuffari mulhaqq, wa salla-llahu 'ala n-Nabiyy wa ali-hi wa sallim."

He inhaled deeply, staring deeply into the scrying medium in the cen-ter of a second room. Had he mispronounced a word? Was it a false ritual?

Slowly, form began to take shape in his dark crystal. Eeraj began to shake in his robes now marked with Quranic text for protection. Soon he was staring at a miniature being of smoke in the shape of a man. Eeraj recognized the Djinn; he had evoked something similar during his time in Sale.

Words entered his mind. *Speak your request.*

Eeraj smiled. "I need knowledge from the mind of a Christian who bears a shield inscribed with planetary sigils."

The words came again. *What knowledge?*

❦ ❦ ❦

Bohun gestured for Aleksandr to join the party, only to watch him col-lapse in an alley. He shrugged; the sorcerer was probably drunk.

Deeply in pain, Aleksandr crawled into a small storage area crammed with oil jars and grain barrels. He was under a sorcerous attack; there was no other explanation for the pain. He began the process of leaving his body. Aleksandr knew he could heal himself in the unseen realms.

❦ ❦ ❦

In his snake form, Aleksandr confronted a smoke being sawing at his person with a Mussulman blade: a djinn! The sorcerer called for an ally's aid.

"Sadko! Defend me against this spirit!"

Slowly the former human took shape and pinned the smoke djinn; an attack represented by rope.

"Who sent you?" asked Aleksandr.

The djinn had no trouble answering; he was not under contract to hide the Tatar sorcerer's identity. "Eeraj," it said, opening its arms to display an image of Aleksandr's new enemy.

"His location?" Sadko asked.

The djinn wove an image to reveal Eeraj's secret quarters.

"What now?" Sadko asked.

"Nothing," said Aleksandr, as he began the headless one exorcism ritual.

※ ※ ※

In his chambers Eeraj heard words from the djinn as the being returned to his realm. *He is coming.*

Even though the djinn was gone, Eeraj shouted and drew his kilij sword. "I will welcome him!"

※ ※ ※

Joseph wandered through the streets away from the celebration. He had to avoid alcohol to remain alert. He watched Aleksandr dart across the street. With the speed of a wraith the Cossack sorcerer climbed onto a one story home and began to run toward the Khan's palace.

※ ※ ※

Eeraj jumped off the Khan's balcony, he used his abilities to dull the pain once he impacted the ground. He covered his kilij in his clothing. The invaders, now occupiers, would kill him if they saw his weapon. Eeraj had other weapons to engage in combat with the pig eater sorcerer.

Slowly the Tatar walked around the wall that encircled Giray's palace, moving into open space, waiting for the Cossack with the sorcerous shield. Eeraj's life lay in pieces, he faced the threats of losing his home and occupation; yet only the challenge of defeating another sorcerer occupied his thoughts.

※ ※ ※

"How soon until we reach the Khan's palace?" Samiylo asked, as he ignored stares from Tatars in various buildings.

"Soon, Hetman," said Grigor.

"Great," Samiylo mumbled as he whipped his horse forward. "Welcome to the Zaporozhian host young Grigor."

※ ※ ※

Aleksandr stepped out of an alley. Eeraj greeted him.

"You've been to the unseen realms?"

Aleksandr was impressed; the Tatar sorcerer looked exactly like Sadko. "Yes."

"How?"

Aleksandr remained silent about the knowledge he had gained from an archangel years ago.

"How?"

"Secrets are for wives, lovers, or even friends," Aleksandr said as he cocked his flintlock pistol. "Not for cowardly attackers." He aimed the firearm. "I will you let you run, though."

Eeraj didn't move.

Aleksandr fired.

The bullet missed thanks to Eeraj's protection amulet.

"You could use it to hammer nails," Eeraj mocked as Aleksandr threw away the gun.

"For your casket?"

"Tell me how to explore the Unseen Realms and you will live," Eeraj said as he drew his blade and used his sorcery to increase his strength.

Aleksandr laughed like a child enjoying a comic vertep play.

Eeraj ran forward filled with rage, his muscles coursing with new strength! As he drew his kilij, Aleksandr brought his shield into a guard position. Eeraj slashed at his opponent, only to have his blade career off, thanks to the shield's talismanic power.

Aleksandr invoked the archangel of war, "Michael! In the name of Yahweh protect me!"

He felt angelic forces come upon him as he drew his sabre. Aleksandr counterattacked, drawing blood on Eeraj's sword arm in a move that was too swift for the Tatar to block.

Eeraj stumbled back, desperately trying to defend himself against Aleksandr's onslaught and remember the correct As-Sihr rituals at the same time. He was away from safe and sterile ritual chambers.

Overtaken by the archangel's sheer might, Aleksandr retreated.

Eeraj used his abilities to suppress his fear, and attacked with a thrust that the pig eater enemy easily parried.

He attacked with his kilij. Aleksandr blocked it with his sabre but instantly sharp though mild pain ran through his arm. The Zaporozhian laughed at the weak sorcery. The Cossack sorcerer used his free hand to grab a dagger from his belt and he threw it at Eeraj. The knife went wide, missing the Tatar by many feet, his amulets at work.

Aleksandr snarled in rage! He darted forward slashing, and his blade sliced through his enemy's forearm. Blood began to soak Eeraj's clothing.

"Soon you'll be rotting like a pig carcass next to other Mussulman scum!"

The Tatar ignored the taunts. He blocked Aleksandr's thrust as he used his abilities to numb the pain from his forearm.

Eeraj realized that he was only a short way from a ladder that would take him to the roof of the sekban barracks. He could defeat his enemy on a space that was alien to the pig eater. He blocked another slash from

Aleksandr's blood crusted sabre, and then used his abilities to once more increase his strength. With renewed stamina flowing through his arms he attacked wildly, driving the Cossack back.

Eeraj used the time gained by his enemy's retreat to flee. He raced to the ladder and scaled it to the empty barrack's summit. He ran to the far end of the building, which neighbored the stretch of markets, bathhouses, and homes near the end of Kaffa's borders. It was an excellent area to escape from. Eeraj waited for his enemy, for he lacked any desire to kill the Christian. He craved his knowledge.

Aleksandr drew a second pistol concealed his clothing, and after saying a short incantation, he began up the ladder. Before reaching the top he fired the pistol; not in any attempt to harm the Tatar but to give himself more time. The Zaporozhian rushed out of the gun smoke swinging his blade wildly; Eeraj barely managed to parry the rapid strokes.

A shot cracked through the air! Yaure stood a short distance away on the ground holding a smoking rifle next to a band of chern.

Eeraj now knew that he had no chance of overpowering and torturing the Christian sorcerer for his knowledge. He attacked, cutting his foe's shoulder, and then began to run. He leaped onto the next rooftop, stopping only for a second.

Aleksandr stumbled down the ladder, tearing his shirt into strips for a bandage while Yaure and the others began to move toward the barracks.

"Let him run!" Aleksandr shouted.

Yaure asked, "Why?"

"We've won Kaffa without losing a single man; don't waste a shot or tempt death by chasing after one man."

The men became silent; a sorcerer's command was more feared than an ataman's order.

Aleksandr finished bandaging his wound. "Now come; we must prepare for the hetman's arrival."

☙ ☙ ☙

From a distance Eeraj watched as the pig eater sorcerer lead the rabble away. He removed a rope from his pack and prepared to scale Kaffa's wall. Eeraj was more excited than terrified; he was about to make a new life for himself beyond the petty intrigues of court life!

☙ ☙ ☙

Throngs of Cossacks cheered as hetman Samiylo entered the nobles' quarter. Though only a portion of the Zaporozhian host had participated in the conquest of Kaffa there were so many chern that they had to gather on the rooftops, since others choked the streets with their sheer numbers.

Tatars stared at their conquerers from Moorish windows; some were even adventurous enough to walk into streets that had once been under the Khan's authority. Ostap heard singing as he rode through the small space in the street that wasn't filled with men from the Sich.

"...nobles all!"

"...to Krym they ride,
The soldiers, side by side–
And over the country wide..."

"...they're dancing–
Our brothers surely are advancing
From prison chains the sad to free.
O swiftly come, over the sea, over the sea..."

❦ ❦ ❦

Men standing on top of a market place fired pistols and rifles at the pure blue sky. Samiylo smiled. With a new arsenal that once belonged to the Khanate they could afford to waste shot and powder. At Marko's order the chern drew their sabres, holding their shining blades high; Samiylo passed so many blades that he almost mistook it for a steel forest. Shoulder to shoulder they stood with other chern, watching as the hetman and the two atamans rode past the crowds, stopped and then entered the Khan's palace, followed by a Cossack unit he left to get a place for the parade.

❦ ❦ ❦

Canibek fidgeted in his seat in the divan chamber. Like the other assembled beys he was uncomfortable and wracked with fear about what his life would become. The bey couldn't imagine living without the bounty of comforts provided by his nobility; he knew nothing else, nothing that could provide him with a living if he had to become a common man. There was the option of fleeing with his wife to Constantinople where his life as an exile dependent on Turkish charity would only vaguely resemble his previous existence as a mighty bey of the great Khanate.

The hetman entered, the beys stood up and bowed. Samiylo, a staunch republican, laughed at their degrading actions. The chern soldiers encircled the divan chamber while Samiylo, Ostap, and Marko became seated.

Samiylo shattered the silence. "I hate ceremony worse than death, so I will be swift." He paused for breath. "Every bey will retain his privileges and comforts; so have your feasts, your hunts, and your concubines."

"Just no power," Ostap quipped with a smile.

Canibek was amazed; the old goat had the dishonor to speak without permission from whatever they called their leader!

"The common Tatars will return to their homes without losing any property," continued Samiylo. "They will pay only a third of what they used to pay in taxes."

"We won't need any more tax money once we have control of Crimean smuggling," added Marko, tracing a finger over miniature art on the wall depicting dancing Mussulman mystics.

Ostap nodded in agreement.

Samiylo made eye contact with Giray. "After this assembly, you will continue as a ceremonial figure, exercising control over the Muslims but unable to carry out any actions without approval."

"And my son?"

Samiylo scratched his dirty hair. "He will be returned to you once Crimea is peaceful."

Mehmed had no words.

Samiylo spoke. "After you are done writing, I will send Tatar speaking messengers to towns and farms telling them that you have fallen, that the Khanate is no more and that they will be safe, free and will render only a third of what they used to pay in taxes." He paused. "If they resist, their homes will seized."

"The messengers carry Sekban helmets and documents bearing the Khan's signature," commented Ostap.

Samiylo clapped his hands. "Dismissed!" The kurultay was over.

Canibek was relieved; his life would continue! He watched the pig eater leader sign a document, putting his promises in writing. For his own sake and his family the bey was now completely loyal to his new Christian masters. He and the other beys would carry out any order; kill anyone to please the Zaporozhians, thus preserving their lives of pleasure.

Samiylo left the kurultay satisfied. Once Crimea was pacified, he would leave, allowing the new Crimean Cossack host to elect their own atamans and hetman. He had decided to allow Muslim men to join; the average Zaporozhian had much more in common with Crimean Tatars than Dacians, English, Turks, and other vile races.

❧ ❧ ❧

The main street leading out of the noble quarter was clear. Tatars on both sides watched the pig eater victory parade from the street, rooftops, or windows. The mounted hetman was at the front of the parade line, behind him Marko and Ostap; the three men sat atop the Khan's best horses. Marko was in front of every man who had participated in the conquest.

Samiylo drew his sabre, and slowly, with much dignity, they began to march. Every Cossack carried a variety of weapons; a show of force to a conquered people. The chern marched with pride for their actions would be immortalized in countless tomes and songs!

Samiylo rode through thick throngs of people cheering him. He could see Sadko, Koshchiy, and Sirin over the city; they had chosen to make themselves visible to him to remind the hetman of the vast debt he owed to the Inspired. He heard Sadko's unnatural voice laughing gently like a small child enjoying a comedic vertep play.

Marko's thoughts turned to what expeditions he would launch after Crimea, would he return to Tsargrad as an emissary instead of a raider?

Ostap realized that he could die in a few days; which didn't trouble him for he had lived a rich enough life for an entire army of men.

Bohun walked slowly, carrying an engraved flintlock he had taken from a sekban. He would not retire on his wealth; the conquest had only emboldened him.

Aleksandr marched past Christians freed from Tatary's captivity. He spied Elena among the crowd, and as their eyes met the sorcerer understood something.

"We all know about the Cossacks that these chivalrous men of our race are of our kin and are true Orthodox Christians... They are the descendents of the glorious Rus of the seed of Japheth who fought Greece on land and on sea. They are the descendents of that warlike race which under Oleg the Rus monarch attacked Constantinople. They are the Same as those who with Volodymyr the sainted king of Rus conquered Greece, Macedonia and Illyria. Their ancestors together with Volodomyr were baptized and accepted Christianity from the church at Constantinople and even to this day they are born are baptized and live in this faith....What other peoples achieve by words and discourses the Cossacks achieve by their actions."
-Orthodox Bishops.

THE END

Glossary:

Artel - An association of hunters, fishermen or criminals.

Ataman - an elected Cossack leader in charge of a kuren.

Bisurmany - a Ruthenian word to describe followers of the Islamic faith.

Bogatyr - a warrior of the medieval states of Kievan Rus and the Novgorodian republic.

Bulava - a mace, a symbol of authority adopted from Eurasian nomads by Cossacks.

Bunchuk -a Hetman's standard consisting of a staff with a horizontal bar and horse tails at the top, adopted from Turkic nomads by Cossacks.

Bylina - an epic about medieval Russian heroes, plural byliny.

Chaika - a Cossack vessel; used mainly for piracy, similar to a Norse long-ship, plural chaiki.

Chern - common Cossacks.

Dacia - in the book this refers to regions of Romania that remain pagan due to a partly successful resistance against Roman invasion in ancient times.

Galleot - a small version of the galley that was easier to man and maintain.

Hetman - the chief elected Cossack official.

Kalpak - traditional hat of the Crimean Khanate.

Kilij - an Ottoman saber, similar to a scimitar.

Kuren - a Sich barracks, plural kureni.

Liakh - An anti-Polish slur.

Lytavr -a large Cossack drum, plural lytavry.

Mamay - a folkloric Cossack character.

Nadziak - spiked war hammer.

Pancerni - medium-cavalrymen of the Polish-Lithuanian Commonwealth's military forces.

Porochivnycia - a y-shaped Cossack gunpowder flask.

Rada - the democratic assembly of the Zaporozhian Cossacks.

Registered Cossacks - Cossacks employed by the Commonwealth that enjoyed a status similar to the nobility.

Rzeczpospolita - the Polish-Lithuanian Commonwealth.

Russkaya Pravda - a medieval Russian legal code, used by the Zaporozhian Cossacks in this setting.

Ruthenia - Ukraine.

Ruthenian - the precursor to the modern Ukrainian language.

Sabre - a common sword in the Rzecpospolita and Cossack lands, influenced by Ottoman swords.

Sich - A fortress that served as the administrative and military center for Zaporozhian and later Danube Cossacks.

Sjem - the parliament of the Polish-Lithuanian Commonwealth with functions that including election the king.

Spoiler - common argot (in the book) for a sorcerer officially employed by the Commonwealth, usually for combat.

Szlachta - the Polish-Lithuanian Commonwealth's nobility.

Szlachcic - a member of the Polish-Lithuanian Commonwealth's nobility.

Veche - a medieval Slavic assembly, comparable to the Norse Thing, Gaelic Tuath or Swiss Landsgemeinde.

Vertep - traditional Ruthenian puppet theatre, often centered around the exploits of fictional Cossacks.

Yatagan - an Ottoman short sword.

Pull up anchor, cast off the mooring lines and drop the sail, the good ship Blue Nymph is about to set sail for adventure once again with her famous seafaring captain at the helm.

Airship 27 Productions is thrilled to present the second volume of brand new stories starring the greatest seaman of them all, Sinbad the Sailor and his international crew of daring adventurers. Here is Henri Delacrois, the deadly archer from Gaul, Ralf Gunarson, the strapping young Viking giant, Tishimi Osara the beautiful female samurai and Omar, the irascible first mate. All of them bound together by their love of action and yearning to explore uncharted lands.

Over the horizon awaits treasure, beautiful exotic maidens and monsters beyond imagining. Dare you sign aboard with Sinbad El Ari? If so, then batten the hatches and have your curved blade ready, heart-pounding adventure awaits.

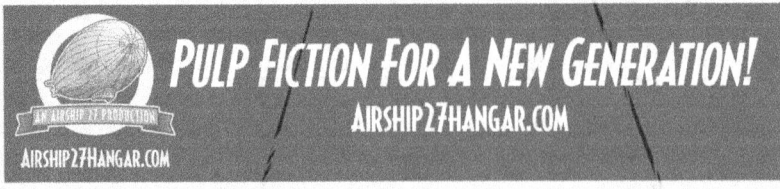